Reflections

A Love Story Through the Ages

MONICA SCHUSTER

PAGE PUBLISHING, INC.
New York, NY

First originally published by Page Publishing, Inc. 2018

ISBN 978-1-64214-042-2 (Paperback)
ISBN 978-1-64214-043-9 (Digital)

Printed in the United States of America

To Mona V. Brown
Without you, my life and this book, would look very different.
Thanks, Mom

INTRODUCTION

This is a work of fiction, and although the story is made up, many of the little bits and pieces that make up the story are based on real experiences that I have had personally or that friends have had, lessons I have learned along the way, and things that I have read about and studied in history.

1

I bolted straight up, drenched in sweat, panicky and smelling charred flesh.

My bedroom focused before my eyes. What the hell? I reached up to pull a lock of hair out of my mouth. Salty? I looked at the dark lock. Wet? Scrubbing the hair and tears away, I tried to recall the reason. I must have fallen asleep. The last thing I remembered, was arriving home from work and falling down on the bed for a minute. *Ugh, why do I feel like throwing up?*

I let my body drop back down while I recovered from … what? The only thing I could distinguish was, the feeling of dread. And charred flesh. My eyes wandered the room, taking in the familiar surroundings, trying to remember what my dream was about. It *had* to be a dream. Right?

Something beeped, and for a second, I wondered what it was, then I wondered why I wondered. I was half lying on my phone, and when I adjusted to retrieve it, I noticed my bladder. As I got up to go into the bathroom, I looked at the screen. Brian. I read as I walked.

Well, crap. I plopped down on the toilet and read it again. Boyfriend? Great. Now my boy/friend wanted to be my boyfriend. Why? They call it friends-with-benefits for a reason! Why did he have to ruin a good thing? I smiled to myself as I got up, aware of the irony. I pictured Brian and snorted my disgust. I couldn't believe he'd actually asked me to be his girl in a text.

Standing there watching the water whirl around, I mildly wished that I could flush my life down the drain and start over. I glanced into the mirror and saw someone with red hair standing there. I jumped back against the wall, every hair on my body standing straight. As I watched the figure, the figure watched me. I moved my head, and she moved as well. The reflection was me, but not. What the hell?

The urgency gone, I gathered my wits again, hair standing down, marveling at how long ten seconds could seem. I shook my head, squeezed my eyes shut, and counted to five. I opened one eye. Brown. The relief came out in a raspy gasp. I tentatively moved toward the mirror and slowly opened the cabinet door. Makeup, toothbrush, face cream … condoms.

Wow. Reality check. I scoffed at myself. I did a quick flip of the door with my hand to see if I was still myself. Self-consciously I laughed and did a quick look-around for the *Candid Camera* folks.

Feeling a little unsure, I did the thing that my reflexes had been doing for twenty-five years. Call Marci. Who better to call than my bestest? As I deleted Brian's text, I figured she'd tell me how to deal with him too.

Marci's message reverberated through my head. "Hi, everyone! Getting ready for my party, so call back. Or, better yet, *come* to my party! Bye!"

Shit.

I had sufficiently blocked out the party. Marci's going away party!

She was going to freaking Africa, of all places. For two years! *Not thinking about it. Not thinking about it* … shaking my head as I went into the kitchen to grab a drink. Bypassing my usual wine, I grabbed one of Marci's beers. Holding the bottle against my forehead, I leaned back against the counter, trying not to think about it, or the fact that a few seconds ago my hair was red! *WTF.* I still have no idea what that was. As I stood, immobilized, my mom called asking whether or not I was coming home for Christmas. I told her I *was* home. Again. Besides, how could I think that far ahead? I told her it was hard to talk about December when it was ninety degrees, so I'd call her about it later.

I stepped into my tiny closet thinking about Christmas, dammit!

Ok, party. *Mmm ... What shall I wear?* I reached for the phone to call Marci. My thumb stilled over the number two. Reflexes fighting brain. *I've been doing this since I was nine. I won't be able to do this anymore.* I doubled over with that realization, feeling like I had just been punched in the gut. Hands on knees, I stayed that way until I could breathe again. I stood up, blindly ripped something off the hanger, put it on, and left the house.

Driving to Marci's house, fighting off tears, I reached up to wipe a lock of hair out of my eyes and saw the scar. I smiled at the small white line, remembering how it got there. We were twelve and full of idealism, even at that age. One night, sitting on our respective window sills, four feet apart, we vowed, as blood sisters, to never be separated, and to always serve others.

I marveled at the memory because even as a child, she wanted to serve. I did too, but the urge was much stronger in her, and she made it easy to jump on her band wagon. We laughed about it years later—how two nine-year-olds, sitting on our sills, would discuss the world's problems—and all that changed as we got older was the size of the world's problems.

I couldn't remember a time in my life when Marci wasn't in it. Her family moved to the city and bought a house right next door, and with her bedroom window facing mine, we sat in our windows and watched the shooting stars, and dreamed. She had wanted to become a Peace Corps volunteer and help others who couldn't help themselves. I wanted to become a lawyer and help others who couldn't help themselves.

I mused at how our lives actually turned out. We did become educators, it just didn't quite look like we had planned. She was an elementary school teacher and I was a history professor at the local community college.

Perusing our childhood put me into a better frame of mind, so to keep myself from becoming a basket case, I thought about a particular pain in my ass. One of my freshman students was giving me fits. He would mouth off to get attention, interrupt class at inopportune times, and he'd begun to occasionally follow me. Not enough to call security, but just enough to give me the creeps. But I'd been a little out of sorts lately, so maybe I was imagining things. I didn't know. I didn't think he was a bad kid, but there was just something about him that made my skin crawl, and I didn't know why. He just made me feel … dirty. Even now I cringed, so … I thought about something else.

Thinking about college, I automatically drifted to one of the new rules of conduct. The college, at the beginning of the year, gave us the ultimatum of teaching the curriculum and nothing else, or else. No side routes of any kind. *Then what the hell is college for?* That one made me so mad I had to set it aside or I'd be raving when I got to the party. Besides, Marci had heard my rants once or twice before.

I parked a block away so I could gather myself before walking into my right arm's going-away party. I stopped at the sidewalk looking at the door that, after tomorrow, I wouldn't be walking through for a very long time. My eyes teared, but I bit my lip. Her wish had finally come true.

I looked at her house, her trees, her garden, and felt utterly lost. The weird thing was though, that I was feeling like this long before Marci had decided to go. I had wanted to talk to her about it, but she was going through her own hell, and truth be told, I wasn't sure she would have understood it anyway. She was always so sure of where her path lay, so for me to say that I didn't know where I was going or that I was feeling like there was something more, it wouldn't have made sense to her. So I kept those feelings to myself.

I looked up at the stars and wondered what was coming.

I stepped into a loud, full house. I caught her attention, and she laughingly came right over. Someone said something sarcastic, and she retorted a little too loud and laughed a little too hard and latched on to me with everything she had. I let her have her moment, then whispered in her ear, "big-girl panties." She nodded, and I could feel her squeeze her tears back into her eyelids. I knew that because I was doing the same thing. We didn't notice that, watching us, others were doing the same.

At the party, I did the best-friend gig for a while; I swirled around and traded bits of nothingness with people. You know: "What do you do? *History professor at Greggors. What about you? Are you married? No. Thank God, but I have been thinking about changing teams, or better yet, going celibate.* Hahaha. *You? …*Blah, blah. I couldn't wait to escape the social hockey game.

I sat on a stool in the corner of the living room, partially hidden behind a fern. From this vantage point, I could watch most of the party and be a part of it, without being part of it. I sighed. It was a little weird to see myself like this because I used to be a social butterfly. Now, all I wanted was to wrap myself up in my invisible cocoon.

I was proud of her. I watched Marci as she said her goodbyes. Watched the terror and excitement on her face meld with sadness, and when she thought she was alone with her thoughts, she let the anger show. Then the anger would turn to excitement and joy. I could have watched her all night just to study the different characters inside vying for the right to feel and be felt.

Watching her made me think. She's running headlong into a living dream working for the Peace Corps. What would I do when faced with life-changing circumstances? I've never really had to deal with anything like that. Would I be able to step up to the plate? Would I let myself go enough to fight that fear?

I studied the faces of the people there. I had met most of them at some point or another. I felt really connected to some of them even though I may not have known them for very long, and yet for some, I felt nothing at all, even though I had known them a long time. Weird. I wondered what that was about. As I observed them my thoughts took a turn. Why *do* we feel connected to some, and not others? Why do some people come into our lives and stay forever, like Marci, and yet others, come and go, and yet you can feel close to them as well? I had no answers.

Inside these new thoughts, I began to watch these people more closely; trying to figure out why some are more … accessible … to me? Was it something they were doing? I started to watch their actions, and then I noticed how they interacted with others. I noticed their faces and what I interpreted on their faces. My thoughts switched again. Why are we even here; in this time and this space? And who are they?

The more I watched, the more my thoughts took other turns. I noticed that some of their actions were not what they seemed. Like Marci, the emotions on their faces didn't really match their actions. The more I watched, the more I realized that maybe I didn't know them at all. Were they hiding, or had I even bothered to look? I began to see them. Really see them, when they thought no one was watching, when they let down their guard. I saw the anger, jealousy, sadness, and loneliness underneath the surface joy. I began to see them in a new light. I realized that there were stories behind the stories in everyone here. Conceptually, I knew that there always had been, but I had never really looked for them before. I thought about who they were. Who they *really* were.

Who was I?

How do people see me? Do they see the real me? Do I let them?

"You should see your face right now." I vaguely heard a woman's voice. Huh? I was startled out of my reverie.

"What?" My first knee-jerk reaction was anger. How dare anyone disturb my peace! And I immediately felt guilty for being caught spying. My stormy brown eyes met green ones. I was so involved in my world of observations and revelations that I couldn't focus. I thought I was looking into a tiger's eyes. But ... aren't tigers' eyes yellow? Where did a tiger come from, and how did it get into Marci's party? In that split second, a thousand thoughts flowed through my head. And then I began to focus. Green eyes, long, dark hair, olive skin, incredibly white, not-so-straight teeth. Goddess.

In a flash I took her all in. Slim but strong shoulders. I could see the lithe muscles in her chest in her low-cut, long-sleeved, olive-green, buttoned shirt. The black, beaded necklace. Casual, black slacks. She was half-sitting on the arm of the couch, smiling at me. Her smile held a slight humor to it, but there was no insult in it.

In a matter of a few seconds, my world changed. I don't remember being so instantly in tune with anyone. And her. I just stared at her. She smiled bigger and brighter.

I was captivated. I couldn't speak. I focused on nothing and everything. The small crescent-shaped scar, right above the left eyebrow on the outside corner of her eye. The tiny mole next to the scar just in front of her temple. It made me think of a crescent moon when Venus rests next to it in the sky. I noticed the gold and brown flecks in her irises, the way her sleeves were rolled up on her forearms, and the long, thin, sinewy muscles that rested in repose there. The way she breathed effortlessly. The smell of her perfume. Musk mixed with ... Tide. The way her hands lightly clasped themselves as they rested against her thighs. The way she so gently, non-invasively invaded my space.

Laughter erupted somewhere, and it catapulted me back into the room. I shook my head slightly. She now had this strange half smile on her face. Half amusement, half inquisitiveness. She opened her mouth and noise came out. It took me a moment to realize that she was speaking.

"I'm sorry. What?" What the hell is wrong with me? She smiled wide again.

"I said that was the strangest look I've ever seen on anyone's face," she said.

I opened my mouth to say something, but nothing came out. Mostly because I couldn't think of anything to say. I closed it. I must have looked perplexed because her eyes held laughter in them while searching with those green tiger eyes.

"Don't tigers have yellow eyes?" I blurted. She let out a short burst of laughter. Obviously that wasn't what she expected.

"Uh, I'm ... I don't know," she said. Her voice was rich, like dark chocolate. Deep and dark, with hints of secrets hidden. With hints of secrets ...? Where the hell did that come from? What is wrong with me? And why do I think of tigers when I look at her? Christ, I've gone off the deep end.

Now, there was concern mixed in with that smile.

"Are you okay?" she asked.

I managed to nod.

"I'm Rhina." She held out her hand. I looked down at her hand, and the air shifted. The room shifted. I shifted. My world shifted. I smelled the stench of death. The hand that held out to me was so thin and frail that I could almost see the blood rushing in the veins through the skin. As I continued to look at the hand, I felt an overwhelming sadness, and my eyes filled with tears. "I'm losing you," I whispered. I reached out with both hands and grasped the spindly fingers. I closed my eyes as I brought them to my face and gently caressed it with the back of her hand.

With my eyes closed, in my mind's eye, I could see the woman that I loved, still healthy and whole and happy. I braced myself to see her in reality and opened my eyes—and I looked into tiger eyes. What? I still held her hand against my cheek. I jerked her hand away and looked at it. Strong, thin fingers, olive skin, sinewy muscles. What? What the hell?

I let go of her hand and looked at her in horror. What must she think of me? My eyes met hers, and I didn't see the disgust that I expected to see. Instead, I saw concern, amusement, understanding, and pain. I'm not sure how one feels and sees all those things at once, but there you have it. Then she did the unexpected. She reached out and laid her hand on my shoulder.

"Are you okay?" she gently asked.

Am I okay? Three simple words, but I felt the absolute desolation of sadness. The gut-wrenching pain of loss, like a knife in the heart. I started sobbing. Without hesitation, Rhina got up and stood next to me and held my head against her while I cried myself out. When my tears abated she kept a hand on my shoulder, but reached over to the couch to excavate in her purse for tissues.

When I started blowing my nose, sensing my discomfort, she moved back to the arm of the couch and retained the pose that she had when I first saw her, and gently, calmly, waited.

Humiliated, I took my time. What the hell was that? She must think I'm an absolute nut case. I couldn't look at her. I squeezed my eyes shut, willing my shameful tears back to their ducts. I felt a warm pressure on my lower arm. My eyes burned in shame and I squeezed tighter. She knew.

"I know you're feeling extremely humiliated and unsure right now, but please don't be," she said. My heart hurt. "I think I know what just happened to you. If it's what I think it is, it's happened to me, but I'd like you to tell me." She gave me a reassuring squeeze. I looked at the hand expecting to find a frail, sickly one, but I saw a strong, capable, warm one. I looked and saw only love and understanding.

"Why aren't you running right now?"

"Because I know you." She smiled slightly at my look of confusion. "When I saw you for the first time, in that moment, I recognized you. At first I thought I'd seen you somewhere before, and then I realized that I had, but it wasn't in this lifetime." As I lifted my eyebrow she smiled wide. "You can explain it away all you want, but can you? Really?" I just looked at her. She must have taken that as a no, so she said, "Okay, so I want you to tell me everything." She saw that I couldn't wrap my head around it. "Let's take a walk. It looks like you could use some air, and I'll tell you what went through my mind when I saw you, and what I was feeling when I watched you watching everyone." I blushed. "Don't worry, I watch people all the time. By watching people I learn about them, and when I learn about them, I learn about myself." Okay, *that* I understand. She saw that I did, so she stood and gestured toward the door. "Shall we?"

As we walked across the room, I searched for Marci, saw that she was well engaged, so without further thought, went out the door. I did not see that Marci had spotted us and watched us leave with a very curious look on her face.

Rhina breathed deep as we walked down the path.

"I love summer. The smells. It makes me drunk." And not the wine? I had noticed the empty wine glass on the coffee table. I kept silent because I didn't feel I deserved to be cynical right now. She walked ahead of me, but when we got to the sidewalk she stopped and looked at the crescent moon. And look, there was Venus. I shook my head. We walked in silence for a while. I recognized some of the scents around us. Rose, Honeysuckle … Tide. I chuckled to myself. She looked at me with a slight smile, waiting. I didn't think that she would appreciate my humor, so I just left it. She looked slightly disappointed but hid it behind a question.

"So, why did you ask about tiger eyes?" This time, it was my turn to let out a short burst. I was kind of embarrassed, so I was glad of the darkness, but I couldn't lie.

"When I look at you I think of tigers."

"Really? Huh." I'm sure my face was beet red, but she said the unexpected. "You know, they say that, at one time or another, we incarnate into many different types of beings. Ants, horses, humans … tigers."

"Really? Huh." I felt slightly better. She didn't seem to think I was crazy. I took a deep breath and relaxed. "So …?"

She sensed my shift, smiled slightly, and pondered how she was going to say it.

"When I saw you, I felt this overwhelming love for you." She did a little shoulder hunch. Now, it was her turn to feel embarrassed. "It made my knees weak. I had to hold onto the back of the chair." I stopped and stared at her. She nonchalantly shrugged and kept walking. I followed. I couldn't say anything so I didn't try. After a half a block she carried on with her story. "I've felt strange things before, but this was something else. I … I looked at you and I knew you. I know you. I don't even know your name but I *know* you." She was visibly shaken, remembering. "I had to hold on tight or I would've fallen over. All these separate pictures of … I don't know, like a movie trailer when they show bits of the movie in rapid succession?" She looked at me, and I nodded. "That's what it was like. They were so rapid, I couldn't get a sense of what the pictures were exactly, but I noticed that they had a similarity to them." She stopped talking. What? I waited impatiently for her to continue. She saw me and smiled at my impatience and said, "I'm trying to think of what that feeling was. I was so captivated by you that I couldn't think about anything else." Now it was my turn to smile. She was captivated.

"It was the oddest feeling. I was standing there watching you and feeling like … 'there she is . . .' and then there were more flashes of pictures in my head, and they all melded into one." She stopped and turned to me. The half of her face that I could see in the streetlight was in awe. Tears shimmered in her eyes. "And you are the amalgamation of them all." This time I reached out and softly placed my hand on her arm. As soon as I touched her, green tiger eyes, set in a black, white and orange face, swam in my vision. Ants, horses, humans … tigers.

"So tell me what you saw earlier," she inquired. Dang, I was hoping she would forget about that. "And no, I didn't forget about that."

"How do you do that?" I asked.

She smiled and humbly said, "It was written all over your face."

"Great." I tried to stall.

"So …?"

"You're going to think I'm crazy."

"Try me."

I told her how I was holding her frail hand, but it wasn't her hand … like I was transported to another time and place. "But it was *your* hand! That's what was so weird. I *knew* it was your hand!" I gestured to her. "But you weren't there!" I was stupefied, and frustrated *because* I was stupefied.

"Sounds like you had a flash back to another life, one with both of us in it." She had said it so calmly that I stopped.

"You're serious."

"Yes." Like it was normal that we should be talking about past lives.

"Like, actually serious?"

"Yes."

"Wow." My legs started moving because my brain sure wasn't.

"So you actually think past lives are real?" I asked incredulously.

"Yes. I do. I've experienced too many things, in my own life, and have heard of too many stories of friends, *not* to believe it."

I stopped again and looked at her with my mouth open. I think I was trying to formulate a question, but didn't know what to ask. Or … I might have been just standing there with my mouth open.

It seemed like such a crazy idea but how *do* I explain it? She just watched me with those patient eyes, seeing that I was trying to work through it.

"Tell me more," I said.

"That's kind of a vast subject."

"Tell me the basics then."

"Well … our souls come back many times to learn lessons, and certain souls end up coming back with us time and time again, to help us. You and I have obviously been together before or we wouldn't have connected so instantly—and not to mention your vision of my frail hand, the one that wasn't mine." She grinned. She was poking fun at me. I stopped walking again.

"I assume that you've given me a rudimentary explanation, and that it wasn't designed for me to have any idea what you're talking about." She laughed at me. "Can we go back to the part where you were captivated? I like that part"—I sighed—"because I am too."

The huge breath I took hurt my lungs, but I needed it to last as I slowly let it out. I stood, looking around me at the brightly lit windows and closed my eyes, soaking up the fragrance on my taste buds as I breathed. I could feel a little bit of acceptance click into place. I turned to her and smiled.

"I'm Kattrina, but everyone calls me Kat." I put my hand out.

"Hi, Kat." She extended hers and smiled. "I'm Rhina."

I hesitated a moment before taking it, remembering the last time we tried this, but the instant my skin touched hers, all I could think of was, "I'm home." My eyes flew to hers. Tears welled up in both of us.

We stood there for a year until we heard a large group of women laugh.

I disturbed our dream world to look over, with half my attention, and vaguely remembered that there was a reason we were here. Marci.

"I think we have to head back. It looks as though we've missed the party," I sadly admitted.

"Darn," she said. I smiled. Yeah, darn.

I wanted to keep her hand in mine, but it felt too forward, even after we had shared lifetimes, or so it seemed. She must have felt the same because after a moment's hesitation she squeezed my hand as a question. I answered with my own squeeze. It felt right.

We meandered back down the block toward Marci's. There was nothing to say so we let the sounds and smells of the night surround us. The women had left so I watched Marci watch us, walking hand in hand.

Marci's face was hidden in the shadows of the elm, but I could tell by the way her head was cocked to the side, and by the way her foot was tapping, that she was trying not to be rude by demanding answers. I was very thankful that she didn't know Rhina very well as it saved me from having to answer questions that I didn't have a clue of how to answer. So ... I let her stew.

"Hey, guys. We wondered where you two went off to." She was practically vibrating with curiosity, but was too well mannered to burst out with it. I smiled, liking the idea of Marci squirming.

"Rhina, Linda and Joe were looking for you. We were just about to make some coffee and look at pictures of their Peru trip." Rhina took the hint. She squeezed my hand and gave me an, I'm-glad-its-you look, smiled and walked inside. As soon as the front screen door slid shut, Marci turned toward me with a pose that said "you've been holding out on me"—lips pursed, arms crossed.

"I have not been holding out on you," I said in my defense. Marci raised the bullshit eyebrow. "I promise," I said. I was too tired and perplexed to even try to explain the unexplainable to her. I held up my hands. "Please, Marc. I don't know how to explain what happened tonight. I met her three minutes ago, and I've known her forever." Marci tried to give me another bullshit eyebrow look but it didn't work because she saw that I was a little out of sorts, so there was a curiosity added to the look, which made me laugh.

"Honestly, Marc. I really have no idea how, or what to say about Rhina, but I do promise that, if and when I figure it out, I will email you with all the juicy details." She squinted her eyes and put her hands on her hips.

"Promise?"

"I promise." And then I couldn't resist. "I can tell you, though, that she has tiger eyes." I started walking toward the house.

"Tiger eyes?" I could hear the confusion in her voice. As I reached for the screen door I heard her say, "Don't tigers have yellow eyes?" I burst out laughing as I walked inside. I grabbed her arm as she walked through the door and we walked companionably, arm in arm, to the kitchen where everyone had gathered.

Linda and Joe were good naturedly arguing over how much coffee to use and Rhina pulled her smile away from them and plastered it on me. Marci felt the hitch in my step and gave me a strange look, and then looked at me, looking at Rhina. She looked at Rhina, then back at me, then at Linda and Joe, and they were looking at Rhina and then at me, then at Rhina again. And then at each other, then at Marci. Rhina and I were the only ones not playing tennis. After several moments of this, Joe decided to take advantage of the moment and dumped a heaping scoop of coffee in the filter and quickly shut the lid and poked the On button. "Yes!" He punched the air.

Linda saw what he did and socked him in the arm. "Ow!" He rubbed his arm. "Hey!"

Marci grabbed the cake and pointed to Linda to grab the pile of plates and forks.

"Shall we?" she said.

Rhina and I didn't move, still lost in each other. The other three rolled their eyes and left us alone, laughing their way out of the kitchen.

In my fog I heard Joe say, "I didn't know Kat was a lesbo."

"She's not," Marci answered.

"Really? Wow!"

We chuckled over the exchange and glided toward each other. I put my hand on the counter and she put hers on top of mine. It was as natural as if we'd been doing it all along.

"You're really not?" she asked.

"No." I shook my head. "It flitted through my mind a few times, but it was never really a serious thought. You?"

"Well," she shrugged, "no, not really, but yes, sort of." She saw my blank stare and laughed when she realized the nonsensical sentence she'd just imparted. "I mean, I've been curious, but not serious. I've never met anyone that I wanted to go there with." She gently squeezed my hand in question. "I don't want to stay, but she's your friend and she'll be gone a very long time."

I answered her question.

"I'll call her tomorrow and meet for lunch. She doesn't leave till tomorrow night, so no worries. She'll have plenty of time to pester me for details until she gets on the plane."

They all stopped talking when we walked into the room. There's a hint.

"I'm going to take Rhina home." Neither of us offered an explanation and apparently none was needed. Marci and I made arrangements for lunch, and Rhina hugged her and wished her luck and we all said our goodbyes.

As I was closing the door I heard Linda say, "Pay up, coffee boy."

I laughed as the door clicked shut. As we walked down the front path, I glanced in the dining room window and saw Linda holding out her hand as Joe handed her a twenty.

"Apparently our exploits are profitable." I told her what had transpired. She laughed.

"Who'da thunk?" she pondered.

"Yeah, who'da thunk." I motioned her to the left, down the sidewalk. We walked arm in arm like old lovers. Neither of us thought it was odd that we had met only a few short ... what ... Minutes. Hours. Lifetimes. ... ago?

"So there were rumblings about the reason Marci was leaving. What's that about?" Rhina asked inquisitively. I thought about how to answer that. I didn't think Rhina was asking out of judgement so I answered.

"Her husband of ten years left her. He left with their joint account, his secretary, her self-confidence and flew off to Mexico." I paused at the instant bolt of anger that came up. Shoving it down, I continued, "She was a mess. I could kill him for that. It took a lot of pints, both ice cream and liquor, to get her back. She's still climbing." I turned pensive and silent.

She laid her hand on my arm and stopped. "If we need to go back, we can. She obviously means a great deal to you."

If she only knew.

"Thank you for saying that, but she'll be fine. I'll see her tomorrow and it'll be good for her to spend time with Linda and Joe anyway. They're close."

"But not as close as you two," Rhina correctly observed.

"No. Few are." I looked at her. "But I can't help but feel that we've hit a plateau in our lives. She's flying off to Africa"—I smiled and shook my head—"and I've just met you. And hey, I'm into past lives now," I jested. She smiled and squeezed my hand.

"As long as you're sure," she countered. I looked at her straight in the eye, and felt the truth.

"I've never been so sure of anything in my life. Even if I haven't a clue why." I smiled. She nodded and pushed a lock of hair out of my eyes. My heart did a flip.

2

hen we got situated in my car, I turned and opened my mouth to ask directions, but when I saw her face I froze. She was looking at me with such love and wanting that my heart jumped against my breast plate. Our eyes held for an eternity and we both leaned in minutely to test the water, then we both jumped in. When our lips met, everything shifted into place. It was like coming home after a long trip and you hadn't realized how much you missed it until you were back. The look, the smell, the feel. Home. That's what I felt. And judging by the murmur of pleasure coming from Rhina, she felt it too. Even the air was different. It was softer, warmer. That soft sensual feel of silk on mine. Then, her lips were all that existed.

My lips gently reacquainted with hers. It had been an eternity. It was yesterday. Time lost all meaning. Lifetimes slipped away. All my fears and questions fell away and morphed into this moment of absolute bliss, of complete and otherworldly knowing, that this is *the* only thing that exists that matters.

We eventually lifted away from each other. For a moment she had a different face. I blinked a couple of times. *Please, be my fuzziness from the kiss.* She blinked once and smiled.

"You too?" she said.

"Uh …yeah. I think." Her smile brought her face back into focus. Phew. "For a second there you looked like someone else." I could barely talk. I felt sluggish. Her kiss melted my brain cells.

"Tell me," she said. I looked at her, about to laugh at the joke, then saw that she wasn't kidding. I cocked my head. God, she was beautiful.

"All right. You had the same general features, but your face was thinner and longer. Your hair was thin, straight and long. Prudish, kind of," I recounted. She was looking at me very intently.

"I'll tell you what you looked like, but you need to start driving. I want to go home. Right now." The look in her eye and the huskiness in her voice made my insides jump. I shifted into drive.

After she gave initial directions, she described who I was in that lifetime. Jeez, *in that lifetime.* Two hours ago I wasn't even sure I believed in reincarnation. I guess I do now. Either that or I am now officially insane. Insanity or reincarnation? I looked at her. Okay, I'll take reincarnation. She told me that I had dark hair and brown eyes, with a dark complexion. I was one of what they call the "dark ones" from Ireland. In her head she could even hear me speak with an Irish accent.

I drove in silence. What does one say to that? I glanced over and almost ran off the road. I thought my heart had jumped, but it was only the rumble strips. "You're going to have to stop looking at me like that or we're not going to make it alive." She smiled at me— sure, that's better.

We made it to her house without a fatal incident. It seemed to take forever, as she lived across town, but we finally made it. Within seconds of parking I was at the sidewalk. She held out her hand and I took it. I remember thinking, very briefly, that I should be feeling really weird about all of this, but especially the fact that I'm about to rip the clothes off of a woman I've met only a few hours ago. A woman. And I *am* going to rip her clothes off. We reached the door and I had some vague recollection that it was wood, with a rounded top and painted dark green. I stepped up and held her against me as she pulled her keys out.

She trembled as she tried to put the key in. "You have to step away from me. I can't think."

We both groaned in frustration as she dropped her keys while fumbling for the right one. There were only two. As she bent over I grabbed her hips from behind and brought her really nice butt into me. She almost dropped the keys again, but caught them. She stood and faced me. Mistake. I plastered my lips onto hers and smashed her against the door. She reciprocated with abandon.

Neither noticed a pair of elderly women, clucking and shaking their heads, as they ambled down the sidewalk.

Rhina finally broke away, gasping. "You're killing me! You have to step away from me." I tried to grab her again. "Stop. Christ, you have to stop. You make my knees weak." I answered by grabbing her keys and thank God she only had car and door on the ring. I shoved open the door and then shoved her through it, then slammed the door and slammed her against it. God, I have never felt so much heat. I couldn't help myself. I ripped her shirt apart.

"That was silk," she said in between gulps of air.

"I'll buy you a new one," I said in between gulps of air.

I couldn't get enough of her skin. Her bra went next. I had never held breasts in my hand, or ever kissed, or suckled nipples but as I did both, I felt like I was home. Like I'd done this so many times before. I sighed with her nipple in my mouth and I briefly remembered that I had never done this before. Rhina gasped in my arms. I had done this a thousand times.

"My turn," she said as she reached under and grabbed my shirt and ripped it in two. Buttons went flying. Then my bra. She grabbed my face in her two hands and devoured my lips with hers. She reached for my breasts, one in each hand. She groaned at the pleasure of touching silk clouds. That moan reverberated right through me. I involuntarily let out a sound that was half-way between a sigh and a growl. My knees gave way and we ended up in a heap on the floor with her on top of me.

"Right where I want you," she said in my mouth. Still in her lip-lock she grabbed both my arms and held them above my head pressed against the floor. She held them pinned there while her lips followed her other hand down. She took one nipple in her mouth and her hand took the other. I screamed in ecstasy. I never thought … all thoughts fled. There was nothing left but her touch. Her lips.

I was lost. And found. All that existed in that moment was her. I broke the hold and grabbed for her. I wanted her mouth. Our lips burned a hole in the ozone. My god, it was hot. I felt like I was being seared from the inside. So hot we sizzled, like two light sabers when they touch. We were sizzling … colors. We stopped kissing and just held on. Held on tight. If we were going to burn then let it be together. I vaguely thought that we were actually melding together.

After the heat dissipated, that wave of electrifying tingle flowed through and the waves of color became the dark hallway once again. Huh. I hadn't noticed the dark hallway. I looked around with only my eyes. My arms still entwined with hers in a death grip. I slowly moved one arm up and down her back, more, really, to see if she was still whole. I stole a brief feel to my own hip. Yep. Still two bodies. What the hell was that?

Rhina slowly lifted her head and looked at me with a what-the-hell-was-that look.

"I don't know," I choked out. She smiled.

"Everything accounted for?" Nothing gets past her. She noticed the lights, or rather, the lack of them and then the disarray and grinned like a Cheshire cat. She leaned up slightly on her elbows and looked down at our bodies. "Better than I imagined." She leaned down and grabbed my nipple with her teeth.

"My god. You keep doing that and we'll never get off the floor." She chuckled with me still in her mouth and the vibration made me shiver. "Oh, man. I'm serious, I can't … wait. I want all of you and I don't want our first time to be on the floor in front of your beautiful door. Take me to your bed." She smiled again, but that seemed to wake her up because she was up before my brain could register that she was. She held out her hand and helped me up.

We stood in front of each other taking the other in. Our eyes, lips, nose, neck, breasts, waist. We looked and lingered. I reached up and lightly drew my finger from her breast bone down to her left nipple. Circled it and slowly, gently continued down to her belly button. Circled it then continued down to her waistband. She watched me do this, both of us fascinated by the wonder called … woman.

We both looked up and into each other's eyes. The dark one and the tiger.

She took a step back, held out her hand and led me down the hall to her bedroom. Though it was dark, the streetlights that shone through the windows let in enough light that I could see a soft, eclectic look. Wonderful and plush looking. Chairs and sofas that really didn't go together. Or it's dark, so what do I know?

She walked ahead of me, pulling me behind her and turned right at the end of the hall. She led me to the bed. The room was much darker and I felt rather than saw the bed at my thigh. Not letting go, she reached with the other hand and switched on the bedside lamp. I was expecting to be blinded, but was pleasantly surprised when the light was softened by a violet translucent cloth that was draped over the lamp. She turned those tiger eyes at me. "You're mine," they said.

"I most definitely am," I whispered and didn't even think twice about it. She still held my hand and with the other she reached up and with her crooked finger, brought my chin to her lips. She let go of my hand and brought it up to join the other on either side of my face. She kissed me long, slow, soft, searchingly. She then kissed my whole face slowly, deliberately. Then followed suit with neck, ears, breasts. Searching, exploring, learning, tasting.

I was so riveted by her touch, her smell, *her*, I couldn't move, and didn't want to. "If I'd known how it felt …" I whispered. She chuckled with her lips nibbling my ear. Did I just say that out loud?

"I concur," she said. I was getting really hot and I guess she was too because she reached for my jeans and didn't waste any time removing them. Although, she had to help me step out of them as I was pretty incoherent at the time.

"I love that I could do that to you," she said against my ear. Her hot breath made even my eardrums quiver. I made an effort to undo her pants but must have been very inept at it because she knocked my hand away and finished the job herself.

She grabbed my hands in hers and stepped back to look at me. I looked at her. Our eyes cherished, then devoured. She shoved me down on the bed then laid down next to me. She slid one arm under me then physically slid me up to her pillows.

I watched her move over me as I reached for her. She closed her eyes as she slowly descended over me, taking her time to feel her skin touch mine. I could see on her face that she felt, to the core, every inch of her body touching mine. I was in ecstasy, watching her ecstasy, as she experienced us touching whole body to whole body for the first time. When she rested and relaxed on top of me, she opened her eyes and there were tears in them. "I can't believe I found you again."

This time it was her turn to cry. My heart ached for and with her. I held her tight until her sobs slowed. She looked at me with such pain and love in her eyes that I started to cry, as well. That made her start crying again. We held each other for a time, then I felt her shudder. I thought that she was crying harder so I held her tighter, but then I heard what sounded like a snort, which of course caused me to laugh. So we lay laughing in each other's arms. When we had laughed ourselves out, she leaned up and propped herself on one elbow and looked at me.

"Wow."

"Yeah."

"You sure know how to give a girl a good time." She smiled and shook her head in disbelief.

"Yeah, well, I believe you're the one that picked me up." I looked up into her face and gently touched her cheek. "You're so beautiful." She penetrated me with those tiger eyes, like she was seeing me from the inside out.

"That's my line." Then she leaned down to kiss me. Her lips were so soft that I almost started crying again, the way some things, so absolutely exquisite, bring tears to one's eyes. She made me want to stay here in this bed, in her arms, forever. I had never experienced anything or anyone like this before. She made me drunk.

Her kisses became more. She moved on top of me and this time there was no laughter. No tears.

She groaned, and in between breaths and kisses, she mumbled in my mouth. "Oh god, you are so, so … I don't know." She bit my lip. I scratched her back. We groped, scratched, tugged, all the while wanting to climb inside each other's skin. All our lifetimes were com-

28

ing to the surface. The absolute love, lust, pain, joy, ecstasy. There, in her lips and mine, was everything we would ever have and ever need. And then, her fingers worked her magic. I screamed and shot up from the bed. She held me to keep me steady.

"Holy cow!" I panted. "You don't even have the right parts and you can do that to me." I cried out as she hit a particularly sweet spot. She had to hold me to keep me from bouncing to the ceiling. I grabbed on, with my arms around her neck so hard I thought I was going to break it, but she seemed to weather it okay as she kept on gently massaging me. Many releases later I flopped my head down on the pillow.

I felt like a spring that had been released of its tension. I was too wrung out to even speak accolades, but I watched her watch me. She had a strange little satisfied smile on her face. She continued to explore my body with her hands, but it was more of an exploration than passion. She watched my eyes, my face, every nuance of my expression to see what I liked, and paired them with every move she made with her hands. Like she was trying to imprint those to memory.

She sat up and continued her exploration. I have never felt so totally cherished and loved. And sated.

I watched her. My eyes roamed over this completely enchanting woman. Everything about her fascinated me. I reached up and lightly ran my hand down her back. I closed my eyes to let the sense of touch intensify. I felt her muscles move under my fingers. The way they shifted reminded me of something that I had heard once about water. Hard as rushing water yet soft as rain—or something like that. She was so soft, yet I could feel the muscles ripple under her skin.

With my eyes closed I felt removed from this world. Even my hand felt dislocated, like it was operating on its own accord. I opened my eyes and looked at my hand touching her skin. Even when I could see it, it felt dislocated.

I must have had a funny look on my face because she asked me, "What look was that? What are you thinking?" Her hands stilled and she gently lifted them from my body and part of me wanted to cry out in frustration that she did, but another part of me felt relieved because I could actually think again.

"Wow! Now that was a face. What was *that* expression?" She laughed at me. "You do have an amazing face. In every way." She looked into my soul again. "So what was that expression just now?" I was embarrassed but I told her about being both frustrated and relieved. She smiled at me again. The smile that takes my breath away.

She asked again about the moment earlier. I told her about being so disconnected that I felt like my hand was operating on remote control.

"Like you were in this dimension and your hand was in another one?"

"Yes, that's exactly it!" She understood. "Have you ever felt that?"

"Yes. Once, but it was nothing like this."

"Tell me." Excited, I sat up and laid my hand on her wrist. I couldn't not touch her. I reached up as she started to speak, to tuck a lock of hair behind her ear. She involuntarily moved her cheek against my hand.

"It was a few years ago. I was babysitting my four-year-old niece and we were sitting on the living room floor playing 'build the blocks.'" She got this little smile on her face as she recounted the incident. "She was building a castle and I reached up to straighten her jumper, and all of a sudden my hand was straightening her clothes, but it was a completely different cloth. A different era. I had the distinct feeling that I was straightening my daughters smock before she went outside. Yet I was still looking at my niece and the building blocks in front of me. It was the weirdest thing." Rhina shook her head in remembrance. "I was looking at two different lives but it was all here. Like one was overlaid on top of the other. I don't know how else to explain it." Her eyes came back to the present and she pinned them on me. Her face softened.

"You are so beautiful," she said. She cupped my chin and brought my lips to hers. "I love that you can lose yourself in me. I love that I can, so totally, lose myself in you. I love that you feel like silk yet can practically break my neck in passion. I love that I have never felt so absolutely … rapturous . . . with anyone else. Not even close." She kissed me again.

I looked at her in absolute wonderment. She must have understood my look because she said.

"I know. Boggles the mind doesn't it?" I nodded.

"How—?" She put a finger to my lips.

"Don't think about it. It'll drive you crazy."

Okay. So I thought about something else.

A while later we lay wrapped in each other's arms. It was still dark, but neither of us needed the light; we were so in tune with each other.

"You know, if you were any one of the men I've dated in my life, I would leave right now, or if they were at my place, I would kick them out," I admitted.

"Really?"

"Yeah. It was really kind of mean, now that I think about it."

"You don't want to go do you?" She lifted enough to see me and asked in a slightly panicked voice.

"What? No. Of course not. No. I just meant that you're different. I don't want to go," I said quickly. "You don't want me to go do you?" It was my turn to be slightly panicked.

"No, no I don't." She laid back down and said calmly. "I've just found you again. I'm not going to send you away."

"Good." I settled into her shoulder. "I didn't think of it until now. Until you. It's the difference you give me. I never wanted a man to stay. I wanted to want it, but they were never you. I mean, not that I think I secretly wanted women, it's just that I never met *that* guy. You know what I mean?"

"Yes. I do." She was quiet for a time then asked, "Are you … seeing anyone now?"

I told her about Brian. My friend-with-benefits. "He wants more but I don't. Especially now. I don't know what to tell him. I don't want to hurt him." She waited for more but there was nothing more for me to say.

"When you have an insight, or someone tells you something about yourself, sometimes not so pleasant, how do you feel?" she asked.

"It hurts, but I grow from it. I feel better after. I feel bigger," I said.

"Let him be bigger too," she said it simply.

I needed to tell him the truth. "Mmm. Thank you for that."

We stayed like that for a while. Just the feel of her skin next to mine took me to a familiar place, which, of course, I whirled around inside my head.

How can this happen? How can I meet someone and instantly feel like this? Much less, a woman? A woman. I pulled away from her just enough to look at her. My woman.

"What?" she asked.

"You're a woman."

"I know. Isn't it fabulous?"

Her smile was a beacon in the night. I just looked at her. It is fabulous. Isn't it? Here is the person I want to spend the rest of my life with—and wasn't that a mind-numbing thought. How does this happen? As of earlier this evening I had sworn off relationships. But in a matter of a few short hours, I not only found someone that I want to spend the rest of my life with—it's a woman! Boggles the mind.

"Yes, it is," I said neutrally.

"You don't sound very sure," she said cautiously.

"Actually, I am. I'm just working my brain around to the fact that you're a woman," I said matter-of-factly. She smiled.

"Yeah. I know. It's new, but not."

"Yes. Exactly." We both settled into each other until my stomach growled.

"Good," she said. "I'm starved too! Some crazy woman got me distracted and I didn't get any of that great food at the party." She planted one on me and popped out of bed, and she looked wonderful doing it. Sigh.

She went into the next room and I assumed it was the bathroom because she came back with a robe and threw it at me. Then she went to her dresser and put on a man's shirt about three times bigger than her.

"Nice robe," I joked.

"Yeah, well, men are good for something I guess." We laughed at the irony.

"I feel that it's my duty to let you know that I love the way you look in that—" I sighed in longing. "So therefore, I may have to rip it off of you."

"I'll be waiting." She grabbed my hand, kissed me, and pulled me to the kitchen.

She turned on the kitchen light, but it blinded us so she turned on the light over the stove instead. Diving into the fridge she pulled out turkey, cheese and grapes. Table crackers, wine and glasses came next. She handed me a tray with the food and she followed me with the wine. We went and had a very cozy picnic in the middle of her bed.

"Before, you said something about lessons. What did you mean?" I asked. Rhina formulated her thoughts.

"Lessons are what our psyches are trying to learn and heal in any particular lifetime, and if we don't learn them in one lifetime they keep coming back until we do." She could see the blank look on my face. "Another way to put it. Our baggage."

"Okay, that one I know." A grape found its way to my mouth by way of her graceful fingers. "Everyone has baggage, but are the bags big enough that they have to come back time after time to heal them?"

"Sometimes, yes. I'm sure there will be a different answer for everyone that you ask, but *my* belief is that there are no coincidences. I believe that *everyone* and *everything* has a purpose. They show us *something*. So if we don't understand a particular lesson in one life-time and heal it, the lessons keep coming back, lifetime after lifetime, until we finally do. And if in any given lifetime, we don't get it, the situations just get worse, until things get so bad that we don't have a choice, *but* to look." I had the deer-in-the-headlights look again. She tried another tact.

"For example: Ever hear people say that they got hit in the head with a two by four?" I nodded. "Well, if they really looked back at their life, they would probably notice that there were small red flags early on in different situations, but they didn't heed them then either. And then the signs gradually got worse. Two by four ... bus ... freight train .... That's what people do for us. They show us where our work is still needed." She stopped to put a grape in my mouth and kissed me. Sigh.

"How do people show us that?" I asked.

"Have you ever dated the same man? Different guys, but same general look, and/or same general characteristics. I mean, you could pick one, and put his name on the rest of them."

"Yes! My god. That's a thing? I just thought it was me!"

"Well, if you really looked at it, you would notice that as each of these men came along, circumstances that surrounded that relationship got worse with each guy. Right?" As she talked, I looked back in my memories and noticed that she was right. I nodded. I had never realized that before. Wow.

"Okay, so if you delved into the reason why the same man showed up time and time again— what they were trying to show you, in other words—then you could figure out what the lesson is. Sometimes you have to dig to find it and it isn't always pleasant, but if you heal it then, then *they* would never have to show up again. In any lifetime."

"So what does that have to do with people coming *back* together, like you and I?"

"Well, I could go into "spirit pods" and other things, but I'll just keep it simple." Thank goodness, I thought, as my head spun. "We help each other with our issues. I don't doubt that you and I are working on some of the same issues in this lifetime. Or opposite issues, which would then complement each other."

I was overwhelmed and my head was spinning, but I wasn't running and that was cool. When she finished talking I just gazed at her perfection. I got gooey in the middle. I'd heard of love at first sight, but I didn't think it was real. I just thought that those people were *trying* to believe it was real. But here I was, sitting across from this amazing woman, and damned if it wasn't true.

She had been watching me as I watched her. I asked about the crescent scar above her eye. A childhood accident was all she said. I got the feeling that there was more to the story, but I left it.

"You are so beautiful," I said.

"That's my line." She reached across the grapes and kissed me. "Please don't tell me that you have to work this weekend."

"Not till Monday."

"Good. May I kidnap you for the weekend?"

"Damn. I was hoping you would kidnap me forever," I said against her lips. She broke away long enough to remove our picnic paraphernalia.

I kissed her slowly, passionately, with absolute love. We kissed all night long. At some point we rolled on our sides and held each other tight. Like, if we let go then it would all be a dream. A cruel dream.

As night turned light we dozed off, wrapped safe and warm in each other's arms. At some point, when I woke, I found that it wasn't a dream at all. I smiled and slid my eyes closed again, and dreamed of another time ...

3

"It's good to be home," I said to the dark skies. It was still early but I noticed the smoke coming from the chimney. It'll be daylight soon. Mam must be up and about, I thought, as I rode up on my horse. It had been a good long while since I'd been home. I looked around at the farm where I'd grown up and noticed, even in the dark, that things were in disrepair. A broken fence, pieces of plows and hay bales scattered around outside the barn. Shame washed over me.

I stopped in front of the cottage, took a good long inhale and slid gratefully off my horse. I pushed away the shame and smiled like a fool. I was so excited to see my mam, but when I opened the door I was greeted by the smell of sickness. I was horrified as I looked at my mam lying like death in her bed. There was an oil lamp lit on the table next to her. I dumped my bundle and ran to her bed. She barely opened her eyes but when she saw me she tried to open them more and reach for me, but she was too weak. She dropped her hand and shut her eyes and slept. Just then the door burst open and the neighbor, Rhenal, came rushing in.

"Stephen. Thank God you're here." She ran to my mother to make sure she was all right. "Travina, look it's Stephen." She was nearly in tears. My mother slept on.

I jumped up ready to give her a piece of my mind, like it was her fault that my mother was sick, but she looked haggard and exhausted so I curbed my anger.

"Rhenal, what happened?"

She told me that, last fall, my mother had been helping a sick neighbor and the cat had tripped her on the stairs; broke her leg badly in two places. They sent for Meerina Buchannon, the best healer in the region. She had set Mam's leg, but it was a very painful ordeal. Meerina stayed for three days to make sure there were no complications, but my mother was strong, so the healer left and then came back every time she was in the area.

Over time, Travina was getting well enough to take small steps across the floor, but the long, cold, damp winter had taken its toll. She had been sedentary too long and had developed pneumonia. Rhenal had recounted the story, but I could tell it had pained her greatly to do so.

"Stephen. This has been so hard on her. You know how she is. Always moving, doing …"

"I know. And you as well. Troublemakers, the both of you, "I joked tenderly. She waved her hand in fun. "She's lucky to have you, Rhenal." I put my hand on her shoulder in support. "Is Meerina coming back?" I asked. She said that she had sent her son to Meerina's village and left word there, but that was last week.

"I'm sorry. I've done all I know how to do." She broke down. "I told him to try to find you as well, but we had no idea where you were. He said he left messages with the villagers along the way, in case you came along."

"Ah, Rhenal. You've done a fine job. I'm glad you're here for her," I comforted. "If Meerina doesn't show tomorrow, I'll go." I sat and talked with Rhenal for a bit, reacquainting myself with things after I'd been gone for so long. Mam was sleeping deep, so I left Rhenal to tend to her and went outside to take care of the horse, and from the looks of it, some mending and fixing.

That night, I told Rhenal that I would take care of my mam so that she could go home and finally get some rest. She hesitated and looked over at the spare bed that she obviously had been using. I figured she was hesitating because she thought that I might not be able to handle it, but then she acquiesced and left.

It was early morning and still dark when I heard a horse galloping up to the cottage. Thinking it was Meerina, I jumped out of bed and ran outside. Clouds of steam billowed off the horse and rider. Obviously, they had been working hard this morning. The rider stepped easily off her horse. I strode quickly to help with her bags, of which she was already untying. She was so thickly bundled that I didn't know how she could move.

"Meerina, I'm so glad you're here. Thank you for coming." She didn't say anything, but I was so happy to see her that I didn't think anything of it. Our paths had crossed from time to time, so I knew her well enough to know that she had a tendency to be a bit short when she was in healing mode. I also knew that she didn't want you under foot when she was working.

"Get the rest of my bags will you." She grabbed a small pack and rushed off into the house.

Okay. I brought the rest of her things and put them in the house. Meerina had shed her thicker outer garments, but she was already going through her checks of my mother. I asked her if she needed anything special and she quipped a no. I regarded her for a moment before I put logs on the fire and poured more water in the pot that hung there. Then I went outside to tend to her horse. That I could do.

The sky was light enough when I finished with her horse, that I could start mending the paddock fence. I went in search of tools. I noticed that one of the stalls had been kicked in and never repaired. I had been gone too long this time. Maybe it was time to stay. Maybe it was time for me to stop playing the Bard O'Malley. "The great storyteller," I scoffed. Mam obviously needed me. I felt shame flow through me in not being here, but what could I do? Every time I came home, Mam made me promise not to stay. I knew she loved me and wanted the best for me, but I still didn't understand. It confused me.

It was early still when I finished my chores and went inside for something warm to eat. I would make porridge for Meerina as well.

"Where have you been?" she demanded harshly. "Get me some hot water." She didn't even look at me. It was quite rude but I needed her. I grabbed a large bowl and ladled her some water. As I walked over to her I could see her profile. She had de-cloaked and I could see her clearly now. This was not Meerina.

"Who are you? You're not Meerina," I demanded.

"I need the water," she snapped at me.

"Who are you?" I did not budge.

"I am Rachael, Meerina's niece. Now may I have my water?" I had heard of Rachael. Meerina had talked of her and she was a very good healer in her own right. I breathed a sigh of relief as I brought over the bowl of water.

"Where's Meerina?" I asked. She didn't answer. I watched Rachael as she ground herb with stone and pestle, then poured water and made a mixture of something. She then took the mixture and made a poultice. She put it on my mam's chest. I was fascinated by her hands and how deft they were. It wasn't until she was done that she looked at me. She opened her mouth to say something, but stilled. Our eyes met, and I lost the feeling in my knees. She was the most beautiful creature I'd ever seen. I couldn't take my eyes off her. We stood like that until my mother stirred. That broke the spell and we were back in this world again. She turned to talk to my mam.

"Travina, hi." My mother recognized her and started to say something but Rachael gently quieted her.

"Don't Travina. It's okay now. We're going to get you up again very soon." She damped a cloth and washed Travina's face. My mother saw me.

"I wasn't dreaming," she croaked as she tried to reach for me.

"Ma." I knelt next to the bed opposite Rachael, whose eyes I could feel on me. "You've always been the lazy one," I joked, but immediately regretted it as Mam tried to laugh, but it turned into a coughing fit. I watched in helplessness as Rachael held some kind of herbal infusion under Mam's nose and let the fumes soothe her. Soon she calmed down and breathed easier. I just held her hand. She watched me with sunken eyes but couldn't trust herself to talk. We stayed like that for some time. She just kept her eyes on me, not believing that I was actually there.

As Rachael watched Stephen and his mam connect, her heart warmed. It was obvious that they were close and that he loved his mother very much. She thought about that moment when she herself locked eyes with him. She'd felt an instant bond. She'd heard of such things but had never believed it could happen. She'd also had a "familiar" feeling, like they'd met before, though she couldn't think where.

Travina started to fluster and fought to say something.

"I'm sorry," she whispered, her eyes boring into me.

Confused, I asked, "Sorry? There's nothing to be sorry for." She went into another coughing fit.

I would have stayed and held my mother's hand, but Rachael shooed me away and busied herself with my mam. She asked me to get some fresh hot water for a tea that would help Mam rest more comfortably. I sat in the corner and watched, wishing there was something I could do to help. Watching Rachael made my heart warm. I memorized her. The way her brow furrowed when she was thinking. The way she would move her lips when she was measuring ingredients, like she was talking her way through it. I knew that she was silently reciting the properties as she pulled out each herb and plant in her bundle. I had seen Meerina do the same thing.

She had a tiny mole high on her right cheek bone that danced as she spoke or smiled. Her pale blue eyes were strong, determined, and a little challenging, daring anyone to prove her wrong. Her reddish blond hair hung in waves down her back. More red than blond. In that moment, my mother must have said something to her because Rachael smiled so bright her whole face lit up. She looked over her shoulder at me. In that moment, I vowed that I would give her reason to greet every day with a smile like that.

That surprised me.

I thought of all the women I'd had the pleasure to be with along my travels. It was rare that I didn't have a warm bed and willing heart to keep me company. I didn't think anything of it—until now. Without even a moment's hesitation, my world had transformed. One where Rachael was the center of it. I watched her with this new knowledge and my blood settled in my veins. I suddenly felt "home."

I watched her with my mam. Her demeanor was sure and gentle, and when she spoke with my mam, it came with a measure of love. I knew that Meerina had felt that her gift was not just about learning herbs and plants, but a bit of the Goddess was mixed in. That otherworldly aspect was always a factor. It looked like she had instilled that in Rachael as well, but it didn't hurt that Rachael obviously knew what she was about and that made me proud. My heart swelled. The object of my musings spoke.

"Can you bring me that deerskin bundle. The one in those bags you brought in?" I nodded. "Thanks." I brought it to her and when she reached for it our fingers touched. It was like a little lightning bug had passed between us. We looked at our hands then each other. She seemed to be just as mesmerized as I was.

Just then Rhenal burst through the door, obliterating the moment.

They obviously knew each other and left me completely out, so I went outside to do some more chores. I didn't see Rachael watch me walk out.

I was chopping wood when I remembered something that I had heard about Rachael. A bolt of hot lightning went through me. I had to stop and lean on my axe. That was unexpected. Someone had told me once that Meerina's niece left hearts broken all over the region. The fact that men wanted her made me ... what? Jealous? That was new. Meerina's niece came outside at that moment, looked around and came toward me. I straightened and must have had a pained look on my face because she asked if I was all right. I said I was fine. I lied.

"I was going to care for my horse, but I see that you've already taken care of that. Thanks for that."

"Well, thanks for caring for my mam," I said, and she nodded. I looked toward the cottage and she interpreted my look.

"Rhenal's looking after her. She needed to," was all she said. Her comment was odd but I left it there.

"Your mam is very proud of you," she said. "She kept trying to talk. She's stubborn, that one." I smiled affectionately.

"She taught me all that I am, so I'll give her the credit," I said. Rachael gave me a look, that I hoped was respect, and it warmed my heart. "How is Rhenal holding up?" I asked.

"She'll be fine. She loves your mother."

"Yes. They helped each other after my da, and her husband died." I thought back to that time. A raid from one of the neighboring villages. A band had come from the north and ambushed my da's hunting party. Even to this day, thinking of my strong mother falling apart … Rachael ran her hand down my arm in sympathy.

"They're thick as thieves, those two. They saved each other back then." I smiled seeing them together in my mind.

Rachael regarded me with a strange look but didn't say anything. She smiled.

"Yes. That they are."

"Where's Meerina? Is she well?" I asked, remembering her aunt.

"She is. More than well. You know the Priestess Hall?"

"Of course. Who doesn't?" The house where the young girls go to become priestesses. There, they are trained in the magical arts, and ritual, and are true to the Goddess. It was the wish of many young girls to go there.

"The High Priestess herself came and asked if Auntie would come to the Hall and teach the healing arts to the initiates. She'll be gone for two years."

"Two years? That's a long time. You'll miss her I expect."

"More than you know," she said. I looked back at the cottage and I thought that maybe I did know something of that.

"The High Priestess herself? That's quite an honor." I was impressed. "Well, it's much deserved. When did she leave?"

"Not long, about a moon ago."

"So I guess you've taken her place then? You'll be the one they send for."

"Yes, well, what else is there? I'm not her, but I'll make do, I suppose."

"That's not what I hear. I hear you're a very gifted healer. In time you'll match Meerina."

"Ah. Where did you hear that?" she scoffed.

"Your aunt herself told me."

"You know her?" she asked incredulously.

"Yes. Our paths have crossed many times."

"Is that so? Where?"

"We met from time to time on our rounds."

"Rounds?" She seemed to remember something. She looked toward the cottage, then back at me. "Travina O'Malley. O'Malley!" She looked shocked. "You're that Stephen!" I smiled, enjoying her shock for some reason. "You're the Bard O'Malley!"

"Yes."

"Well …." She paused, not knowing what to say. She drew back, I thought, but it might have been my imagination. I felt cold. "I have to go back in. Rhenal made stew if you're hungry." As she walked back to the cottage, I watched her with a heart that wasn't as foot loose and fancy free as it was when I bolted out of bed this morning. She did something to me inside. She seemed angry though. I wondered about that.

I brought an arm full of wood with me as I came in for supper. I placed it next to the hearth and when I turned around Rhenal was there to hand me a bowl of stew.

"It's a mess, isn't it?" She nodded toward the barn and fences. "I'm sorry, Stephen. There just hasn't been much time."

"Rhenal." I set my bowl down and wrapped her up in my arms. "Please. I don't care. Just take care of my ma. That's your job. All right?" She nodded and started to cry.

"It's just been too much." I held her as she cried herself out. I looked at Rachael and she was regarding me with a funny look. I couldn't tell what it was. Rhenal dried herself up and went back to gently bathing my mam. Rachael let her do it. I ate, then went back outside. I could be of use out there.

I stayed outside until it was starting to get dark. I was happy with my accomplishments that day. I was tired, but it felt good. I hadn't used my muscles that way for some time. I noticed Rachael first thing. She was sitting next to my mother cutting up a cloth in small sections. Our eyes locked when she looked up. I tripped. She fumbled her knife, but caught it before it landed in my mother. I laughed. She didn't.

Rhenal looked up from dishing the remainder of the stew and looked at both of us in turn. She shook her head and continued on with what she was doing.

I brought my bowl to the bed and sat in the chair opposite Rachael. Without looking at Rachael, I set my bowl up on the bed and ate with one hand while holding my mam's hand with the other. After I finished, Rhenal reached for my bowl and I promptly laid my head down and fell asleep.

Rachael watched him, his dark hair and dark eyes. He handled his mother with such loving care that she was taken aback. She had just assumed that the Bard O'Malley, "the great storyteller," the man with, at least one woman in every village, would be a lazy, selfish, womanizing pig, but the man before her was none of those. Travina had talked about her son, but Rachael hadn't put the two together. She hadn't realized that Travina's Stephen was the same as the "Bard." She was having to rearrange her thoughts.

Rachael steamed. She really liked this man, but when she found out who he was, his reputation, well, she couldn't be with a man like that, and it made her angry. Of course, she finally had met a man that she liked, but it turned out that he was a ladies man.

Watching Stephen sleep so lovingly next to his mam made her insides coil. The longer he slept the more upset she got. Rhenal was sitting on the spare bed with her back against the wall, and had dozed off herself.

Rachael couldn't stand it anymore. She grabbed her shawl and went outside. She walked around the yard in the dark, then heard her horse whinny. It was much darker in the barn, but she let the sound of her horse lead her to him. She settled somewhat, running her hands along his fine lines. She leaned up against him with his head hanging over her shoulder. He belched which made her smile.

By the time she walked into the cabin she was calmer but the moment she saw him, carving by the fire, she coiled up again. She forgot all pretenses of fighting it and let herself be mad. She had just met him so why was she acting like this? So what that she liked him?

It didn't give her the excuse to be a petulant child about it. She only knew that since the moment she had looked into his eyes she was lost.

She sat next to Travina and began her mental healing checklist. Stephen came over on the other side and sat down as well. She cringed inside, but continued. He watched her for a bit then asked.

"How is she, Rachael? Will she be all right?"

She wanted to snap at him for being so caring, but held it in.

"She'll be fine. We caught it early enough. Rhenal has done well enough to keep the sickness at bay, and your mother's strong," she said, trying to be kind.

I sighed. Shame shot through me again.

"Oh, Ma. I'm so sorry that I wasn't here," I said, almost forgetting that anyone else was there. Rachael lost it. She couldn't stop herself.

"Yes. Why weren't you here?" she heaved the insult at me, "She'll be fine, no thanks to you."

I sat straight up. Shocked.

"Rachael. I—"

Rhenal woke when they began talking and was surprised at the accusation.

"That's the problem, isn't it? You weren't home taking care of her. Instead you're out—"

She stopped. Realizing what she was saying.

"I'm out what?" I asked angrily. I felt bad enough I didn't need her to add to it. "Making a life?"

Rachael didn't say anything, feeling guilty that she had said anything at all. Rhenal was intrigued with the dynamics. She knew what was going on, and why. She needed to make this right.

"When your father died you both were wounded so deeply." Both Rachael and Stephen whipped their heads around. "We all were, but at least I had all my boys. It was just the two of you; you were so strong and determined to make it work. She loved him so much that to work this land meant working with him. He was part of this land, and you worked it right along with her. Then one day she realized that you would stay here forever. For her. She didn't want that for you. You were always such a gifted artist. She knew you were destined for larger things." She looked at Rachael.

"Do you know what she did?" Rachael shook her head. "She brought out her best horse, loaded it with a week's worth of rations and told him to go out in the world and make something of himself." She turned to me. "She had me come over here that day. Do you remember, I was here?" I nodded. "She did that because it broke her heart to send you away, but she had to do it for you. She brought me here to pick up the pieces after you left." Tears came to my eyes. She looked at Rachael again. "That boy did fight though. He did everything he could. But when she sets her mind to something … well … you better just do it." She laughed.

"I had to. Don't you see?" My mother had woken. She grabbed my arm. I could barely feel it. "You never would have left."

"Oh, Ma."

"Travina," Rachael said. Mam pressed on.

"Please forgive me. I did it because I knew you would never leave your mother." I looked at my mother with new eyes. I had always had immense respect for her, but this … I knew it must have killed her to send me away.

"Oh, Ma," I cried, "You're such a fool." We smiled at each other.

"Listen to your mam." She looked for Rhenal, who crossed the room. "Rhenal and I have each other. We're just fine. You come home once in a while, you fix things, leave more money than I need, and you're doing what you love, bringing joy to those around you. And your carvings are so beautiful. What more could a mother want?" She reached for Rhenal.

"We're fine. We two old ladies can take care of ourselves quite well. Can't we old girl?" I looked at their clasped hands, then at my mother, then at Rhenal, then back at my mother. They had eyes only for each other. I looked at Rachael, who had come to her own conclusions, which she confirmed in her own eyes to me, with a sweet smile on her face. The moment passed, and Rhenal self-consciously said that she should be going home to give us time together.

"No." I stood up. I gave her a look that said "I know and I understand." "You stay. Rachael and I will go get some more wood."

I looked questioningly at Rachael and she nodded. I got up, kissed Mam on the cheek, and then Rhenal, and squeezed her shoulder. Rachael and I left the cottage and walked slowly across the yard, in our own thoughts. We finally made our way to the wood pile and sat quietly in the dark.

"You know, I felt so horrible for leaving her here to manage the farm, but each time I came home, she made me promise to not fight her. I never understood it. I felt helpless somehow. Now, it makes sense." I started laughing. "And especially now. Now I know it was for another reason as well." Rachael started laughing as well. "Who knew?"

We laughed, then we both sobered.

"Rachael. Have I done something to offend you? I would apologize if I knew what I did." I turned to her in the dark. "Why were you so angry?"

She didn't answer for so long that I sighed in resignation, and started to get up. "I feel a fool. You're going to think I'm daft."

"Well, I already think you're daft, so you might as well give it a try," I joked. She snorted.

"Well, I can't dance around it, not being in the same space, so I'll be honest with you." She shifted slightly away from me. "When I first saw you I couldn't breathe," she said quickly. "And the only reason I'm telling you this is because I think that you had the same reaction, and then I found out who you were. Your reputation precedes you as a ladies man. I liked you, but I didn't want to be one of your women. Provided, of course, that you even wanted me."

Well ... didn't that punch me in the gut. The Buchannons were definitely known for their candor. She sounded a little shy, but to have the courage to open her feelings like that made my heart swell. I opened my mouth to say something.

"Oh," was all that came out. She waited a beat for something else.

"Oh? I flay myself open at your feet and that's all you can say? Bard O'Malley, my arse." I huffed out a laugh, then I started laughing in earnest. She followed suit. "Bard O'Malley, ladies man."

That sobered me.

"You make that sound like a bad thing." I was confused.

"Isn't it?" she demanded. "Aren't they your conquests?"

"Not to me." It was dark but I could see well enough to know she rolled her eyes. Anger sparked. "You don't know me. Women are … they're the world to me. I watched my ma and da run this farm. Her as much as him. They were … together. And when he died, she worked her fingers to the bone. I watched Rhenal do the same thing. I respect women so much. You have no idea. All I knew growing up, were women who were stronger than most men I know." I shifted to her, trying to convince her of what I was saying.

"Women are amazing. They're soft and warm, and so willing to make me feel that way as well. And on a cold winter night, yes, I'll take it. Why would I turn that down? I don't go looking for it, Rachael. They come to me."

She didn't say anything. I wanted, no, needed her to understand that I felt the same way toward her.

"Rachael." She didn't say anything. "Rachael?"

"Please, Stephen. Don't," she begged. I moved to kneel in front of her. Even in the dark I could see the mistrust in her eyes.

"Rachael. You weren't imagining things. I felt the same as you. The first time I looked into your eyes I knew that I would never again want to wake up with anyone else but you."

Tears came to her eyes, she so wanted to believe him. She reached out to lay her hand on his cheek.

"You idiot. We just met." She sniffed. I covered her hand with my own.

Before we could say anything more, Rhenal came out. Mam had started a coughing fit and Rachael got up on a run.

For three days, Rachael stayed and brought some relief to my mam, who was actually getting to the point that she could hold her own spoon. During that time, when Rachael wasn't by my mam's side, we went walking. Both, to give us time, and to give Mam and Rhenal time together. It had been a hard winter on them. Rachael didn't trust me so I used that time to win her over. We found that we had a lot in common, and after three days I'd felt like I'd never not known her.

We soon realized, however, that life continued on. On one such walk, a young man about fifteen years old, galloped up to us on an old horse. Rachael was needed immediately in the next village. A farmer, Dutch McDonald, had been run over by his wagon and plow, badly cut and broken. His son, David, had heard that there was a healer in the village and had come to fetch her.

"Who is watching him now?" Rachael asked.

"Mary. A neighbor."

"Where's your mother?"

"Ma died last winter with the lung sickness." Fear radiated off him in waves. Rachael nodded, then turned to me.

"I have to go, Stephen."

"I know."

"Your mother seems fine enough for now. I'll go and then come back as soon as I can." She looked at the sky. It would soon be dark. David was waiting, either, to send a message, or escort her to his village now. She stole a look at the cottage, then the boy. I knew she was weighing, leaving my mother, or leaving with the messenger.

"If I may," I interjected. "I could take you. Send David away. Tell him what you need so they can have it ready when you get there. You can tell Rhenal what Ma needs, then we can leave immediately." She hesitated. "I have business there anyway. It would be perfect."

I knew then that sometimes, as a healer, the options of who gets help now and who can wait can sometimes be a choice of life or death. The thought solidified my love for Rachael.

I could see her weighing her options and then she turned toward the messenger.

"We'll follow Mr. O'Malley's plan." She turned to me. I nodded. She told David what she needed and sent him off.

Mam was awake when we went inside. Rhenal was holding a bowl of soup and my ma was feeding herself. I was pleased. Rachael told them of the plan. We all agreed that Mam would be fine. I went to prepare the horses while Rachael gave Rhenal directions and packed what she needed.

When she walked outside, I was waiting with the horses. She was a little nonplussed to have everything ready.

49

"Okay then," she said. She got on and took off at a run. And I'd follow you anywhere, I thought, as I watched her ride off in the dark. I took off after her.

The speed in which we rode kept conversation to a minimum. We followed the directions that David had given us and he was waiting for us when we arrived.

"I have everything ready that you asked for," he said, scared and eager. Rachael was calm and gentle and directed him inside.

"That's great, David. Let's see what we have, shall we." Mr. McDonald was sleeping, but was feverish and murmuring. As per her directions there was a fire going and water boiling over it, and a small pile of clean rags. There were a few pots, filled with some kind of mixture, setting on the table as well. She sat in the chair that was sitting next to the bed and started peeling back the shredded clothes and bloody rags that someone had used on the wounds. There was a young girl of about David's age who had backed off against the wall when we came in. She was covered in blood. Rachael had immediately recognized the fear in her eyes. David hung back by the door. She interpreted the situation quickly.

"Did you do this?" Rachael nodded to the rags. The girl warily nodded, afraid she had done something wrong. "You did just fine. You stopped the bleeding. You might have saved his life." The girl heaved a sigh of relief. As Rachael began her healing checklist on the farmer, she talked to the girl. "Are you Mary?"

"Yes."

"Well, Mary, I need your help." The girl, eager to help, stepped closer. Rachael looked at me and then at David and back at me. She knew he wouldn't hold up. He'd already lost his mother and his dad was ripped to pieces. I nodded and had David come outside with me to collect more wood.

"Listen, Mary, in a little while, I need you to take David outside and keep him there for a while. Take the horses and put them in the barn. Feed them, brush them. Whatever it takes. Okay?" Rachael looked around the room in mock secret mode, bringing Mary into the importance of it. She nodded at her patient. "His leg is badly broken and David shouldn't see this next part. Stay out as long as you can. Can you do that for me?" Mary nodded eagerly, feeling important. "Good. But first, before you do that, I need you to rip one of these into strips for bandages." She nodded toward the rags that David had set out. Rachael immediately mixed up a powerful tea to keep her patient asleep while they realigned his leg.

David and I walked in, each with an armload of wood. To keep him busy, she directed David to get a large bowl of hot water. She directed me to start unloading her tools and medicines and lay them out on the table next to her. Like a true leader, she directed us all. While we waited for the effects of the medicine to work, she showed Mary how to treat and bandage the wounds. When she was ready, she nodded to Mary, who took David outside. He didn't want to go but Rachael smoothly talked him into it, saying she could concentrate better if she knew her horse was looked after. He nodded, and they both left. She turned to me and the look she had on her face made my stomach churn.

"Have you ever fixed a broken bone?" she asked with the tone of voice that one asks to pass the butter. Shite.

"Grab the rope," she said. "Put it near you."

"What's the rope for?"

"Maybe nothing, but have it close in case." She wasn't looking at me. "It's for leverage. In case you can't get a good hold on the leg." Something about that made me pale.

She directed me to the proper handholds and how to pull. She would manipulate the bone into place if needed. There were two breaks so we needed to make sure both of them maneuvered back into place.

"Ready?" she asked. As ready as I'll ever be. I nodded. "Okay, now."

I grunted and cursed. The first break slid into place nicely, but the second didn't want to cooperate. My hands were slipping from sweat so I had to stop. I replaced my grip and braced one foot against the bed. I nodded when I was ready.

I pulled with everything I had and with Rachael's help it slid into place. I almost let go but Rachael yelled to keep the tension. She grabbed the splints that David had made and tied them quickly, then nodded for me to let go. I collapsed against the wall.

When we both got our wind back she looked over at me with renewed respect. I looked at her with awe.

"You were amazing," I said. "The way you know how to do that." She grew embarrassed with my praise.

"Matter of fact in my family," she said humbly.

"Yeah, well, to the rest of us peons, it's amazing."

"Well, thanks," she said in acceptance. "You didn't do too bad yourself. We didn't even need the rope. You were so strong," she said mockingly. She reached out and squeezed my arm, but when she did it was no longer a joke. The contact made us both conscious of each other in a way that was indisputable. The energy was rocketing back and forth between us.

We heard footsteps so we broke apart. David and Mary came in. Rachael directed Mary to help her and I helped David make us something to eat. None of us were hungry but it gave him something to do.

When they were done, Rachael asked David where they would all sleep. He seemed embarrassed that there was no other room than the one we were in. We would sleep on the floor here or in the hay loft in the barn. I put a hand on his shoulder.

"Don't worry. It's just like the cottage I grew up in and I've slept in many a barn along the way." David seemed to relax. He and I would sleep in the barn and the women would stay inside and look after his father. Rachael gave me a look of thanks and sent us off to bed, telling us to let the women take care of things. I knew she was really taking care of David. I was laying in my bedroll and David had yet to come up. I presumed he was keeping Mary company, his object of affection.

I had been laying there, thinking of Rachael, when the object of *my* thoughts came up the ladder with a lantern and two cups of hot tea. It was a feat for sure that she made it up with that in her hands. Impressive.

"I thought you might like something hot before bed. The air has a bit of chill with it."

"Thank you. You didn't have to." Our fingers touched when she handed me the cup and we were speechless.

"'Tis nothing," she finally said.

Neither of us could think of anything to say, so out of embarrassment, she looked like she was going to get up.

"How's Mr. McDonald?" I hurriedly asked. She happily settled in again.

"He's resting as comfortably as he can be. Poor man. At least he's got a son who loves him."

"And a young girl who loves the son," I remarked.

"Oi. You noticed that too?" She laughed. "It's good. I'm glad."

"You're so beautiful," I said simply.

"You're so blind," she countered and blushed.

"I mean it. You're beautiful."

"Stop it. Stephen O'Malley, don't you toy with me. You don't get to," she said very seriously. Her voice broke in fear.

"I'm not toying." I sat up, set my tea down and took her hands. "You're strong, smart, capable, *and* beautiful." She pulled her hands from mine and got up.

"Don't play with me," she said as she turned away.

I watched her descend and knew that she was going to be my wife. All I had to do was to convince her of that.

A while later David came up and laid out his bed roll. We chatted for a bit then we both rolled over, although it was a long time before I fell asleep. There was a certain red head that had crawled in bed with me.

The next morning I went inside for something to eat, and to see if Rachael needed anything. Her demeanor was a little cold, but this time I knew why. I had only to prove to her that I meant every word. I didn't know how I was going to do that but it was a worthy challenge indeed. The day was spent with Rachael showing Mary the art of healing, and I, helping David with some chores.

We stayed that night, and I was disappointed that there were no callers with tea, but it only served my resolve.

The next day I had to go into the village and tend to some business.

"I've got business in town, I'll be back mid-day. Do you need anything?" I asked her. She looked at me with a blank stare. "Do you need anything?" I asked again. She shook her head. "All right, I'll see you then."

Rachael's stomach churned when he mentioned town. She knew that women would be there. Probably some that he'd been with already. He said that she was *the one*, but how can one change just like that. She didn't believe him. She wanted to, he seemed earnest enough, but she'd known too many men that were otherwise.

In town, I took care of business and then was drinking a pint out in the town center. Someone wanted to hear a story, so I obliged. I recounted a story of the trolls that used to roam the land. By the time I was finished with that one, the word had gone out that the Bard O'Malley was in town and people were flocking in.

While Stephen was regaling the crowds, Rachael remained back at the farm. Fuming.

"Great storyteller, my arse," she sputtered. She was so angry she pummeled the herbs in her little stone bowl until a fine powdery cloud wafted.

"Are you all right?" Mary hesitantly asked. Rachael shot her head up, forgetting that anyone else was about. She blew a lock of hair off her face. She looked into the fine powder that she'd made and went to place the bowl on the table. She miscalculated and the bowl fell and broke. Shite. Mary reacted.

"Oh no! Do you want me to go to town and get you another one?" She was so eager that Rachael had to sit back and take a breath.

"Oh, thanks Mary, but I think I need some fresh air. I'll go. You'll be all right here?"

"Oh yes!" She was so eager, Rachael smiled.

She could have sent Mary, or David, but if she was truthful to herself, she wanted to know what Stephen was up to. In short, she was spying on him. It made her feel small and she didn't like it.

While in town, she'd found a shop that had a few other tools and supplies that she'd been wanting, so she ended up with a rather large bundle. There was a large crowd in the center of town so she assumed Stephen was working his magic. She found a spot in the back of the crowd and sat down with her bundle to watch.

She watched him take command of the crowd. He led them down dark hallways, into scary woods, up snowcapped mountains, into hovels and castles, and into the minds of the rich and the hearts of the poor. She, as much as the crowd, got swept up in his velvety, rich voice. She had a sudden craving for dark chocolate. Listening to him captivate those around him, she fell hopelessly in love. She prayed that he meant what he said because she didn't know if she could bear it if he was toying with her.

The sun was high in the sky as Stephen finished his last story. Rachael stayed where she was while he bid everyone adieu and stood shaking hands while they filed by with kind words and hellos.

As the crowd dispersed, Rachael's stomach coiled into knots when she watched a young woman saunter over to Stephen. The two talked for a short bit, then the woman stomped away angry. Rachael was slightly mollified. She started toward him, but then stopped when another young woman came up to him. The young woman tried to put her arms around him but he stopped her and shook his head and said something. He just happened to look over in Rachael's general direction and did a double take. He stopped talking and stood there mesmerized. He said something to the young woman.

The woman looked over at Rachael, then stomped in Rachael's direction with Stephen slowly following.

"Bitch," the young woman snarled at Rachael as she passed, which left Rachael with her mouth hanging open.

My heart leapt when I saw Rachael. As I walked toward her, she became my world. In another part of my brain, I registered that people wanted to talk to me, but I was so enamored with Rachael that I was completely deaf and blind to them. Then when Sofia had called her a bitch, I had to smile. Rachael had no idea why the woman was upset.

"They're mad at you for sure."

"At me? Why me?" she exclaimed, completely clueless to what was happening.

"Well, it might be that I've told them that I'm a married man now," I said simply. Rachael's mouth dropped.

"You've made me an honest man, Rachael. I want to marry you."

Rachael didn't move. I believe I could have knocked her over if I'd had a feather. I walked to her.

"I know you don't trust me. Yes, I have a reputation, but I will do whatever it takes for you to realize that I am now your man. And only yours."

Rachael's heart skipped a beat. She was stunned, and just couldn't believe.

But she wasn't going to run either.

"Well, then you can carry this for me." She gestured toward her bundle and walked away with a big grin.

"Gladly, my princess." I smiled.

We headed back to my mam's village the next day. Mr. McDonald was well enough for us to leave. Rachael had taught Mary enough that she could manage most things. In fact, Rachael recognized in her, an untapped healer, and had spoken to her about becoming one of Rachael's apprentices. So we left with the directive that Mary was to send for her immediately if needed.

On the way home we were both giddy. We took our time and ambled along wanting to spend more time with just us. The warmth of the sun felt wondrous, and the gentle sway of the horses relaxed us. I gazed at Rachael, so beautiful with her red hair shining in the sun, her skin glowing. She stole a glance at me and blushed.

"What are you looking at, you fool?" she asked with a smile.

"The most beautiful woman in the world," I said with complete sincerity.

"Aah. The Bard O'Malley, with the golden tongue." She thought of something. "Do they call you that because of your stories, or because—"

"Oh, please, Rachael." I knew she liked to see me squirm, talking about my women. She said it was pay back because it made her heart burn every time she thought of me and my women. She had told me enough to know that she'd been hurt too many times. I told her that I would gladly spend the rest of my life relieving her of that fear.

"How did you become a bard anyway? Did you study?"

"Well, that's a story for sure, and no, I didn't."

She waited for me to tell the story.

"Well, you know already that Mam threw me out on my ear."

"Ear my arse. I'm going to tell her you said that," Rachael joked.

"Anyway ...," I continued on, "when I finally quit kicking and screaming, I decided that if I couldn't help Ma at the farm, then I'd get rich and give her everything that she'd ever wanted. I went from town to town doing the odd job and selling some of my carvings. I got a few commissions here and there. But things didn't start happening until I started drinking in the pubs." I smiled thinking of those times. "I would drink and talk a good story. One night, the drunken bastards I was with, started calling me the Bard, as a joke, you know. It stuck. When you're drunk, everything sounds like a good idea." I looked over at Rachael. "You're so beautiful." She was embarrassed but smiled.

"Anyway, when I moved on to another town, one of the boys from before, recognized me and called me Bard. One thing led to another and word got around, then soon, everywhere I went I would hear someone yell out "Bard, tell us a story!" I began to tell old stories, then I picked up new ones and embellished them, about ordinary people doing extraordinary things. Their plain, simple lives lived on in everyone's minds.

"I started carrying messages, letters and small packages. People wanted me to come to town. I never had to spend money on lodging or—"

"Oh, I bet!" she said.

"Even if ..." I gave her a look of mock sternness. "Even if I didn't spend the night with a woman, the merchants would put me up ... because the Bard O'Malley is good for business," I said in mock importance. She rolled her eyes.

"The rest is history, as they say." I paused and finished in self-deprecation. "I'm more of the average man's Bard. Yes, I'm known in the region, but I'm sure that if I went into a major town or city like Dublin, or Galway, that I'd be thrown out on my ear and laughed all the way home."

"Oh, I don't know about that. A year ago when I traveled to Edinburg, with Aunt Meerina, I heard your name come up."

"Edinburg? Really? Me?" I was incredulous. She nodded. "Huh."

We stayed at my mam's for three days and then set off together. By this time, we knew there was no other option for us, but to travel together. We had found each other and wouldn't be apart. When we departed from the farm, we decided to head cross country instead of taking the road. It would make our journey longer but we weren't interested in speed. Only us.

We rode in silence. I knew I didn't know what to say and I presumed that she was of the same thought. We were entering a new phase of our relationship. I couldn't stop thinking of her body next to mine, but she'd been hurt so many times before that I didn't want to push her. It would kill me but I would gladly wait forever.

"You might as well say what's on your mind. My head is ringing from you thinking so loudly," she broke into my thoughts. I smiled.

"Well, why don't you tell me what I'm thinking then," I joked, "if you're so good at hearing things."

"Okay then. You're thinking about the first time you get me into your bed," she said it so matter-of-factly I sputtered. Or I might have sputtered because it was true.

"How did you come up with that?"

"Well, it's not because I can read minds, but rather, it's just noticing that there's a particular part of your anatomy that's talking," she said smiling. I looked down.

Shite.

"Stephen. You don't think that I haven't thought about it as well?" She was serious now. "Let's just see what happens. Okay?" All I could do was nod. Just mentioning what was on our minds lessoned the tension, so we talked about nothing, and everything.

I suddenly remembered that I had made something for her. I reached into the folds of my garb and pulled out a small bundle wrapped in deerskin. She unfolded it and gasped. In her palm was a small statue of a tiger. She looked at me with shock.

"How did you know? Tigers are my favorite."

I just shrugged, pleased that she liked it.

"I don't know. I just thought it was something you might like," I said humbly. She leaned over and kissed my cheek.

We stopped for lunch at a small stand of aspen, their leaves quaking in the brisk breeze. After lunch, as there was no hurry, we decided to stay for the night. We both remarked how easy it was to have two people do the work. A stream was flowing on the far side of the stand and it was here that we decided to make camp.

I unloaded the horses and gathered wood, as she put out the bedrolls and made camp. While I was gathering wood, I noticed that the wind had stopped. I stood for a moment in the quiet.

When I reached the clearing with my first armload, she mentioned that in the silence, she had heard the sound of a waterfall upstream.

"I think I'm going to go investigate." She began walking in that direction then she turned and gave me a deliberate look. "In a bit, when you're done, why don't you come and join me." Then kept walking.

The pile of wood, in my arms, fell right where I stood. Her husky laugh rang through the trees.

I finished gathering enough wood that would last all night. I created a small pyre in the make-shift fire ring, so that it was ready to light when we got back from ... the waterfall.

I took my time, enjoying my anticipation, and listening to the birds. Following the thrum of the waterfall, I touched each tree as I passed, and came out next to the stream by a large flat rock. The waterfall, about the size of a man, was to my right, upstream. Rachael had been doing laundry I saw. I noticed a root, used for soap, smashed on the rock. Next to the root was a small pile of herbs and plants that she had picked. I recognized a few that I assumed were going to be part of our dinner. Her wet clothes were spread out over various branches, but she was nowhere to be found. I decided to follow her lead and undressed. I washed my clothes and then myself. Rachael still hadn't shown up so I just floated in the small pool at the foot of the small waterfall. The feel of the sun on my bare skin, the coolness of the water, the sound of the falls, and the thought of Rachael, put me into an, almost, otherworldly state. I drifted in *this* world, but felt myself in another.

I heard the slight crack of a small twig and opened one eye. She stood on the rock above me with the sun behind her, giving her an ethereal goddess look. I opened both eyes and watched her slowly step into the pool. Her body was exactly as I pictured. Strong, lithe. As she neared I brought my knees down and knelt at her feet. My goddess. She stood in front of me and I leaned in and smelled her skin, my forehead against her belly. I felt her hands on my head holding me there, both of us relishing the moment. I looked up into her eyes and I saw tears in them. Disbelief was there as well. I slowly stood. I wanted to remove that disbelief.

"I'm yours forever. Only yours." I brought my lips to hers. It was like I entered another time. I felt, in that moment, that there was no other place on earth. That we were all that existed. Somehow, my arms had wrapped themselves around her body, and somehow her legs had wound themselves around my waist. And somehow, we found ourselves by the rock. I couldn't let her lips go. I laid her down gently with my body on hers.

I raised my head up so that I could look into her eyes. A jolt shot through my heart at the love I saw in those blue eyes. I prayed that I would never fail in keeping it there.

"That's a very serious look you have there, Stephen," she said, quietly. She inquisitively cocked her head.

"I was praying that I always be the man that you need. That I never fail you in that. That I will always see the love in your eyes, that I see right now." Hope dared to peak out from her eyes. I teared up, watching her finally realize that I meant what I said. Tears leaked out of the corners of her eyes and rolled down across her temples. I wiped them away with my thumbs. We stayed like that, just staring into the other's eyes. I got lost in those blue points of light. She reached up and caressed my cheek.

"Ah, Stephen. What you do with my heart," she said with a sigh and lifted her head to kiss me. Her lips explored mine, then more demand grew in her kisses. I felt that she was giving me her blessing. I complied.

My lips slowly followed a trail down and explored. My hand began its own exploration. Her skin was like silk, and with the heat from the sun, it was like nectar to the bees. My lips explored her breasts, then I kissed my way down to her belly and beyond. I tasted her whole body, wanting to imprint to my mind, every taste and every muscle. Her hands roamed over my body, and every place that she touched felt like she had left a trail of molten lava in the wake of her fingers. It was like nothing I'd ever experienced before.

My fingers found their way home and she shot up latching onto my neck. My lips found hers again.

"More," she gasped. "More. I want you inside me."

I entered her and we moved to the rhythm of the water. The pounding of the falls matched the sound of my heart as it pounded in my chest. She let go with a cry. The birds let out a flurry of birdsong. I followed with my own.

As our breath evened, I rolled over, as she had rough granite under her. I grasped her hand and we lay there for some time, letting our skin bake in the hot sun. After a while she sat up, and kissed me tenderly.

"I love you, Stephen O'Malley." She looked into my eyes, and for a moment, she wore her heart in her eyes. Hope and fear. Then the moment was gone and she got up and strode into the woods. The sure woman once again. A few minutes later when she came back, she walked to the edge of the rock, dove in and swam to the waterfall. She sat and let the water run over her head and body. I grew hard as I watched the silver streams transform her body into slivers of light gleaming in the sunlight. I slid into the water and slowly swam toward her. She opened her eyes and watched me slowly come to her.

I reached her and she reached for me. I entered her with water flowing over us, between us, inside of us. I made love to her as the mother flowed and thundered around us, our bodies enveloped with liquid silver. When we came together, it was like a blessing from the Goddess. We held each other long after.

Finally, chilled, we swam back to the rock. Rachael checked our clothes, turned them over and laid down next to me. We slept until the sun started going down behind the ridge. We gathered our clothes and herbs and walked naked to our campsite.

We put our bedrolls together and made love, and talked, way into the night. I thought of the pagan marriage ritual.

"I want to have a hand-fast ceremony when we reach the next village. I want you to make me an honest man," I told her. I saw her white teeth in the dark.

"You're such a fool. We just met." She reached up and touched my cheek.

"Is that a yes then?" I asked.

"Yes." She laughed her happiness. She rolled over on top of me and kissed me. "That's a yes."

So within the week, she was Rachael O'Malley. I was the happiest man alive. Rachael was sorry her Aunt Meerina couldn't be there, and I thought about my mam, but under the circumstances, I think they'd both be proud. Meerina was too far away, and Mam was too sick to stand up. We decided that we'd have another ceremony in a few years when Aunt Meerina got back, and my mam could be there as well. For now, we couldn't not be husband and wife.

I woke in the dark and for a moment felt disoriented, then I saw the unfamiliar fireplace and the old armoire and I remembered. Aunt Meerina. She'd been back since the last half moon, and she had sent for us to come home. Rachael was so excited she couldn't be contained. I had been hesitant, however. Meerina and I had always had a good rapport with each other, but now that I was married to her niece, well … that was a different story. I had been nervous.

We'd been traveling for two years. The bard and the healer. We became as famous together as we were apart. The stories about our love reached Meerina, even way up north in the Priestess Hall. She had sent a message of congratulations, reserved though it was. I had the feeling that it was because she knew my reputation and didn't trust me. Rachael had told me not to worry, that once Auntie got to know me, she would love me despite what my past was like. Laying there, I hoped that it was true. We had arrived only yesterday so it was too soon to tell.

I thought about Meerina. She had been the surrogate mother since Rachael was a child. Rachael had lost her parents in a war with invaders. Her father had been a soldier, and her mother went along to heal the wounded. She would leave Rachael with Meerina as her apprentice, and follow her man. After the fighting, her mother would wander the fields of red to treat the wounded. One day, marauders hid in the forest and when least expected, they attacked, leaving Rachael alone. Meerina had been mother ever since.

Looking down at Rachael, I frowned, as she was still sickly looking. About two months before Meerina had come home, a horse of one of Rachael's patients kicked her, cut her badly, and then, like all good healers, didn't take care of herself. She had gotten septic and then very sick. She was recovering nicely, but had lost a lot of weight and was still trying to put it back on. The thought that Meerina might blame me for not taking care of Rachael, had weighed heavily on my mind.

Though Rachael was still pale, they looked like each other, Rachael and Meerina. Their coloring and their features were the same. Golden skin, reddish hair and blue eyes, but for all their sameness, her aunt had eyes that looked straight through you until you squirmed; must have been those years with the Priestesses.

Growing up, Rachael was Meerina's favorite protégé. Her soft hands, quiet demeanor and quick mind made her one of her aunt's best assistants, but over the last two years Rachael had come into her own as a healer. Meerina had noticed and mentioned that. Rachael was floating when her aunt told her, but Meerina was also quick to remind Rachael that what made a great healer was the fact that they remained humble. That they were only the conduit for the Goddess to work her magic. Rachael took the hint, and was suitably admonished. So saying that, she told Rachael that she had learned some healing techniques at the Hall, and she wanted Rachael to learn them.

Days flowed by easily enough and our nightly routine developed. It consisted of me carving in front of the fire, and those two standing at the table for hours as they discussed herbs, and practiced their craft. With the two of their heads together, sometimes I shook my head in wonder and felt I was the luckiest man alive. I had a smart, beautiful wife who loved me, and work that fed me. What more could a man want?

One such night, about a week after we arrived, I was sitting by the fire, and instead of carving I just watched them. Rachael felt my eyes on her and looked up. With a smirk on her face she pinned her eyes on me. My heart skipped a beat for the love in them. Her aunt admonished her for not paying attention, but then gave me a quick approving glance.

On the following day, Meerina walked up next to me as I was repairing a basket. She said that since healers traveled a lot she was glad that Rachael had found someone who knew what that entailed. She also liked that I didn't mind that my wife was as well known as I was.

"You know, Stephen, it takes a strong man to let his woman be his equal," she said to me. "I hope you keep that strength. She's strong that one." She nodded toward her niece. "She needs to be loved by someone who can handle that strength." I had the feeling that Meerina knew something of what she was saying. I watched Rachael, very deliberately and selectively, picking some herbs.

"Well, I don't know if it's strength, Meerina. Is it strength to love someone? I just know that to lose her would mean that I would be lost. She's my home." After a bit, I looked back at Meerina and saw that her eyes were shiny. She stared a hole through my soul, gave a barely perceptible nod, and left to do her business.

After that, she accepted me without qualm and treated me like her own, instead of treating me with reserved kindness, like a guest. She would mock me and admonish me for something that I did or didn't do, like she would her own. Rachael noticed the shift and seemed to settle. Like she had been holding her breath for her aunt's approval.

"She likes you," Rachael said after we went to bed one night. "I've never seen her take to someone so fast." She reached up to touch my cheek. "She's reserved, that one. You must have charmed her." She smiled. "Like me." I kissed her.

"Nah, it was just the carving I gave her." I had given her a figurine of the Goddess with designs all over it. Each one represented some aspect of nature. "She seemed to like it." Rachael leaned up, pushed me down and leaned over me.

"Like it? She put it in her traveling bag. She said that you had reached down from the stars and plucked out each part of her soul and put them in that little statue." She leaned down and kissed me. "She said with magic like that I had better hold on to you or you'll be spreading that magic all over the countryside."

She sat up and straddled me. With her hands down at her sides she just looked into my eyes. For the longest time she just stared. Her eyes roamed over my face, like she was memorizing every part of it. She had the most intense look on her face.

"What are you doing?" I asked her. For a fleeting moment, she looked pained, then it was gone and she replaced it with a sly grin.

"I'm soaking up that magic just in case you decide to start spreading that magic elsewhere."

I looked at her in astonishment. Did she really not know? That I would give everything that I have, that I am, to be by her side? That I would rather die than leave her?

"After all this time do you still not know?" I asked. She gave me a quizzical look. "Do you not know that you are the magic in my soul? That to leave you would mean that I would leave that magic behind?" Tears came to her eyes as she heard my words. "I'm sorry I've not let you know that every day. I'm sorry that you've thought that even once."

"Ah, Stephen." She reached down and laid her hand on my cheek and whispered, "I love you more than life itself."

"You are the other half of my soul." I reached up and put my hand over her heart. She put hers over mine. We looked into each other for a moment of forever. Then she stretched her body over mine and softly kissed me.

We woke to birds singing and our bed was covered with a shaft of sunlight. The blue sky held promise of a glorious day and the grass glistened with dew. The trees and flowers dripped from the downpour in the night.

Toward the end of the week, Meerina had announced that she wanted us to go with her on her healing rounds, and since we had no pressing business we were able to accompany her. The night before we left, a courier from the Castle Pembroke, brought a message that Lady Pembroke was in a bad way and would Meerina make her way there as soon as possible? Although, it was a "request" we all knew that it was not really a request. Lord Pembroke could make our lives miserable. Even someone with as much stature as Meerina—not that she would refuse someone in need anyway. It was a two day ride, so before light the next day, we packed up the horses and mule, and set out.

We arrived at the castle at dusk and were hustled directly into the inner sanctum as Lady Pembroke had taken a turn for the worst. When we arrived at her chambers, my two ladies were ushered in, while I was told to wait outside in the hallway. Sometime later the chamber maid brought me a chair.

I sat and paced the great hallway long into the night. At some point I heard shouting from the lady's chamber. I tried to listen through the thick oak door, but all I could hear was the sound of voices; Meerina's and a thick, deep male voice, which I could only assume was Lord Pembroke's. Then the shouting stopped suddenly, and I presumed the lady had told them to stop. For whom else would the "lord" shut his trap.

When the faint signs of daylight showed through the slit in the stone walls, I got up. I couldn't stay within those walls any longer. I found my way through the maze of the castle, and went to check on the horses and to see about getting something to eat for us all. They had to come out eventually. Didn't they?

I found the horses and made sure they were being cared for properly. As I briskly passed by a stall I overheard bits of a conversation about someone being tortured and burned. I thought I was mistaken, just hearing part of the conversation, so I didn't think twice about it. Before going in search of the kitchen I grabbed a piece of sanded wood out of my saddlebag. A good time to work.

As I was charming one of the cooks for some hot porridge and bread for three, I heard some of the other cooks talking about witches and fire, or some such thing. I wanted to ask them more but then a loud bell resounded through the air and everyone scrambled. I assumed it was breakfast time. I grabbed our food and spotted one of the servants from the lady's chamber and asked her to tell Meerina and Rachael that I would be waiting for them right outside the gates of the castle.

I found a nice grassy knoll upon which to sit. I was hungry but I wanted to wait for my two ladies. I pulled out my carving knife, which I always carried in my belt, and started to carve. After a short time, however, I found I wasn't in the mood. Not having the motivation to carve, I laid down. If I was this tired, what must my two ladies be feeling? The sun was just peeking over the hills and I watched the sliver of orange until my eyes could no longer behold. A slice of doom, ripped through my body. I shivered but it left just as instantly as it came. I wondered briefly what it was about but promptly forgot about it as I fell asleep.

"Typical man. Eats and sleeps while the rest of us work our fingers to the bone." Rachael nudged me awake with her foot. I reached up and took her hand and gave her a slight yank and she landed on top of me, right where I wanted her. I looked past Rachael's hair and saw Meerina looking down on us with a sweet smile on her face but her eyes were sad. I knew she had lost the love of her life some years before, but it seemed more than just lonely pain I was seeing, but I couldn't fathom what else it was. We held eyes and had a moment. In that moment a conversation took place. In essence it was, "You take care of my girl." "I will." For a brief moment, she looked desperate, then it passed.

"Good morning, Meerina."

"Good morning, Stephen. You've found yourself a nice bit of green, have ya?"

"I couldn't wait within those stones any longer."

"Well, I understand that." She stretched and raised her face to the sun and breathed in the morning air. I asked about Lady Pembroke and all she said was that she should have been solicited long before this.

"I've got porridge and bread. Although, it's cold." We sat up to allow me to get the breakfast to them. She sat down with us.

"Well, they fed us a bit sometime before light but I could eat some more, cold or not. Thank you. That was thoughtful." She sighed. "I don't relish going back in there right now."

Neither seemed inclined to talk about it so we just sat in silence and watched the world wake.

They had given us a room to use while we were at the castle. It was near the stables, for which I was glad. Exercising the horses gave me an excuse to get out of the castle. On the third morning, before light, a messenger had come to our door. Lady Pembroke had gotten worse. The three left immediately.

I couldn't get back to sleep so I saddled my horse and went for a ride. It was mid-morning before I returned. When I did, there was mayhem in the castle; bells clanging, people shouting and rushing to and fro carrying their belongings. What the hell? I tried to make it to our room, but was unsuccessful. Fighting upstream against the throng of people, I decided to go find Rachael and Meerina instead. I fought the crowds until I saw my girls rushing toward me. There was panic in Rachael's eyes, but it was the deathly fear in Meerina's eyes that made my insides turn to ice.

4

$\mathcal{I}$ popped open my eyes and fought the bolt of panic that shot through me. I saw Rachael's face and for a moment I thought it was still the dream. Then, the world took shape and I blinked as Rhina pushed a lock of hair out of my eyes. Whoa.

"And you still have the most amazing expressions. Are you okay? You look scared," Rhina said concerned.

The dream hadn't quite left me but Rhina's face brought me back. The love I felt between Rachael and Stephen was so strong it was palpable. I looked at Rhina and felt that same palpable energy. I no longer doubted the concept of past lives, and the overwhelming love I felt for Rhina/Rachael stabbed me thru the heart and I sighed.

"Wow. That's a sigh if I ever heard one. No regrets I hope," Rhina probed. I looked at her in astonishment.

"How could you think that?" Stephen's words rang in my head and I shifted over her. I kissed her until I could even out. The dream still had a hold of me.

"No. No regrets. For the first time I've found something I have no words for," I said softly. Tears came to Rhina's eyes. "And I'm finding, that with you, I don't need any." She reached up and touched my face so tenderly, my eyes teared as well. Then we sobered and just looked at each other, eyes searching for something we couldn't believe we had found.

After a long moment of saying nothing, the physical present brought itself forward and I sighed.

"What?" she asked.

"I have to pee," I said it so despondently that she started laughing.

I reluctantly got up, feeling her eyes watch me as I crossed the room. Talk about a foreign feeling, having a woman watch me. Foreign, but absolutely delicious.

We laid in each other's arms for a while just experiencing one another. It was so languid and peaceful, I tried to think if I'd ever felt like that before. I didn't think so because it was so scrumptious I would have remembered.

We finished the tray of food that we had started the night before, and added strawberries and dark chocolate to the mix. We topped it off by drinking Mimosa's. Such luxury. You have to love a woman who has champagne hanging around. While we ate I told her about the dream, and the panic I felt at the end. She didn't have much to say about it, but was very pensive. I asked her about it and she said it was hard to say since I woke up in the middle of it.

"It does give us at least one lifetime together though," she said. "It explains why we feel the way we do toward each other."

"You know," I said off-handedly, "if a guy ever got too close too fast I would drop him like a hot potato … have you ever dropped a hot potato? I haven't. Anyway … I love your smile. No. I just love your whole face. Come here." I leaned over and gave her a chocolate kiss. "And yet, this with you, feels like the most natural thing in the world." She nodded her agreement.

"I know. This goes beyond anything I've felt before as well. Or understood," she admitted. She reached up with her thumb and wiped a bit of cheese from my lip and slowly bought it to her mouth. Oh my. I swallowed hard.

"Holy crap, what you do to me!" I took the tray and put it on the floor and then I took her mouth.

I arrived at Marci's and let myself in. She was in the kitchen still going over details with the couple who were subletting, so I wandered around her living room. There were so many memories here. I found myself in front of a shelving unit covered with photos. Family and friends. I smiled, remembering. I was in most of them, or I had taken them.

I looked around me at her open suitcases on the floor, and realized that, had I stood here twenty-four hours earlier, I would be in the middle of the floor and Marci would be mopping up after me. But ... it *was* twenty-four hours later.

Rhina had happened.

I watched Marci say goodbye and shut the door.

What a metaphor.

She started toward me. I gestured toward her suitcases.

"So ... I guess you're ready to go."

"Oh no, you don't, missy," she demanded. I laughed. I knew she wouldn't let me off. She wiggled her fingers at me. "Don't you dare deflect. Details girl."

I tried to joke it off but I found that I couldn't. I felt that if I did, it would do Rhina a disservice. And Stephen and Rachael for that matter. I didn't know why they mattered, but somehow they did.

Marci could see the struggle on my face, and not knowing the reason, she became concerned.

"Hey ... everything okay?" She reached out and lightly grabbed my arm. I looked into her eyes.

"Actually, Marc, everything is just right."

She got this squinty-eyed expression and scrutinized me with it, but she must have finally concluded that all was well because she hugged me.

"Okay then. We'll just go eat salad and you can tell me all about it," she said simply.

As we ate I told her everything. How I've never really made love until I was with Rhina.

"I mean, I've had a lot of great sex, but looking back, I've never felt anything remotely close to what I feel with her," I said, trying to convey my feelings for a *woman* that I've just met.

"Do you think it's because it's a woman, or because you haven't met the right guy?" Marci asked, not really grasping, but trying.

"I don't know." I smiled slyly. "I haven't really had time to question."

Marci watched with eagle eyes, and thought to herself, that maybe it was just as well that she was leaving.

"Well, honestly, Kat, I don't know what to think. She's a woman, but I've never seen you like this. Happy. Giddy. You were always so … almost indifferent," she admitted.

That brought me up short. Indifferent. Huh.

I saw her passport and traveling papers on the counter and decided to change the subject. I didn't know what more to say anyway.

"So … I don't know how you can be sitting here so calm. You must be jumping out of your skin," I stated. She let me change the subject. It was a bit out of her realm anyway. Marci finally let her guard down.

"It's all I can do to keep from calling my sponsor and can-celling," she confided quietly. I reached over and took her hand. I couldn't even imagine.

She talked about her flight plan, and what was supposed to hap-pen on the other end, and what her job was going to be … it was nothing that I hadn't heard from her before, but she needed to talk. I held her hand and kept her grounded. I don't think she realized that my fingers had gone numb.

At one point she stopped talking and sat there looking at me with eyes like saucers. It reminded me of the artist who painted all his subjects with those huge soulful eyes. I got up and held her to me, much like Rhina did for me at the party.

"Kat, I am so scared." She started crying.

"I think if you weren't you'd be an idiot," I said sardonically. She laughed through her tears, blew her nose then composed herself. And we were back. "Besides, there seems to be a lot of that going on lately," I jested.

We talked about nothing and everything until Linda and Joe showed up. They were going to take her to the airport later. They looked at me expectantly, but I figured Marci would fill them in so I left them hanging.

When we said goodbye, Marci and I cried and hung on for dear life. As I watched her drive away with a heavy heart, I sniffled and remembered who was waiting for me. I stood up straight and walked to my car. Marci was going to pursue her dream, and I was going … home.

I walked up Rhina's front walk and her beautiful front door opened.

There she is.

I stopped and stared at her. Home.

She held out her hand. When I reached her I grasped it. "Okay?"

"Yeah," I sighed. "Twenty-four hours ago, I wouldn't have been."

She nodded. "C'mon. I made some iced tea." She led me to her bright, sunny kitchen.

And just like that. Everything was just right.

With the exception of the few hours I took to meet Marci, we stayed inside all weekend. We talked, ate and … well … a few other things too. Time stopped for us. Two days seemed like two weeks.

It was Sunday evening and we were sitting on her couch having wine and conversation, when she sat up all of a sudden.

"Oh man!"

"What?" I sat up in alarm.

"I have to work tomorrow," she said flippantly. I sat back in relief. I must have had a questioning look on my face because she looked chagrined.

"I just meant that I had completely forgotten that we had another life a couple days ago." She smiled and I realized that I hadn't thought about my *other* life either. I ran straight into a wall. Ha. So to speak. My *other* life. It seemed so far away. My everyday normal life. My job, my friends, my family, my boy/friend.

I felt a light touch on my arm.

"Are you okay? You look very pained."

I told her all of what I was just thinking. She just listened with a still face. I tried to read what she was thinking in her eyes but she had closed them off. Shit. Just as well, I guess. I'm not sure I wanted to know. I had such a straight life. How was she going to deal with that? Better yet, how was I going to deal with that?

I'm sure that I looked at her through all my doubts, but in the end, her lovely face was all I saw. The love in my heart burst through and I leaned over and gently, softly, kissed her.

"We'll figure it out." I smiled. She let out her breath and sighed her relief. Her eyes came back to life and I saw relief, and love, and regrettably, a little pain, in them.

Later, we were standing in her closet trying on her clothes. "Wow. Who knew that having a woman lover can be so advantageous," I said with stars in my eyes. She laughed.

"Then I can't wait to get into your closet," she said suggestively. Then she looked at me with a quizzical look on her face.

"What?" I asked.

"You've told me that you're a professor but I don't know which subject. We never got around to it." She grinned.

"How the hell did we miss that one?" I asked dumbfounded. "I guess we had a few other things on our minds."

"Maybe it would be too close to the 'real' world," she joked. She smiled and I laughed, but thought that that might be a little too close to home. I saw it in her eyes as well. That's when I thought that I might have a bit of a time with this. I looked at her.

"Bring it on," I challenged. But then I teared up.

I looked at the love and understanding that poured out of her eyes and I thought of Marci. I sure could use some of her courage right about now. I looked into Rhina's eyes, through my tears.

"I've known you for five minutes, but I know without a doubt, that I love you, but I'm scared shitless." She opened her arms, and I stepped into them. She held me tight until my tears trickled. I stepped away sniffling.

"How do you do it? Aren't you a mess?" I asked.

"I was already halfway there. My life is very flexible; it doesn't really matter who I'm with. I have a lot of friends who are gay, so no, I'm not a mess about this. You are everything I asked for," she paused. "Believe me, I get messy in other areas. I have no doubt you'll see that soon enough, but about this, no, I'm not messed up."

The thought of fucking this up and losing her again scared me. It sobered me right up. My other life seemed doable. So what if I lose my job, my friends … because … I'm gay now. I blew out a breath. I had a quick flashback of being within those dark and damp castle walls. At least it's a different and more open time. I hoped.

"You look good in my clothes," she said as a tension relief. "You look good without my clothes too." She reached for me. "Let's get through tomorrow, then we'll deal with all the other tomorrows after that. Okay?" I took a big breath and let it out slowly.

"Okay."

"Good. How about a nice romantic comedy to take our minds off tomorrow," she offered. I nodded shakily.

"Sounds good." I had a thought, and got some of my spunk back. "But only if we watch it in bed. I don't want to wear your clothes anymore."

As I drove to work I felt as if I was in another world. It seemed so surreal. Sitting at traffic lights. And more traffic lights. It was like I had stepped into another dimension. I was looking at the world around me with a clarity I'd never had before. Even the cars, and the stone and steel buildings seemed weird. Cold. The world didn't fit anymore. My friends, my boy/friend, my life. My whole life was quickly flashing before my eyes. I had recently begun the soul-searching process, but now I was looking at things on a whole different level.

In a brief moment, I saw my life as a series of things and people to get me through to the next moment. My job was the only thing that kind of still seemed to fit. I thought I had really liked my life. As I was driving, though, I began to shift and see that what I had thought was fulfillment, was just a way to ingeniously disguise the moments in between. Those moments when I didn't have to look, or feel too close. I blew out a breath. In a moment's time, my world as I knew it, had been destroyed.

I parked in the furthest spot from the building to give myself time to think and pull myself together before class. Thank God, or Goddess rather ... jeez, even my deities have changed. Halfway across the lot I suddenly realized how the concept of past lives fits in so well with my History and Ancient Civilizations classes. Who knows, I might be part of my own history lessons! It still boggles my mind how we spent the whole weekend talking about ... everything. I have never spent that much time talking to anyone.

Sitting at my desk, I watched my freshmen straggle in. I saw them in a new light. One of these pimple-faced babes might have been Lord or Lady Pembroke. Or Meerina. I gave a small shudder. I became aware that they were looking at me expectantly. I returned their gaze and looked at each one, as if I could see King Arthur, or Tut. I chuckled to myself, shook my head and walked around to the front of my desk and sat on it. By this time they were sitting up straighter and giving each other the *WTF* look. I sat and looked through them, at them, around them. Some had fear in their eyes, probably thinking I'm popping them a quiz. Others, had curious grins; something was different. Maybe something cool?

"What do you guys know about past lives?" I burst out. Shit! Did I just say that out loud?

Half the class expelled a long bated breath. I laughed. "No. There will not be a pop quiz." They laughed and they brightened and sat even straighter in their chairs. Their faces became animated. Yep ... this was indeed a different generation. I hadn't expected to blurt that, but now that I have, I'm running with it. In for a pound!

"So who can tell me something about past lives, or reincarnation?"

"You mean, like, if I was King Tut in another life?" asked Sam. The class half laughed. Interesting that he chose Tut, I mused. My troublemaker.

"Well, that's part of it, I guess. But what I was really after, is do any of you know how it works?"

"What brought this on Miss Sykes?" Sam again. "Met your soul mate and wanna know if you've done the dance before?" The class laughed, but I knew his crush on me was the reason for the question. He was very interested in the answer, and I was very interested in him not knowing the answer. It wasn't that he was that bad, it just ... there was something about him. Dangerous. Yet he wasn't. That's what was frustrating. I couldn't put my finger on it.

"Yes, Sam. That's exactly what happened," I said *very* deadpan.

"Okay, guys. Give it up. Reincarnation."

"You come back as different people, right?" asked Amanda.

"Everybody's famous at one point, right? So we know how great we are?" Sam questioned.

"Yeah. Except you." The class laughed.

"Hey now. Play nice," I admonished. "What else?"

"Well, he said we're all famous once. Maybe it's to feel greatness, but what if it's someone like Hitler. He was a great leader, but he used his greatness for evil."

"Good point, Angela," I said. "So anybody—"

"So what does that mean? We're supposed to be bad people so we get to go through some, what-goes-around-comes-around bullshit?" Josh asked heatedly. Okay that hit a nerve. Good to know.

"No. I just meant that what little I've read, we come back as many different types of people. Good and bad," Angela said defensively.

"Why?" Josh demanded. Before I could diffuse, Alex spoke up.

"Dude. Relax man. It's just a discussion." He looked back at Angela. "Okay, so why do we reincarnate in the first place?"

"Karma, man!" Sam blurted.

"What the hell does that mean?" Angela demanded.

"You kill someone in one life, you get killed in this one," Sam said. The class was silent for a second.

"Okay, same goes. What for?" This time from Janet. "Why do we have to kill and get killed over and over?"

"To learn." This time from Joe.

"To learn what?" Janet shot back. "To learn how many different ways we can die and kill people?" This was becoming interesting. I just sat back and let it roll.

"It's not all about killing or being killed." The whole class turned their heads in shock, toward Penny. Normally, she would only speak whenever I would ask her a direct question, so this was interesting. When they all turned their attention on her she flustered but plowed through anyway. "It's not always about being good or bad." She stalled a little but God bless them, the class listened quietly. Kids can be such asses, but at times they can be pretty amazing too.

"Sometimes, it's just existing. Feeling everything there is to feel. And sometimes it's to experience how we've treated someone else." Penny paused, settling herself from all the attention. "When we can learn from a lifetime where we've been a horrible human being, we can have compassion for someone in this lifetime who may not be so nice, because we've been there."

"Walking in someone else's shoes?" Angela asked.

"Yeah, kinda."

"But why?" Angela asked again.

I'm with Angela. Why?

"I thought compassion was a nonviolence thing, like Gandhi," Mary said.

"No, compassion is empathy. Like feeling what other people are feeling," Joe said.

"Like someone is robbing you at gunpoint. Feeling that?" Sam said sarcastically.

"Well, actually kind of," Joe suggested. "You may not like that he's robbing you and you do what you need to in that moment, but you don't have to hate him for it either. You could ask yourself why he feels the need to do that."

"And what if he kills someone while you're being so compassionate?" Josh asked angrily. Joe just shrugged and nobody else had an answer either.

"I think you're both right," Penny said. They all turned to her expectantly. "I think it's about compassion, or empathy, and putting ourselves in someone else's shoes. But Sam's right too. What do you do with that compassion when it hurts? Like if the robber shot your sister, or mom." No one said anything for a bit.

"Yeah, AND …?" Grace piped up.

This is getting *very* interesting.

"You get to kill him right? That karma shit and all." Sam blurted. Everyone snickered at his comic relief. I guess even jerks have their place.

"Okay, Penny, you seem to have the answers. What about it?" Angela asked.

"I don't know if I have answers. They're more just thoughts, really," Penny said.

"Well, you seem to have more thoughts than anyone else here. Out with it."

"Well ... I think it's different for everyone. And it depends on the reasoning behind him shooting ... let's say your sister." She shifted in her seat, warming up. Good for her. Thank you, Angela.

"Okay, it also depends on what the shooter's reasons were. If he didn't care and was just an asshole, it would be easy to hate him." She gestured toward Sam. "And what if, in another life, your sister in another body, raped and murdered your wife and your daughter, and it's karma.

"Or maybe the shooter was just a teenage boy that was taking care of his three young sisters on his own and he lost his third job because he slept in one too many times, because he was exhausted and rent was due, and he was already two months behind. Maybe that was the only way he could think of to make rent. And maybe he was so scared he accidentally fired the gun. He didn't mean to kill her. What do you do then? How do you react?"

"Kill the motherf—"

"Sam!" I stopped him.

"Sorry." He gave me a shit-eatin grin. He turned back to the class. "But he still killed your sister," he said indignantly.

"Yeah. But he didn't mean to," Janice voiced.

"Yeah, but my sister's still dead."

"Can't you feel sorry for the guy *and* hate him for killing your sister?" Barry chimed in.

That brought a reaction from the whole class. About half said yes and the other were indignant, with either buts, or noes. I let them go for a bit to see where they would take it. Who were these kids? I'd taught them this whole time and who knew that this was in them. After a few minutes of discussing it I could see that it wasn't going anywhere so I was about to step in when Angela yelled out.

"Hey, guys! This is all fine and well, but what does this have to do with past lives?" Funny, the whole class swung around to Penny. She'd certainly jumped into the fire today. She looked at me for help, but I shook my head and motioned for her to continue. She needed this, but also because I didn't have a clue how to answer that. I believe they call it "passing the buck," and I was just fine with that. She took a breath and steadied herself. A light seemed to shine from her that wasn't there before. I looked at her in amazement. She seemed to transform before my eyes. I watched the rest of the class watch her as well. I don't think they were conscious of it but their bodies shifted, as in respect. Very interesting.

"Well, I think that's why people look at past lives, because it's easier to look at things that are far away. Like it's easier to talk about this right now because it's not about *us* right now. Looking into past lives, are a look into our own lives, but what they were then, not now. But it can parallel what's going on now. It's not the situation really, but how we perceive it. It's just a way we can put ourselves in another's shoes and react from there, rather than react from only our one-sided knowledge and opinion. Past lives teach us that we can, and most likely have been, that which we hate." She finished talking and gave a little head shake, like she'd been in a trance.

"Who are you and what have you done with the shy girl?" Angela asked. Everyone laughed including Penny. "How do you know this stuff?"

"My mom facilitates past-life regressions." The class erupted in a chorus of "Really?" "Wow!" "No freakin' way!" "I wanna!"

"Okay, that's great, but the question still stands. Why do we go through it all anyway? Life after life after life?" Alex asked. They all turned back to Penny. It was kind of comical really. Many things had been altered that day.

"We live all these different lives because God wants us to experience all the facets of Him before He calls us home for good," Penny explained simply. The whole class, including me, stared at her for a good long while. It was so simple and so eloquently spoken that no one had anything else to say.

I could have hugged her at that moment. All the anxiety and overwhelm that I had been feeling just melted away. It resonated with me so much that my skin tingled. Seeing the class still turned in their seats, I could see that Penny was starting to feel uncomfortable. That snapped me out of my musings. I looked at the clock.

"Okay everyone. Time is almost up. Just because we had a break today doesn't mean it's a total vacation. Your assignment is to read pages sixty-three to ninety-three, before Wed." She weathered the groans, "*And*"—louder groans—"I want you to write a paper …" She waited until the outburst calmed down. "On past lives." There's more than one way to do research, I chuckled to myself. They still groaned but not as bad. "I don't care what or who. You can write about dear Aunt Sally or just esoteric knowledge about reincarnation. It has to be at least two pages. Single spaced." They started to get out of their chairs. "Whoa. Whoa! The assignment is to read the pages I've assigned, and the past-life paper. Paper's worth twenty points. But …" More groans. "But … if you can tie in the past-life stuff with what we're learning about the Roman Empire," I gestured to the board, "then you will get fifty extra credit points." They stopped for a second. "Yes, fifty big ones. Tie it in somewhat, you'll get some credit, but you have to tie it in. EFFECTIVELY. None of this half-assed crap, Sam." They all laughed.

"Thank you, everyone. It's been an enlightening morning." I saw a couple of them talking to Penny as they walked out and it warmed my heart.

This class … my *freshman* class no less … gave me so much satisfaction that I didn't feel the need to pursue the topic of past lives with my other classes. My thirst for knowledge on this topic was so strong, I would have disrupted my whole day if needed, but as it was, I didn't need to. So … it was business as usual for the rest of the day. Well, as usual as it can be when I've just fallen head over heels in love and have a permanent smile plastered on my face.

I felt better about this new life, in which I was embarking, because at some point during the day, interacting with my students, I realized that I really loved my job and that no matter what happens with the rest of my life, I will always have this. Then, I had a thought. They can't fire anyone for who they sleep with. Right? I decided not to think about that.

I was on my way to my house, to grab some things before going to Rhina's, when I received a text from Brian. The boy/friend. Crap.

What the hell am I going to tell him? Somehow, I don't believe "I met a woman" is going to go over too well. Hmm. Is it easier for a guy to hear that the woman you've been sleeping with, has fallen in love with a woman, or another man? Hard either way, I think.

Jeez, all these things I've never thought of before. I never thought of myself as sheltered before … but maybe I was. I'll put him on hold for the moment.

I thought of Rhina, and a smile came to my lips. Never have I felt like this. I am totally bowled over by this woman. I never believed that love at first sight really existed, but I'm certainly glad I've been proven wrong.

Then I thought of past lives. Are all couples, who love each other a by-product of past lives together, or are there other factors as well? And the fact that until three days ago I wasn't even thinking about any of this, makes me feel like I should check myself into the nearest hospital. Yet there's something … inexplicably explainable about everything.

That night in Rhina's kitchen, we talked about all that had transpired that day. I told her what happened. I also told her how it could jeopardize my job.

"Why?" she asked. "It's not that big of deal."

"At the beginning of the year we got word from the school board that we're not supposed to go outside the curriculum, for any reason. The taxpayers were crying that their kids are to learn nothing but what they're paying for. No forays into other areas of knowledge other than what's in the curriculum."

"What?" Rhina exclaimed. "It's a college! It's supposed to be free thinking!"

"Preachin' to the choir," I said, resigned. When the dean had told us, it felt like he had pulled the rug out.

"What happened to put that rule in affect?" she asked indignantly.

"Supposedly, some teacher … somewhere … started teaching yoga in the class. A little, just for a warm up, you know. Some of the parents got wind of it and complained. So the board decided that that wouldn't happen here. I have no idea what the specifics are, but it's just one more thing that pigeon-holes our kids into a certain way of thinking. Or lack of thinking, as the case may be." Both of us, disgusted, decided it was best to speak of Rhina's day.

Her day consisted of clients as usual. During the weekend, when she had told me that she was a massage therapist, *and* a Reiki practitioner, it didn't surprise me. No wonder she knew all about this. I put all that stuff in the same genre. Woo woo.

"So how was it for you today?" I asked her. "Was it as eye opening for you as it was for me?"

"Well, I don't know if I would describe it as eye opening, but yes, it was definitely different. I had a smile plastered on my face all day," she admitted. Then she thought for a moment more. "My life is set up differently than yours. More forgiving, I think ... maybe that's the wrong word to use, but people I've aligned myself with are probably a little more open to ... differences ... shall we say." She paused. "Maybe *accepting* is a better word."

"Did you do that on purpose, you think?"

"I don't think so. Not consciously anyway. I just know that, personally, I have a mindset of inclusion, rather than exclusion, therefore it would make sense that the world around me was that way as well."

"I never thought of it that way before."

"Why would you?"

"Today, I had the thought of being very sheltered. It makes me think that I haven't been very open. I haven't given any of this a second thought. Until now."

"Again. Why would you?" She shrugged. "You are surrounded by students every day. That in itself is pretty damn open. You have to keep up with the times when you teach. Teaching is hard. And an opportunity like this has never presented itself before. I have no doubt that you adapt when you need to."

"Yeah, but I've never even thought about opening my world like you have. I know that at least some of my kids have to be gay, and yet I've never thought about it. I feel conceited or a hypocrite or something."

"Why?"

"I haven't done anything to open my mind like you have." I was getting frustrated with myself.

"Listen." She took my hand. "I've thought about it because a lot of my friends are gay. Just by nature of association makes me think about things differently."

"Yeah, but—"

"Stop," she said gently. "You are a professor in a college. You have to be open minded or these kids would eat you alive. They can tell if you've got an Achilles heel. But it sounds like you've got a good rapport with them." She smiled. "I can't believe you brought that up in class."

"I know. Crazy huh? I didn't even know that I was going to do it. It just came out of my mouth, and when I did, I couldn't take it back. I can't believe Penny. Talk about blossoming."

Rhina saw that I had calmed myself so she let go and started peeling potatoes.

"You know, that's a perfect segue into something I was going to ask you." She got kind of nervous, I could tell, so I just let her go on. "You don't have to," she said hurriedly, "but would you like to get our past lives read together?" She didn't look at me. Interesting. Here's some of her messiness. It touched me. What does that say about me that her messiness makes me feel better?

"Of course." I didn't have to think twice. She let out a sigh. "Did you think I wouldn't?"

"I wasn't sure," she said self-consciously. Huh. There's definitely something there.

"Honey, after these past few days, I am a firm believer. You have converted me." I got a wicked gleam in my eye. "In so many ways." She laughed.

"And aren't I lucky," she said and leaned over to kiss me. Nervousness gone. Okay. That's for another time.

"I think that's a two-way street. Do you have someone in mind?" I asked. She looked perplexed. "For the past-life stuff."

"Ah. Yes and no. I mean, I know people, who know people, but I don't personally."

"Well … as it happens. Who'da thunk?" I told her about Penny's mom. "Would you mind if we used her mom versus one of your people? I think it would go a long way for her ego." Rhina smiled. God she was beautiful.

"And you say you're not open to people." I must have looked at her funny. "You just do it in a different way. You already are open to your students being who they are. Now you're just tweaking it a bit. Expanding the search, as it were." I thought about that. I supposed she was right. Which is why I never thought about being close-minded before. I just had different words for it, that's all. I felt better about myself. Something inside me let go.

"Hm. Thanks for that," I said gratefully. "I'll ask her on Wednesday."

"Why not look up her mom right now? Does she have the same last name?" I shrugged. "Why don't you have a go"—she nodded at my laptop—"while I finish dinner."

So ... I did. I found "Pam" and left an email.

"Okay, that's done." As I shoved my laptop away, Rhina shoved a plate under my nose. "Whoa. Hey. Perfect timing. That looks great." I smiled at Rhina as she sat. "I love this." I just looked at her and shook my head. She just waited. "Today's Monday. We met on Friday night." She nodded, and knowing where this was going, she just smiled.

"I have never had my world, so totally, shifted on its axis. Let alone in such a short time. You have put me in an alternate universe. I am absolutely so scared to death, yet ... yet ... I have never been so ready and willing to jump into the void with anything ... or anyone ... as I am with you." With tears in her eyes, she nodded.

Tuesday went as usual, the same yet so different. I had wandered through the day with different colored glasses. Penny's mom had returned my email and we had an appointment with her on Saturday morning. Wednesday, I stopped Penny, as she came into class, and told her about the appointment. She brightened, and I was glad I had contacted her mom. Angela said hi to us both as she walked in. Penny turned and gave me a big smile. I gave her a quick wink.

As the last student entered the room and put their paper on top of the others on the pre-ordained corner of the desk, I grabbed them and asked, "Anymore?" At the nonresponse, I shoved them into my briefcase. "I am very excited to read these." They had no idea. "Okay, everybody turn to page sixty-three." The class groaned.

"Hey, aren't we going to talk more about past lives?" Sam asked. The class agreed.

"Yes, we are. Turn to page sixty-three. It's called history. It's the past." More groans. "You guys had a vacation on Monday. After I read them we might … might talk about them on Friday." More groans, but they had hope in them. "Okay, who can tell me …"

5

On the way home, I was so excited to read those papers that I almost dug one out to read while I was stuck in traffic, but I thought that might not be prudent. Frustration at the slow speed had me edgy. The downside of staying at Rhina's was that it was across town.

When I got to Rhina's I found a note saying that she had a house call. She had also booked another massage while she was in the area, so it would be late when she got home. I had the house to myself. I wasn't sure how I felt about that. Excited, sad, or a little relieved. I wanted to spend time with Rhina and my heart ached when I wasn't with her, but I also wanted to read the papers, so the excitement and sadness worked themselves out. Relieved because I wouldn't have to choose.

The ache was new. Whenever the "boys" had left me alone I had felt relieved. But I so desperately missed Rhina when she wasn't here. Is that normal? Is that healthy? Well, I guess we'll figure it out. In the meantime it felt good to ache for someone. Papers!

The coffee table in the living room, became my office. Over the years I had developed a system. The first paragraph usually gave me an idea what kind of paper it was going to be. I made three stacks—fluff, mediocre, and the good stuff. I read the fluff, gave the minimum grade and moved to the mediocre. When that was done I had a small stack of papers that had some meat to them. I was about to start reading when Rhina called. There was a tanker accident on the freeway, and she was stuck and didn't have a clue how long she was going to be. I fixed something to eat and put a plate of leftovers for Rhina in the fridge. I grabbed my small stack, took a shower and headed to bed. Tucked in, I began to read.

My god. Who were these kids? There were about eight papers that were unbelievable. I'd have given them a hundred points. One was from someone I didn't expect. At all.

By the time I finished reading them all, I was fighting my eyelids, but I was so fascinated that I snatched them up again. I also had an ulterior motive. I wanted to hold Rhina while I was still coherent enough to do so.

Rhina was so excited to get home. *Not* sitting in traffic had very little to do with it. She couldn't wait to wrap her arms around Kat and just hold her. She'd never felt like this with anyone. She dumped her things on the kitchen table and followed the pale light emanating from the bedroom. She was totally taken by surprise by what awaited her. She didn't know what she had expected, but she certainly didn't expect this, or the overwhelming feeling of love that flooded her being.

There Kat lay with papers all around her, and one on her chest, as she lightly mumbled something in her sleep. Rhina felt such an ache of love that she thought that this is what a heart attack must feel like. She grabbed the door knob for support. When she was steady again she quietly went to shower.

Kat had still to move when Rhina was ready for bed. Leaving the one on Kat's chest, she silently gathered the papers that sat in disarray around her girl, and put them on the table on her own side. Rhina slid slowly into bed, not wanting to wake Kat. She retrieved one of the papers in the pile and started reading. She was curious.

Rhina was halfway through the short pile when Kat finally stirred.

"Hey, you."

"Hey. You're home." Kat yawned. "You should have woken me."

"Are you kidding? I wanted to read these. But … if you'd been up I would've wanted to do this." She leaned over and gave Kat a long, slow, sensual kiss. "Mmm. I've been dying to do that all day."

"Mm. Well then ..." Kat flung the paper from her chest and replaced it with Rhina.

On Friday, I was surprised to see my kids come in early and raring to go, sitting straight up in their chairs by the starting hour. Huh. Interesting.

"Good morning, everyone. Hope your week has been good. Let's turn to page—" The groans and complaints were deafening. I started laughing. "All right, all right. It's Friday. You guys indulged me on Monday, so I'll indulge you today. We'll spend the first half talking about these"—I patted the stack of papers that were sitting on the corner of the desk—"then we have to talk about silly stuff like, you know ... the curriculum."

"Okay, the usual. You put the minimal effort in you get minimal grade, blah, blah. No matter what, I appreciate the effort that you put into this so I gave you all a little extra." I picked up the top paper.

"There were a few extraordinary papers that went beyond the point scale. I would like to read one aloud because it ties in really well with what we were talking about on Monday, as well as what's going on with the Romans." She hooked a thumb toward the blackboard.

They all wanted to know who wrote it. "I've already gotten permission from the author, so I don't want you to worry about who wrote it. I want you to listen to the words. Let them sink in." When they were quiet and listening I started reading ...

I had a dream the other night. I dreamed that I was a small boy and I was hiding in a trap door in the attic. I could see through the small cracks. I was the youngest, not quite five. My family had me hide when the soldiers came. They didn't have time to get anyone else out. The soldiers beat my brother and father, and forced them to watch as they took turns with my mother and sisters. My sisters were eight, twelve and fifteen. They used them, then slit their throats. My brother was gutted while my mother watched in a pool of her own blood. Then they slit her throat. They tied each of my father's limbs to four horses and then they made them to scatter. He was drawn and quartered.

The room was dead silent.

In my dream, I kept seeing my real-time brother's face superimposed on the Roman Sargent's face. The Sargent who led the band of soldiers that did these horrible things.

Three years ago my brother was beaten and knifed to death in front of me. I was watching from the second story window. The guys who did it were never brought to justice. Until that dream I was angry at God, and the world, for taking my brother. Now, after the dream, I see it as a universal justice system. I ask myself, "Why am I seeing this now?" They (angels) tell me I am now ready to see it. I am ready to learn. Learn what? I see the small boy peeking from the attic and wonder what I'm supposed to learn. What am I supposed to learn by watching these horrible things or watching my brother being knifed to death? They were the victims weren't they? Aren't I a victim too? What is a victim supposed to learn?

Ah. How not to be a victim. Got it. How do I do that? HOW DO I DO THAT?

I look back at my dream and I remember that some of the soldiers did not want to partake in these horrible deeds, but when the Sargent (my brother) ran one of them though with his sword, for fear of their life, they joined in.

I think of our analogy on Monday, about the shooter killing the sister. I look differently at that situation now. Not only at what the shooter was really doing there, but why he shot the sister. We talked about different scenarios on Monday, but also, I looked at who the sister might have been in some past life.

Looking at past lives helps me see the lessons I have to learn in this lifetime. Like, being the victim. I can continue in this life as a victim, or I can choose not to. I can take one of the Roman soldiers, who were forced to hurt that family, and put the face of the shooter on the same body. Are they not victims too? Anyone can be strangled, and anyone can be the strangler, in any given lifetime. Putting myself in either's shoes lets me see how else it can be done. What OTHER choices can I make? I can choose to be a victim and continue the cycle, or I can choose NOT to be a victim and maybe find a way to stop the violence.

I laid the paper on the desk. No one spoke. It was just as powerful now as when I read it the first time. Even more so as I saw it in
the eyes of every student. The energy in the room was palpable. And
the amazing thing was that these kids recognized it! The room was
silent for some time.

"Holy shit," Sam broke the ice. I chuckled. The rest of the class
laughed. Thank you, Sam. He was good for something.

"Whose was that?" Alex asked.

"I don't want to say just yet. Let's discuss it first." No one said
anything.

"I know. Pretty deep huh?" I admitted. Still no one said anything.

"Okay. So since no one has any thoughts right now, let me ask
this. How does this make you feel?"

"Like my paper sucked wide," Ryan piped up. We all burst out
laughing. There were a couple of agreeing "Mine toos" in there as
well.

I smiled and thought for a moment.

"Okay. Since this was extra credit, I'll give, those who want it,
a chance to up their grade. Not mandatory, but I would happily give
you that opportunity. Due on Monday." They liked that and gave
their approval.

"So ... let's hear it."

"I feel like I just got sucker-punched," Sam confided. There
were agreements all around. He didn't say anything more. The rest
were more than willing to let him talk. They couldn't—didn't know
what to say.

"Say more about that please, Sam," I directed.

"Well, first of all .... whoever ... hits you between the eyes with
the whole, rape, torture deal, then with the brother deal, and how his
brother was actually the Sargent, and how it's this universal justice
deal. And then the whole victim deal. How some of the soldiers did
some bad shit, but they were forced to do it, or die too, so they were
victims too. Then ... the shooter/sister thing. It's crazy how someone
can be so bad, doing some nasty things, and yet they can be as vic-
timy as the victims they're doin." Some snickered as Sam's grammar
curtailed, but his point got across.

"Thank you, Sam, for breaking the ice, and for so noneloquently getting to the crux of the piece."

"I never thought of it like that before," Angela spoke up. "I just always thought that bad people did bad stuff and only good people were the victims. Now I see that even bad people can be good people too."

"How do you know the difference?" Mary asked.

Wow, excellent question!

No one spoke for a bit, then they all turned in unison to Penny. I stopped myself, just in time, from laughing at the irony, and the shear synchronicity of it all. Four days ago, they barely knew she existed. She was so surprised that I thought she was about to bolt and run, but bless her heart, she stuck. She gathered herself and did herself proud.

"Uh ... Well, I don't think that you do. Not right away anyway. I think that every situation you have to look at separately and ask yourself, 'What's really happening in the moment?'" She looked around and saw that people were actually listening to her. She seemed to settle in. Good for her.

"When it's close to home it's hard. Like the person who's brother got killed. It's hard to be objective when you're hurting, but when time goes by maybe we can learn to look deeper than just the actions of one person."

She shifted in her seat and got into story telling mode. "My mom has a friend, who's very intuitive, and at one point in her life, she was really, really bothered by the whole Hitler thing." She gestured to Angela, who brought him up the other day. "She kept asking herself why that happened. If everything has a reason, why did that happen in our history? Then one day, when she went into her meditation, the answer that she'd been looking for finally came to her. She was told in her meditation that she was finally ready to see."

Penny was so involved in the story that she had no idea the effect she had on the other students. Some were in rapt attention, some were looking with respect, and some were looking at her in a new light. I'd bet a month's paycheck that she'd get a few dates after this, I mused. Penny continued on.

"What she saw was that, way back in ancient times, a few thousand years ago, the 'Jewish' priests killed all the priestesses. You see, back then, it was more of a matriarchal society, and the priestesses were the healers and the spiritual leaders of that time. But changes were coming. The priests wanted to be the power in the land, so they had all the women of power killed, and all those connected with them. Over the years, they killed hundreds of thousands.

There was a collective releasing of breaths, including my own, from the classroom. The ramifications of that thought process was staggering.

"Is that really true?" Maggie asked.

"Well ... the vision was true. I was sitting in the room when she was telling Mom. But ... as far as the reality of it," she just shrugged. "I don't know, but you just have to look at history," she gestured to the blackboard "to see that that kind of stuff happened all the time. Plus, if you want to look at the universal justice part of it, it makes a lot of sense."

Jeez. Even my head was spinning. The kids, one by one, slowly turned back toward the front, each in their own thoughts. These were eighteen and nineteen-year-olds, and generally speaking, I thought that they were sort of irresponsible, lazy, want-something-for-nothing kind of kids. I looked at them now with a respect that I hadn't thought possible. Maybe some of that old thinking is true, but these were not the same kids that walked into this room on Monday morning. I saw it in their eyes. All they needed was a chance to prove that they were bigger than, even they, thought they were. Bigger than we think as a society for sure.

I wanted to continue that train of thought, but I felt that nothing could top that. I thought of Rhina and wished she were here. That gave me an idea.

"Okay. Penny, that was ... extraordinary, but I think before we get off track onto this, I need to start segueing into what they actually pay me to talk about." I gestured to the board. They started to groan.

"Hold on, we're not going back yet, but I do want to tweak the topic a bit and lighten it up." I paused for effect. "True love." Everyone brightened. I reminded myself, and was a bit surprised, that this was the very reason I started this whole business anyway. I hadn't realized how it would affect me and everyone else.

"How does a past love affect the present?" I asked, I hoped nonchalantly.

"What? Like if you loved someone in another lifetime you'll love them in this lifetime?" Sam asked.

"Sort of. What else?" I gestured. Everyone seemed gung-ho for this topic.

"If you were scorned in another lifetime you scorn them?" They started firing off questions so fast I could barely keep up.

"When you love someone regardless 'if you should,' because you've loved them in another lifetime?"

"When the king loves a pauper even though they're not of his class?"

"Like the Hatfield and McCoys? They couldn't help it. Maybe they were lovers in another lifetime." They were having fun now.

"Miss Sykes and her lover, who she just met, were king and queen in a past life!" Sam yelled over everyone else. Everyone laughed. It was a good release.

"Okay, smart-ass," I joked. "Answer me this. You have this great love affair in another lifetime. And you meet the same soul this lifetime. Only this lifetime you both came back as men. You both feel attracted to each other, but neither one of you are gay. What do you do?" Everyone eagerly waited for what he had to say. He squirmed at being in the hot seat.

"Do you love the soul or reject the vessel?" Angela asked.

"Exactly," I said. "Very eloquently put." All the males yelled, "Reject the soul!" and all the girls yelled, "Love the vessel!" Shocker.

"Okay," I asked. "Same scenario. What if it were two women?"

Everyone shouted, "Love the soul!" Then they all laughed and good-naturedly started the "girl against guy" argument about the double standard and guys' fantasies, etc. I let them go on with that topic for a bit and get it out of their systems. I felt it was a good place to stop. They were laughing, and I didn't want them to guess.

"Okay. This is a good place to stop." I listened to their moans, and as I walked around to the blackboard, took a quick glance at everyone. They were in a good place. I felt good leaving it there and I didn't want them scarred for life. As I was perusing faces I noticed Sam giving me a strange look, and it really wasn't a pleasant one. I didn't react but a tingle went up my spine and it was accompanied with a touch of fear. *Shit. That little pissant knows.* I realized then that he might have a touch of intuitiveness. Maybe that's why he's such an ass half the time, to hide that fact. Huh. Good safety tip.

"Wait, Miss Sykes. You forgot to tell us who wrote that paper." Ben said. Ah. The paper.

Without a word, I stopped what I was doing, reached over, and grabbed the stack. I grabbed the top one.

"You mean this one?" As I held it up everyone sat straight. I could have fun with this at least. I slowly walked over to the wall and down the side to the back. Straight toward Penny. I'm sure everyone thought it was hers, but when I got to her I paused, then I turned and walked back up the aisle. I heard a few groans and "C'mons." I reached the front and paused again.

"C'mon, Miss Sykes," Alex said. I smiled, then shifted back one desk and handed the paper to Josh. There was a collective gasp.

"Josh!" "Holy shits" all around.

"Dude. That was awesome!" Alex sounded out. "Man, no wonder you got pissy on Monday. Sorry about your brother man."

"Did you really have that dream?" Angela asked.

"Yeah, I did." I handed the stack to Josh and told him to pass the rest out while I continued with class. I knew they wouldn't pay attention so I just went through the motions of teaching what we had already covered. Even though it had been an amazing journey, for all of us, I needed them back on track. I had derailed them enough.

I got to Rhina's house and found she was in session in her massage room, so I went into her living room and sat at her computer. I needed to catch up on some emails as I'd been a little preoccupied lately. I also wanted to email Brian. I knew it was a chickenly way to do it, but honestly, I didn't want to see him again. Rhina was so large in my life that I didn't want to go backward. I wanted to tell him the truth, however, he deserved that much. I left him a very detailed, very honest letter, and hoped he was well. I felt good. Before, I might not have given him the whole truth, to spare him, but I've changed. And I'd like to think that I've changed for the better.

Marci had sent me two emails. One was to say that she'd arrived in Sudan, and went on to describe her world. With tears in my eyes, I read about her adventures. My heart swelled with love. I was so proud of her. I was certainly going to miss her, but I guess it was synchronistic. With me spending so much time with Rhina I wouldn't be spending it with Marci. It wouldn't have been the first time that friends suffered for relationships, but it didn't make it any less lonely for the friends. Besides, if it wasn't for Marci's going away party, I wouldn't have met Rhina. Life was a trip.

Marci's second email was peppered with questions about Rhina and me. Jeez ... even from thousands of miles away she was relentless. Take the girl out of the country ... I sent her as many details as I could. In love, going great, women are amazing, blah, blah. I decided not to mention reincarnation, or my class exploration yet. That would take too much time. With a promise to write more, I finished and turned off the computer. I turned to get out of the chair and saw Rhina leaning against the door jamb, just watching me. She had a little smile on her face. Seeing her, I returned the smile with my heart skipping a little.

"I love watching you," she said.

I couldn't believe how giddy she made me feel. I walked across the room with the intent of not stopping until I was in her arms. She held them out with what looked like an acceptance of that intent, but when I reached her, the door down the hall opened and her client came out and stepped into the bathroom. She looked at me and it seemed she knew what I needed. I'm glad one of us did.

"Why don't you wait for me in the bedroom," Rhina said, then gave me a kiss that melted my bones.

My god, how does she do that? As I floated down the hall, I debated whether or not to get undressed and wait for her in bed, but I decided that it was much more fun to undress each other. So I spent my time fumbling through the CDs, finding the perfect one. I'm going to have to get this girl some kind of iPod or MP3 player or something. I had just pressed play when she walked into the room. All thought of musical devices fled.

One look at her and all the emotions from the day just flooded in. I practically ran into her arms. I was planning on seducing her slowly and taking off one article of clothing at a time ... but ... well ... shit happens. Instead I slammed her up against the door-jamb. It took her by surprise, but thank goodness, she adjusted and was more than happy to oblige me. We ripped each other's clothes off. This could get expensive, I thought briefly, then there was nothing but her.

A flame burned inside that I'd never experienced before. I just wanted her to put it out. I pummeled her against the wall, she paused then something came over her. She threw me onto the bed.

The tiger was free. We kicked, scratched, clawed, pushed, pulled, and thrust. Those yellow eyes seared into me. She was the wild animal taming the wild beast. It was like my passion gave her permission to let the wild animal out of its cage.

We both lay exhausted staring at the water spot on the ceiling. I briefly thought, "Huh. So that's how two women fuck." I chuckled to myself. Then I sobered. What the hell had just happened?

"I'm not sure whether to say thank you, or apologize," I said as my breath evened out

"Apologize for what?"

"Well, I was a little exuberant."

"Yes, you were, and I was fighting it the whole way," she said dryly. When we quit giggling, she turned on her side. "I have never had sex like that before. I mean, I've had some pretty steamy sex, but nothing like this. And you're a woman! Well, I've always wondered how two women fuck." She said. I burst out laughing.

"I just thought that exact same thing!" I leaned on my elbow and pushed a lock of hair away from her face. "I've never done that before either," I said tenderly. "I've never known that was inside me." I gave her my best grin. "I guess I just needed to tame the tiger."

"I'd say you did a pretty good job of it."

"You know I could have sworn that I was looking into the face of a tiger," I said. She reached up, pulled me to her and kissed me tenderly and then held me tight.

"It scared me a little, letting go like that. Exhilarating, but scary." There was a minuscule tremor to her voice. I pushed slightly out of her arms so that she could see me.

"Me too."

"I scared you or you scared you?" She tried to sound nonchalant but didn't quite pull it off.

"Both," I said shyly. She nodded. "I don't think I've ever let my passions go like that either." I thought about it for a moment. "Any passion, for anything, for any reason. You?" She thought about it for a second and shook her head slightly. I pulled her to me. "No wonder."

There was something so sensual about watching her cook breakfast. I sat at the kitchen counter, drinking coffee, just watching. My heart melted even more. How many times can a heart melt before it's gone? Maybe it was just the contrast of our extreme … what was it? It certainly wasn't making love. Was it? Well, we certainly made something.

It seemed that unlocking those parts within us, that had been withheld we expanded somehow. Like opening up in that primal way, we expanded our hearts as well. At least, I had anyway. Just the simple act of her making breakfast turned me inside out. She must have heard my thoughts.

"Having you watch me like that makes my heart grow." She turned, with spatula in hand and leaned back on the counter. "It's not like I've never made breakfast for you before, but it's different this morning."

"I love how we're so in tune." I smiled. "I was just thinking along those same lines." She leaned over the counter and kissed me then turned back to the task at hand.

"Tell me," she said as she flipped the omelet.

"I was just thinking that watching you cook breakfast has such a new feeling to it. I've sat here before and have loved every minute of watching you move." Rhina smiled to herself. "But this morning … it almost feels like you've given me … I don't know … *love potion number nine* or something," I joked. "I feel warmer, deeper … sweeter."

Rhina didn't say anything for a bit, then she stopped, turned and said gently. "Yeah." She gave me a slight smile then turned back around.

"So … what brought on such beastly behavior?" she asked flippantly. So while we ate I told her what had transpired that day in class. All the up and down emotions: my new experience of history, the look that Sam had given me, my utter astonishment of those kids, and me wondering if they were the spirit of King Tut or Cleopatra or Genghis Khan. She listened as I told her everything.

She remained silent when I finished; there was nothing else to say. Soon she got up, laid her hands on my shoulders, kissed the top of my head, then cleaned up the dishes.

When she finished I was still staring into my coffee cup. She came over to stand next to me. I wrapped my arms around her waist while she held me. We stayed like that for a while then she patted my shoulder and said gently, "C'mon. We have an appointment with our past in an hour." Pam. Penny's mom. Scared or excited? Both, I decided. I got up and we walked arm in arm down the hall.

6

We were silent on the way to Pam's house, just holding hands and holding vigil for our thoughts. Pam, thankfully, looked normal. Her jeans and a nice tee took me pleasantly by surprise. The long, flowing caftan and the turban that I had expected was thankfully non-existent.

She greeted us graciously, and exuberantly went on about how I brought reincarnation into the classroom. I asked if Penny was here.

"I asked her not to be here. I told her you might be nervous, but really, I knew you were bringing Rhina and I didn't know … I didn't want there to be any problems." She looked at us pointedly, and we nodded. "So, she's out with Angela." My heart warmed. Pam told us that a few of Penny's classmates had come to her for past-life regressions. I was surprised and pleased.

"I love that you discussed that it's more than being someone famous. That there are consequences—"

"You know, I wish I could take credit for that, but honestly, I was just along for the ride. Those kids—still shocks me when I think about it—they're the ones who brought all this stuff up. Especially Penny. She's the one who steered the conversation. You should have seen her; it was as if something came over her as she talked. They really responded to her."

"I love that you just said all that, but make no mistake." She stared through me till I squirmed. "You let it happen. You created the space to let it happen." She got up and went into the kitchen while I pondered that. Rhina just sat there with a big grin on her face.

"Oh shut up."

Pam came back in, tray in hand, with cups, tea pot, and a plate of fresh-baked chocolate chip cookies. I smiled as Rhina's eyes got big at seeing her favorite cookies.

"We'll get started in a minute but I just wanted to thank you."

"You don't—"

"Yes, I do," cutting me off. "I know that you may not have meant it, but what you've done this week, with that classroom …" She spread her hands. "It's unheard of. Penny's pretty aware and sensitive, so she's told me about the difference in the class. The changes in those kids. All because you were willing to set aside the rule book for a minute." I tried to tell her it was only due to circumstances and my own selfishness that I did it to begin with. She didn't listen.

"It doesn't matter. How many people do you know who would throw in a topic of past lives into a college curriculum? For whatever the reason." I had to admit that nobody I knew would step off the cliff like that. Hell, I didn't know anyone who even knew of the subject. What if one of the students went crawling to the dean? Oh boy. Sam ran through my head briefly. I shooed him out. "So there. Take the compliment. Now. What exactly may I do for you ladies? She looked at us in turn, several times and we had the distinct feeling that this woman knew exactly why we were there.

So we told her why we were there.

"So you're curious about the lives in which you were together as lovers?" We nodded.

"That's how it works, right?" I asked.

"Sometimes." At my perplexed look she explained, "It's different every time. You may never have had one at that level of intimacy. You may have had ten. It's all what your spirits came to do."

"I know that we've had at least one life together." I briefly told her of my dream and how vivid it was.

"Great! You want to see if there are more?" We nodded. "Okay, then let's get to it." She led us to a room down the hall. The muted colors and soft music soothed my anxious mind. Somewhat. "Do either of you need anything before we start? Water? Bathroom?" We shook our heads.

"You two sit there on the couch." We sat on the couch and she took the wicker chair in the center of the room, with the coffee table between us.

"Okay, then we'll go ahead and start. If you'll indulge me a few moments to gather myself." She closed her eyes and then after a few moments she opened one eye and looked at me. "It's not going to hurt." I let out a breath that I didn't know I was holding. I looked sheepishly at Rhina. She just smiled at me.

With her eyes closed, Pam started to speak.

She started with a small prayer for clarity and highest good. Then she launched into the many lives when we were together in other capacities other than intimate lovers: mother/son, general/valet, brother/sister, to name a few. She didn't go into any details, as it wasn't what we were there for.

"Ah, here we go. I'm sure you two will figure out who's who, so I'll just tell the story as I see it.

America. I see ... mmm ... late 1700s. I see a young white man. Blonde hair, light eyes. John. He's a Scottish immigrant"....

John admired the landscape from his perch on top of the new, two-story barn he was building. As an indentured servant from Scotland, he had not expected that he would find anything that equaled his home of birth. But here he was doing work that he loved, and he knew well from growing up as a stable boy and the son of a carpenter. He had a job in this beautiful country, a place to lay his head every night, and food in his belly. That's more than he'd had in Scotland. At twenty-two, he felt he was on top of the world. So to speak.

He was an indentured servant; which made him subhuman in the eyes of those around him. And though they gave him the worst jobs at first, and very little pay, he was content enough. After about a year his gentle, easy way, and his exacting work had won them over.

After two years, in spite of his young age, John was the man to go to when they were in need of a master builder. And when there were horses to be broke, he was the man. He loved working with his hands, and taking care of the "Beasts of the Gods," as he called them. He felt that, although he missed his home, he couldn't ask for anything better. He was a happy man indeed.

But life can change.

One morning, John was in the pasture, talking with one of the new fillies, smoothing her over to his side of things, when he noticed Lord Wilmington talking with the head stable master. When they started walking toward him something tightened in his gut. He tried to think back to anything he might have done.

"John." Lord Wilmington nodded toward him.

"My lord."

"Smithy here, tells me you're a fine horseman." John let out an inward sigh and as he looked over at the filly his face softened.

"Aye, well, it just takes a wee bit of listening. Doesn't it now my friend?" The young horse laid her neck over John's shoulder and snorted. Lord Wilmington made up his mind.

"My daughter, Annabelle, wants to learn to ride. Smithy says you're the best."

John just nodded. He didn't say that she was constantly down at the stables getting in their way and a complete pain in their arses.

"Every morning and every afternoon, I want you to give her a lesson. I want you to work her hard."

"Yes, Sir. I can do that."

"I can't talk her out of it, so I want you to work her out of it. I want it to be her idea that she quits. Understand?" John's gut clenched again.

"Yes, Sir. You don't want her to be riding, but she's very strong willed, that wee one. Do you think she'll actually quit?"

"It's not lady-like!" Wilmington puffed up. "I don't want her riding and it's your job to see that she doesn't." John couldn't help but notice that his lordship felt a little emasculated by her ten-year-old willfulness, but said nothing.

"I understand, but what if I can't discourage her. I've seen her out here, watchin' the beasts." He ran his hand gently down the filly's nose. "Horses have powerful energy." Wilmington brought himself up to full height and loomed over John.

"Just see to it." He looked John straight in the eye. John understood the ramifications if he failed at his mission, yet could not turn down the offer.

"She'll be here this afternoon. See to it that you're here." John watched Lord Wilmington huff off with the self-importance of someone who thought that he was a great man.

Smithy walked by and gave John a look of pity, then he became the stable master again.

"Be sure you don't fail, Laddie. I don't want to have to train someone else."

Alone with the filly, John took a deep breath, as he stroked her nose.

"Well now, my friend, I believe this is what they call a rosy situation. Beautiful on top but filled with many thorns." Too many he thought.

That afternoon, a skinny little girl with a mane of blonde hair about ten years old, came skipping out to the stables where he was waiting. She came in happy and bright and excited. He hated to squash that.

"You're late. What are you wearing? You expect to ride in a dress?" Her smile faded. His heart twisted, but he'd be damned if he was going to let a spoiled little girl ruin his life. He shored himself up.

"Do we get to ride now?" She brightened.

"No. Do ya walk before ya crawl?" he asked unkindly.

She frowned again and for a moment her little face scrunched, and his heart softened.

"Take this halter, and I'll show ya how to put it on," he said as he handed it to her.

"I know how to put it on," she said defiantly.

"Oh do ya now?"

"Yes," she said confidently.

"Really? So you're not willing to do it right?" He hated this. He wouldn't dare treat a horse this badly.

"I know how to do it right!"

"And how do you know that?" John asked, crossing his arms.

"I've been watching you do it." She stood her ground. She took him aback. He had no idea that she'd been watching him.

"Okay. Then do it."

She reached up to put the halter on, but hesitated when he said, "if you do it wrong, you're done. I won't teach ya anymore."

The little ten-year-old steeled herself and proceeded to correctly put on the halter, and with him looming over her it couldn't have been easy. His heart grew with pride as he watched her. He felt a jolt of anger that he couldn't encourage her, but he had to take care of himself. He steeled himself. Again.

During the whole lesson he treated her with disdain, but she kept coming back and doing everything he asked, without a word. She wasn't happy about it but she didn't quit.

For almost a week this went on and he taught her well, but he acted like he didn't want to. For the life of him he couldn't figure out how to sway her. He tried everything he could. It seemed she was even more determined to learn, than he was to discourage her. His mood got worse as the week went by because this little wench was going to cost him his job and way of life.

When the week was up Lord Wilmington called John to the main house. His stomach was in knots. He felt powerless. He had tried everything he could and still he had failed. Part of him was so proud of her, his heart expanded. He imagined that this was what a father felt like when his child accomplished something great. Then there was that side of him that hated her for ruining his life.

Lord Wilmington was sitting at his desk when John walked into his office. Wilmington didn't even bother to look up at him.

"You're to remove your things, and yourself, from this property immediately." John's heart dropped to the floor.

"My lord—"

"That will be all," Wilmington said sternly and still hadn't the decency to look up.

All the stress that had been building all week spewed out. What had he to lose?

"No, my lord. You will hear me out!" When Wilmington finally looked up and looked like he was going to speak, John continued quickly. "My lord. At your command, I have done everything in my power to dissuade the girl."

"Then why is she still interested in riding? I gave you a simple chore and you failed. So therefore, you are out. Now go!"

Before John blew up, he took a breath and settled himself. Getting himself hanged for insubordination wasn't on his list of ways to die.

"My lord," he said softly. Hoping to touch the man's heart. "She's really good. Strong, confident, and she understands horses." Wilmington tried to interject but John plowed on. In for a pound, he thought.

"Why don't you let her do what she's good at. After only a week, she's already a better rider than some of the lads, despite me being a bastard. She loves being a horseman. If you love her you'd let her do what she loves—"

"That's enough!" Lord Wilmington snapped to attention. "You leave at once or I will call the guards and have you hanged for sedition!" His face turned purple. "You will not tell me how to love my daughter! Get out!"

Beaten, John bowed.

"My lord." He left the room. Neither knew that there was a little blond girl listening outside the door.

In a helpless haze, John gathered his belongings and with the few shillings he had, went straight to the nearest pub and drank himself into the gutter.

The next morning he was rudely awakened by a bucket of ice cold water and Smithy's ruddy face looming over him.

"Get up, Laddie," he said gently. He reached down to help John up. John almost came up swinging, but the sorrow in Smithy's eyes stopped him.

"Come on," Smithy said wiggling his fingers. "Don't let the bastards win." Smithy waited patiently while John decided that Smithy's face didn't need to be peeled off, then continued, "I talked to the stable master over on Baron Halstead's lands. He's expecting you."

Smithy sniffed. "But first we'll be stopping off at the river. Smells like you've been sleeping with the pigs."

Smithy got John squared away and was preparing to leave when John stopped him.

"Master."

"Call me Smithy, son. I am no longer your master."

John nodded and said, "Thank you. For everything." They shook hands.

"You're a good lad. You didn't deserve that."

As he watched Smithy ride off, he felt guilt roll through him; he knew that Smithy had counted on him. He knew that it wasn't his fault but he couldn't help it. For some unknown reason he felt it for Annabelle too. He scolded himself. Why the hell am I feeling guilty for her? She's the reason I'm in this mess. But he couldn't shake the feeling that he had somehow failed her, and that made him even angrier.

A month later John was working in the arena with a foal, when he noticed a little blonde head streak by. His insides tightened. Nope, just a stable boy, he told himself, and he hoped it was true. He turned away, not wanting the reminder. He just stood there roaming his hands over the foal to calm himself.

"So are you going to just stand there, or are you going to teach me something?" John whipped around. What the—?

There she was, the object of his broken heart.

"What the bloody hell are you doing here?" he asked angrily. "Haven't ya done enough? And what have you done with your hair?" Her beautiful blond hair was cut short. "You look like a boy." His face was hot with anger. He swung around, in panic, looking for guards. "My god, girl. Don't you know that I'll be hanged? You can't be seen talking to me!"

He stalked to her, took her arm to drag her to the stable master to take her home, but she dug in. She broke away and with hands on her hips she calmly stated that her father knew she was here.

"He what? Bloody hell!" He whipped his head around again, thinking that this was some kind of joke.

"He knows I'm here, and I have his permission." John sneered at her and the smug smile on her face, and he thought to himself, this little tart is enjoying this.

"You just march yourself out of here right now, or I'll take you over my knee!"

She wouldn't budge. He waived his arms around him. "I'm here because of you!" Frustrated. "And why the bloody hell did you cut off your hair?"

"It was the only way that I'd get to ride again," she said matter-of-factly. That brought him up short. "I finally persuaded my father to let me ride. I didn't speak to him for a month, but it was my hair that finally did it. I had threatened to cut it, but he didn't think I'd do it." John stood there dumbfounded.

"So what are you doing here?"

"I told him I wanted you to teach me. You're the best there is." She giggled. "I thought he was going to pop when I told him, but I think he was just glad I was talking to him again, so he said yes."

She walked toward John. "I tried to get him to take you back, but he stood fast on that. He said it would make him look like a fool if he brought you back. So he said I could come here. He said he would clear it with the baron." John came out of his shock, sort of.

"So just like that, he let you come all the way here? It takes all morning to get here. I sincerely doubt he said yes to that," he said angrily. He didn't know if he was angry or moved, that she would do this.

"That's if you take the road around the mountain." She then pointed to the mountain. "If you go over, it doesn't take any time at all."

John looked at the mountain and then at her, shook his head, and walked back to the filly that was still in the ring. He snittered to the filly, "she's only ten. How much trouble is she going to cause when she's fifteen or twenty."

Annabelle, or Annie, as he called her, showed up twice a week for two years. They were only allowed one hour, after John's regular duties. John also stipulated that one of Lord Wilmington's men accompany her to and from. He didn't have the time for that, as well as her lessons. He had another reason in mind as well. Since John had been hired here, he had seen that Baron Halstead had a habit of taking what wasn't his to take. He wanted her protected. He had seen Halstead watching from the stable one day, and it made his insides twist, so he had started meeting Annabelle and her escort on the ridge before it dropped into the valley.

He felt guilty enough at the things that he saw and couldn't do anything about. The landowners would hang him for sure if he acted against the baron. If anything would happen to Annie, he wouldn't have time to kill himself over guilt; he was sure that Lord Wilmington would do it for him—in the most painful manner possible.

As Annabelle grew older, her duties as a maiden of the Wilmington household were numerous and her time was limited. She went on numerous trips with her father. She was a beautiful young woman, and she made a good showpiece for his business. He also took her around to the other landowners to promote goodwill with them. The only time they had for her lessons were on Sunday afternoons, his half day off. They made the most of those afternoons.

Long ago she had started complaining about women being nothing in the household. Even at her young age, she had realized that women were just chattel along with the servants. That infuriated her. It was a constant barrage of insults to women. Women were just another form of victim in this world, no matter how pretty their clothes were. Her father painted the picture of her being his partner, but she knew the reality was that she was just a toy in the world of men.

John just listened to her on those days. He knew what she felt, even though his clothes weren't nearly as pretty as hers.

They were reaching the point where he could not teach her any more. Her riding skills were equal to his, but he did not want to give up the lessons. He desperately thought of new ways for her to absorb the same information. He didn't know why, but he had to continue the lessons. *He had to.*

One night, lying in bed, he heard the sobs of yet another servant girl being used by the baron. Anger roiled through him. He wanted to bash the baron's head in. If it were another man, he would have, but Halstead was a landowner. They stuck together and took whatever they wanted. He felt guilty that he was too afraid to stand up to the establishment. It made him feel helpless, and he hated the baron for that as well.

With guilt and helplessness in mind, he thought of Annie. He sat straight up. He knew what to do. He got up and started working. Every night he worked by the light of the moon.

On Sunday, before Annabelle showed up for her lesson, he was working with a young stallion that the baron had just purchased. John couldn't wait to show Annabelle what he'd been up to. Occasionally, she would be early and wait for him at the stables. Fear of Halstead's proclivities, he admonished her for it, but it didn't stop her. He actually wished that today would be one of those days. He was so excited, the stallion, sensing his chaotic energy, wasn't behaving. John finally gave up and started to play with the young horse.

Annabelle had loved John for as long as she could remember. Her young heart beat solidly against her breast as she watched him from the trees. She knew that John would, yet again, chastise her for meeting him here at the stables, but she couldn't help it. She loved watching him with those big hands smoothing and calming some young filly. She often fantasized those hands smoothing over her. Although, today something was different, he seemed agitated.

A smile came to her lips as she thought of the first time she had laid eyes on him. She was eight when she had found herself down at the stables. She hadn't wanted to go, the horses were smelly, but her father made her. He needed her to summon Smithy as all the servants were busy with other tasks. Smithy was a growly old man, and he smelled like horses, and well, he scared her and she didn't like to be scared.

She had been wandering around looking for Smithy when she rounded the corner and saw John for the first time. There he was talking to a young foal and its mother. Thunderstruck, she watched him with her mouth open. It wasn't until Smithy had asked her three times, the question of what she was doing there, that she became aware of him. She looked at Smithy, and stammered the summons to him. Embarrassed, she ran off. She didn't notice Smithy chuckling to himself as he looked at John, and then back at her retreating little legs. He turned back to his new stable hand and thought idly that he *was* kind of a good looking young lad. If he were a young lady, he supposed that he himself would swoon after John. He turned and strode toward the main house.

Week after week she came and rode with him, and as the years passed her feelings grew stronger. It grew far beyond an infatuation of a young girl. She was a woman now, and she envisioned herself as his wife and making a life with him. She shoved the part of his being a servant to the back of her mind. Anything is possible when you love someone. Right?

As she stood in the trees, watching him, she felt that familiar pull between her legs. He did something to her as a woman, but what made her so loyal to him was that he made her feel strong. When she was with him, it was the only time that she felt the power of herself. He made her feel like she was more than just a woman. He made her feel like she was *somebody.*

Not being able to stand being away from him any longer, she pulled herself out of the trees. When he saw her, she expected a torrent of curses for her coming here. Instead, he did a double take. She noticed that there was something in his eyes. It made her smile. He stopped for a brief second, and then it was gone, and he was teacher and friend once again. But she had seen it. His realization that he felt the same.

"Oh, good, you're here," he said. She cocked her head in suspect. No torrent? "Come on. I've got something to show you."

He was like a kid with a new toy. She followed him as he led the young stallion toward the barn.

"Wait here, I'll be right out." She waited for him. She looked around for the baron. She hated the fact that she wasn't safe. For years, she had been hearing about the baron, and it made her mad. It made her insides wrinkle with fear, and loathing her father because he would do nothing. Just last week she'd had a row with him about it.

Just then John rode his horse out of the barn. She watched him coming toward her. Being with him made her feel safe and strong ... and woman.

They rode up into the hills around the mountain, far away from the dwellings. He led her to a clearing. It was a clearing that they had gone to before, working through drills. Today was different, however. She noticed that there were pieces of equipment spread out. She noticed low jumping rails and small rings scattered about. Some were hanging from trees, some were stationary, mounted on posts. There were also long poles.

"Are those jousts?" she asked incredulously. He just smiled. There were knives, swords, dummies; which were nothing more than burlap sacks filled with straw. "What? How?" Annabelle was speechless. She finally found her voice. "What is all this?"

"I wanted you to be able to defend yourself." He was embarrassed now. "I also know how useless and helpless you feel. I want you to feel powerful." He shrugged. He didn't say that it was also the only thing he could think of to keep her coming and learning.

"How did you get all of this?" Annabelle asked.

"I built it," he said simply. "I also went to the armory and saw that they had wooden practice swords. I asked if I could borrow them. They didn't ask what for. The same with the knives and the jousts. If we need to protect our lands, the more the merrier I guess. They let me take them." He shrugged again and got a little smile on his face. "I took a few things, then later that night, I went back and 'borrowed' a few more things."

Annabelle was astounded and excited. She couldn't wait to get started. She jumped off her horse and started over to the swords.

"How did you learn all this?" Annabelle asked.

"Growing up we had to learn the basics. I told you that my father was a carpenter and that I grew up working with horses, but I didn't tell you that it was at a military encampment. There were always skirmishes of some sort so we had to learn. I'm not an expert by any standard, but I know enough."

He watched as she walked to a sword and picked it up, then held it in front of her with both hands. As she stood there holding that sword, her whole demeanor changed. He was rooted in fascination as he watched the power flow through her. If he had believed that it was possible, he would have said that he could see blue. He had never seen anything like it.

She glowed. That's the word he would use. She grinned at him. He felt something inside. A warmth. He talked himself into believing that it was only satisfaction that he felt. He had found an avenue for her to place her helplessness aside.

"Let's get started then," he said.

One day, as he watched John and Annabelle ride off into the woods, Baron Halstead scowled. He didn't like John taking time for the Wilmington whelp but it kept her father happy so he let it continue. But he did stipulate that it was to be on John's half day off. Let the boy deal with that burden. He idly wondered whether John was taking "payment" from her. She was fourteen, wasn't she? A fine looking fourteen too. Why else would he let the lessons go on? He must be getting paid somehow.

He also thought that maybe someday soon, he should exact payment as well. It was *his* man doing the lessons. Was it not? It was the same thing. The more he thought about it the more he warmed to the idea. He pictured the pair coupling and he became angry that that stupid stable boy was receiving *his* rewards. He got up to follow and take his rightly share, but he thought of that pompous Wilmington. There will be another time, he thought. That dangerous seed had been planted.

He saw a young servant girl heading back to the main house. He called to her.

"You there. Come here." Something in his voice made her tremble. He saw it and it excited him even more. He recognized her as the daughter of the servant bitch that he used often. She was *almost* the same age as the Wilmington bitch. He dragged her into the barn.

The stable master came in as Halstead was walking out buttoning his trousers. "Clean that bitch up. She's disgraceful." He didn't see the stable master ball his fists with rage as he found the girl beaten and bloody. Later, John had heard about what happened and he radiated guilt. How could he not stand up for that girl, and all the others? He pounded the stable next to him and thought, *I'm a fucking coward!*

He pictured Annabelle in the baron's grip and he burned with anger. He vowed never to let Annabelle anywhere near Baron Halstead. But what could he do? If he did anything to protect her he was a dead man. The landowners were the law of the land and the rest of us were just cattle. He only hoped to God that if Annie was being threatened, he would have the courage to fight the establishment.

One Sunday, before her lesson, Annabelle dropped by Baron Halstead's manor to deliver an invitation to a ball that her parents were having. The baron and the baroness were having tea out in the courtyard.

The baroness reached for it, and Annabelle went to give it to her, but the baron told her to bring to him instead. Everyone in attendance paused, and held their breath, even the servants, as this was not man's business.

Annabelle, warily, stayed a dutiful distance away and reached out to hand him the invitation. He instead, grabbed her hand and pulled her to him. He took the invitation, while with his other hand, he reached up under her dress to claim her woman. Or at least he tried to. No one knew, but she had started to wear riding breeches under her dress. One cannot ride in a dress, can they?

His failed attempt infuriated him.

"Get away from me, you little bitch. I shall tell your father of your outrageous behavior." He got up and stomped away from the table.

Annabelle was shocked and saw sheer terror in the eyes of the servants, probably in wait for the sexual assault that he would render to one of them instead. She then looked over and saw jealous hatred in the eyes of the baroness. She would not receive sympathy there.

She felt dirty. Shame, like she had never known, washed over her. She was going to be one of the ones they talked about. One of the ones they pitied. So much for all her training.

When she rode into the pasture, she simply sat in the middle and waited for John. He started to admonish her for being there, but after one look at her face, decided it could wait. He normally didn't indulge her. He loved her and was proud of her, but she was still a spoiled, privileged, little rich girl. The look on her face made him jump on his horse, sans saddle, and follow her as she trotted out the gate.

Once out of the gate, she spurred her horse into full gallop. She rode hard, too hard for the horses, but the familiar twinge in his gut kept him silent.

When she reached the meadow, she stopped. He stopped a little ways from her, giving room for the tempest. The horses were heaving. She seemed, for the first time, to remember her horse. She gave the mare a gentle pat on the neck and whispered something. The big horse took a big breath and sighed. Both calmed.

John dismounted and, warily, started toward her. She sat and looked around her. John stopped and watched, sensing something. She looked around at all the practice equipment. Gates to jump, dressage lanes, poles with rings, dummies, lances and swords. He saw what she saw, or did he?

For the first time, in the storm in her eyes, he saw the woman she was to become.

Before he could comprehend what that meant, she spurred her horse forward, once around the ring, grabbed a sword and headed straight for the dummy. She speared it, and with all her fourteen-year-old might, carried it, with sword, and chunked it into a tree as she rode past it.

She whirled her horse around and trotted around to the front of the tree. The dummy dangled there like a corpse. She seemed to have taken satisfaction with that. She had that warrior look in her eyes and her horse fed off that energy. John watched them both hungrily prancing around in circles. She looked at him with eyes of a warrior queen. He was glad he was on her side.

She then reached into the folds of her garb and brandished a long dagger. *Where the hell did she get that?* At that instant, her horse reared in triumph. She held the reigns with one hand and wielded the dagger with the other. His warrior queen. In that moment he fell in love with her. He didn't want to know that in his heart, he had fallen a long time ago.

The horse settled, she settled. He did not settle.

The duo stood in one place. John could see the anger slowly seeping away. He watched as his warrior queen faded to the frightened little girl once again, full of pain and hurt.

Well … shite.

He strode to her. She reached for him as a child reaches for her father. He grabbed her under the arms and gently pulled her from the saddle. He hugged her to him and let her cry it out.

His emotions were in turmoil, but he'd been a father figure for much longer than the warrior queen's suitor, so he decided he would do what he could for one, and put the other aside for a few years. He sighed and tried not to think about her being royalty, and he was … nothing.

She broke away and told him what had happened. Relieved, he didn't think that it was that bad, considering the *other* things that had happened in the hands of the baron. He knew that she knew that the baron was a bastard. He could almost see it on her face, until today, it was only happening to one of the servants. *Only the servants.* Now, with the baron's actions, he knew that she was only one step away from that. Coming to that conclusion herself she started crying again. He stepped to her and wrapped his charge in his arms.

As he held her he looked around the ring and felt a fool. What good is all this if they were never going to use it. Subservience was too ingrained in both of them.

She had just composed herself and was about to extricate herself from his fatherly hug when Baron Halstead, on his horse, rode out of the woods into the clearing.

"Well, well, well. What do we have here?"

They hastily broke apart.

"I knew there was something going on." Halstead leered at her, then that leer turned to something evil. "You will stop your payments to him and make them to me from now on."

"Payments? What are you talking about?" Annabelle and John looked quizzically at each other.

"Don't you lie to me, boy! I know that she's been servicing you like a whore. Why else would you give lessons to her all these years?" His face was ugly.

Warning bells screamed in John's head. He tried to reason with the baron.

"You've got it all wrong. I've been teaching her to ride, nothing more. Perhaps she could show you—"

"The only thing that bitch is going to show me is what's between her legs." He stepped off the horse and started forward. John slid Annabelle behind him.

"You will not touch her." He knew he would die for this but he couldn't let this monster win. Not this time. All the anger that he had squelched these past few years came to the surface. He had seen too many broken bodies. The baron's face twisted into an ugly grin.

"Good. I will enjoy hanging you. But first, I'll whip you to a bloody pulp." He laughed.

"Please, don't do this," John pleaded. "She's just a girl."

"Don't be stupid. I know you just want her for yourself."

"No. That's not it. I—"

"What do you care? She's just a little bitch, and you're a nobody. No one will know, or care, if you're dead."

"You will not touch her." John stood his ground.

The baron swung his riding switch across John's face. The baron was faster than John gave him credit for, but John stood his ground.

"Get out of my way!" Halstead yelled, his face turning bright red.

When the baron raised his switch again, John shoved him back.

"Over my dead body!"

"Gladly. You're dead anyway. Why not let it go?" the baron tried to change tactics. John realized in that moment that the baron was a coward. He'd only survived this far because of his title. "If you let me have her without a fight, I'll kill you quickly."

"No."

"Then you'll die a very painful death." He charged as he said this last word.

The baron came ahead but John was ready for him. All he could think of was to get Halstead away from Annie. He took a running push, and in his momentum, pushed the baron back across the field. There was nothing the baron could do but back pedal. When they got to the edge of the clearing, Halstead tripped on a rock and fell backward. He hit the ground and lay still with his eyes open.

John stood ready for a trick, expecting Halstead to spring up. When he noticed blood seeping from the back of the baron's head, he approached cautiously and reached behind and felt a good sized rock. Shite. He turned and looked at Annie. She stood at the ready, with dagger in hand, and with fear and war in her eyes. Love shot through his heart. Shite. Love was never going to happen, because he was a dead man.

It was only when she saw the blood on his hand that she fully understood what had happened. He watched her face as it changed from the shock of seeing a dead man, to the shock of realizing the ramifications for him. They would hang him. If he was lucky.

"If we leave him maybe they'll think his horse threw him," she said in desperation.

"Yes. If it wasn't for the fact that he lies within our practice ring, I'd agree with ya." He sighed, "But as everyone knows we practice here, there's no reason for him to be here. They're going to make a connection."

"Then you'll have to leave. Run, and never come back." She ran to him. The love on her face shown through. He had refused to see it before, but now, with his own blinders off, he couldn't see anything else.

"That'll make me look guilty, as sure as you and I are standing here."

"But it wasn't your fault. You were saving me. It was an accident," she cried.

"Do you think that matters to them? Your royalty sticks together. He was a bastard and no one did anything about it!" he said angrily. "Do ya think they'll be celebrating?" he yelled at her. "I'm a dead man and you know it," he said, resigned.

She didn't say anything, knowing it was true. She thought for a moment.

"My father!" she said excitedly.

"Your father what?" he shouted at her. Again, he was in an impossible position because of her. Knowing it wasn't her fault didn't matter. He had to blame someone. "Your father hates me, and wants to strap me to horses and gladly send my body parts to the four ends of the earth."

"He does not hate you."

"Right. I made him look like a fool. He'll be glad I'm gone."

"He doesn't hate you." He snarled at her words. "Not that long ago, he told me that he came here once, to see if you were behaving yourself and actually teaching me. I guess he assumed that because the baron was a ..." Her voice hitched. "He wanted to make sure you were behaving. He begrudgingly said that you were a good teacher." She had a slight smile on her face remembering how difficult it was for her father to say that. "High praise, coming from my father."

John was shocked.

"And—" she continued. "I also know for a fact that he thinks Baron Halstead is a barbarian and wishes he wasn't here." That shocked him even more.

"And still no one did anything!" he exclaimed.

He looked at her. Turned to watch the horses, the grass, trees, mountains—anything but the vision in his head. The one where his body and blood was spread to kingdom come. He knew what she was trying to say, knowing that he had no choice in the matter. If he ran they would hunt him down like a dog.

"What do ya have in mind?" he asked, resignation filling his whole body. He looked at this child, becoming a woman before his very eyes, yet still very much like a child. He made up his mind. He was a dead man anyway, he might as well make it sooner than later. And make it on his own terms. Maybe he'd carry a little less guilt with him to the afterlife; knowing he'd done *something*.

They left the baron where he was. They rode silently to her father's lands. As he rode he felt lighter than he'd felt in a long time.

Acceptance of his fate let his shoulders ride high. He felt free. It amazed him that the closer he rode to his death, the freer he felt.

They arrived in her father's office by the back entrance. They withstood the initial outburst of Lord Wilmington, wondering why they were in his office. Annabelle told him what had transpired that morning at the Halstead manor.

"And what, please tell, has that to do with *him* in my office?" He pointed to John.

Annabelle started to tell him the events but John stopped her.

"Annabelle. Please," he said softly. "this part is mine." John's demeanor intrigued Lord Wilmington and he remained silent. He decided not to throw John out. Not yet. John told him what had happened, calmly, with no embellishments.

"It was an accident, but I killed Baron Halstead," he ended the story.

Wilmington jumped up. His first reaction was to call the guards, but John's demeanor gave him pause. Besides, wasn't it just two days ago that the landowners gathered to manage the problem of Baron Halstead. Most of the landowner's took … certain liberties, shall they say, but the baron's brutality was getting out of hand. And now, his very own daughter! He looked long and hard at John and made up his mind.

"The punishment for this is death." He opened his mouth to continue speaking.

"But you—" Annabelle screamed.

"Silence!" Lord Wilmington bellowed. John's heart sank. "As I was saying! Punishment for this crime is death." He raised his hand to stop another one of Annabelle's outbursts. "But as you've assisted in helping with our little problem …" He paused, looking at John, made another decision. "Baron Halstead had become a liability. Now, he is not. And as you have saved my daughter from his … hands, I will extend to you your life."

Annabelle squealed, almost jumped for joy. In a rush of air John released the breath that he hadn't realized he was holding. But he knew there was more coming.

"See, I—" Annabelle turned to John and started to shout.

"There is, however, one stipulation," Lord Wilmington said. Here it comes, thought John. Too good to be true. His insides clenched. "You must leave these lands. Forever."

Annabelle exploded.

"Forever? You can't do that!"

"I can and I will!" he bellowed. "He stays, he hangs. He goes, he lives. That simple." He looked at John with smugness in his eyes; finally rid of you, they said. Then, the look changed to one of sorrow and thankfulness. John saw it. It was just a moment but it was there. For one moment in time they were just two people. The moment passed and master and slave were back.

"I will arrange for your servitude to be paid in full. You are free to leave. You're dismissed."

John nodded and turned to leave. He was granted a reprieve and was not going to wait around for Wilmington to change his mind. He left the room and heard Annabelle starting to argue with her father.

He didn't hear everything but he did hear Annabelle scream, "Fine, I'm leaving too then!"

"You will not leave these grounds!" Wilmington yelled over the top of her.

John walked outside and took a breath of fresh air. As he walked to his horse, every breath felt like freedom—like a noose around his neck.

When he reached his horse he heard her dress rustling as she ran toward him. He turned and saw the desperation in the eyes of the child, and the love in the eyes of the woman.

The force of his love for her was a blow to him and he almost doubled over from it. Now that he was losing her, he allowed himself to feel what he had always known. Love.

She stopped a few feet from him. They stood staring. Finally, she broke the silence. She needed to break it.

"My father says that he'll send Smithy straight away to make it right with your stable master. He'll tell him he's paid your servitude …." She faded off, knowing she sounded stupid but had to say something.

He nodded. His heart and his head were exploding.

"I love you!" he blurted. She smiled.

"I know." And then she said hopefully, "maybe someday—"

"No. Don't. You know it'll never be. I'll always be the Scottish help and you'll always be Lord Wilmington's daughter."

"But—"

He stepped toward her.

"Ssh. Please. It's better this way. We'll always have love this way. It'll be nothing but pain any other way." A loud snap broke the silent bubble around them.

Lord Wilmington had been watching, holding his riding switch in his hand.

"I've got to go," he told her. She jumped in his arms. He held her for as long as he dared. Then he let her go swiftly and jumped on his horse and bolted.

His horse flew across the turf. The guilt that was released by killing that monster was replaced by the guilt of leaving her. He was a free man but he knew that he would never be free. When he was far enough away so that he could trust himself, he stopped and turned. There she was. His woman/child. He reared his horse up in salute and turned and galloped off. His face became cold from the wind in his tears.

She watched him gallop away and felt her heart break into a thousand pieces. She had loved him since she was eight. She watched him long after he couldn't be seen. Her father walked up behind and laid a gentle hand on her shoulder.

"It's better this way," he said softly.

Somewhere in her brain she knew he was right. She knew circumstances could've turned out very different, but she didn't want to listen to his logical mind right now; it was easier to be mad. She didn't say a word and after a moment just simply walked away.

Helplessness hung like a blanket on her shoulders. The rage she felt couldn't be put anywhere. It burned like a flame to the point where she couldn't be trusted around anyone. She didn't trust herself to see her father. She walked for hours in the hills. Helplessness grew heavier with every step. Why are we punished? We didn't do anything. I'm the victim, aren't I? And John? Baron went after me! Why is it always me that has to do without? Just because I'm a girl. I'm the victim.

"Why is this happening to me?" Her screams echoed in the trees.

In the silence that followed, her heart ached so much she heard it break. That brought rage, victim, helplessness. Her mind whirled. Victim, helpless. She repeated that mantra in her head over and over.

She couldn't bear the thought of living the rest of her life in those terms—she was only a woman, after all—She took out her knife. She wouldn't live like that. She brought the knife to her wrists. "I won't live like this." A brief flash of doing this to Baron Halstead entered her head. That made her pause. Thinking about that made her feel less helpless. That thought grew. She stared at the knife and in that moment she knew that if the baron weren't dead already, he would be shortly. She knew she wasn't a killer but she did want justice. It was too late for her but she could get justice for others. All those times in the practice ring were worth it. She wielded the knife in her hand with assurance and hefted it against a tree and it stuck strong.

The ache and rage in her heart, were shoved down until she felt nothing. She made an about face and strode tall and strong. She no longer was a fourteen-year-old *girl*. She was a woman with a mission.

She would never be helpless again.

7

When Pam opened her eyes, they were moist. She looked at us and grinned. We were arm in arm, with tears and makeup running down our faces.

"Well now, that was something," she said, as she handed over a box of tissues and waited until we collected ourselves.

"Thoughts? Questions?" she asked, after we had composed ourselves.

I chortled. Questions? That was an understatement. Pam smiled.

"Well, I guess that's a good reason why we feel like we can't lose each other again," I surmised.

"Maybe," Pam said. "That's one reason."

"There's more?" I asked incredulously.

"I don't know, but it's possible," Pam answered. She waited for a response and when there was none, she said. "Listen. You guys look wasted. Why don't you go home, let it settle in, and when you have questions, call me." We nodded and got up. Pam led us out. When we reached the living room, Pam must have noticed that we were a little ragged. "Are you guys okay to drive? You're welcome to stay here for a bit." We nodded, but didn't say anything. Pam gestured us to the door, but I had a question and stopped.

"So what's it all for?"

"What's what all for?" Pam asked.

"We have all this information, but what's it for? What do we do with it?"

Pam thought about that for a moment.

"Well, you can use it to learn and grow."

"What do you mean? How?"

"For starters, past lives are a doorway into something that we're working on in this lifetime." Rhina had said the same thing. I must have had a blank look on my face because Pam smiled at me. Jeez. Just like Rhina. "Like for instance, with what we've just experienced, and what little you've shared about your other vision, I can extrapolate and say that both of you are working on a piece of the puzzle called," she raised her fingers in quotations, "not worthy. Or helpless. And a big piece of that is the victim. Those are just the pieces that I see right now. There are probably more. There usually are."

"What if we're not?" I blurted. Who wants to be a victim?

Pam looked at me, with compassion. I was starting to feel a little frantic. I looked at Rhina, who had a nondescript look on her face. There was love, but also something else, in her eyes. It confused me but Rhina wasn't complaining, so I wouldn't either.

"Okay." I resigned myself.

Pam smiled and opened the door.

"Call with questions. It's been a pleasure."

"For us too. Thanks a lot," I said.

When we got settled in the car, I turned to Rhina.

"You're awfully quiet."

Rhina was facing forward and didn't react. A twitch of her eyelid was the only movement, enough for me to know that she had heard me. I waited patiently, on the outside, but on the inside I was worried. This wasn't like her. I think. What did I really know? Everything was too new, too deep. I didn't know what to think about any of this. She was my rope-in-the-wind with all this. What if all this digging reveals too much for her. Too much for us?

"Rhi. You have to give me a bone okay? I'm dying here." There was a slight upturn of her lips. She turned and I could see tears in her eyes. I had never really seen her this rattled, and it scared me. I didn't know what to do. It got me out of my own funk. Sort of.

"Okay … I'm not sure what's going on, so I'm going to just drive until you're ready to talk." Rhina nodded slightly. "Hold my hand. Okay?" Rhina nodded again and grasped my hand. I sighed a big inward sigh. What the hell is wrong with me? I have never been this needy. What the hell?

We both immersed ourselves in our own thoughts as we drove across town.

"I have a very busy week. I have a new client and she has MS. I'm going to have to take the weekend to do some research. It would also give me time." Rhina kept facing forward as she spoke. She stopped me as I drew a breath to speak. "Please don't." I didn't. "I know you have questions." Uh ... understatement. "But I can't deal with this right now."

"Deal with what?" I demanded in panic. She smiled slightly. Damn she knew me so well.

"Don't worry, it's not about you. This is about my life before I met you. I have to work it through."

"I thought 'us' meant working through stuff together," I blurted out before I could stop it.

"Listen!" She quipped in irritation but stopped herself. I withdrew. Shocked. She started again more softly. "Listen. I would love to talk with you, and I plan to, but right now I just need to be alone."

Alone.

She saw the panic on my face. "For now. Just for now," she said. Yeah, that's what they all say. She reached up and laid her hand on my cheek. Relief brought moisture to my eyes. Rhina softened even more.

"Remember when I told you that I get messed up too?" I nodded. "Well, this is my messy." I couldn't react. All I could do was just drive, and not react. "Kat?" She tried to make me understand. "This session brought things up in me that I can't even begin to articulate. I want to be able to articulate them."

I just nodded tightly. I felt hurt. I was lost too! "Kat, please. I'm only asking for some alone time to let it rattle around in my head. Then, when it sorts itself out—"

"What if it never sorts itself out?" Jesus. I sounded like a kid.

"Why are you being like this?" she asked gently. "I'm just asking for a day or two."

Why *am* I acting like this?

"I don't know," I cried. Things were much easier when I was dating guys. I never felt like this.

"Kat, please forgive me, but I can't do this with you. Not yet."

I nodded curtly. She sighed.

We drove in silence for five minutes until we pulled up in front of her house. I looked straight ahead. I could see her peripherally, looking at me but I couldn't look at her, and I couldn't fathom why. Why was I acting like a petulant child?

"Do you have anything inside that you need?" I curtly shook my head. She sighed. "Okay." She got out, but before she shut the door she leaned in. "Kat. Kattrina. Look at me." I turned toward her. The love shining in her eyes made my eyes water. She opened her mouth to say something but changed her mind. Her shoulders shrugged and she said. "I have to do this." My shoulders let go. She said. "I love you. Please know that. I'll call you Sunday night. Okay?" After a moment's hesitation I nodded. She shut the door and I watched her walk away. As her front door closed the flood gates opened.

When my tears abated I put the car in drive. As I negotiated traffic, I wondered what the hell had just happened. I had never felt, or acted, like that. What the hell? It was clingy and needy and I didn't like it.

I thought about John and Annabelle. Did they ever meet again? I think not. Is that why I feel like this? Because she, or he, is walking out of my life again? I knew, intellectually, that Rhina wasn't walking but it sure felt like it. It felt like it was happening all over again.

Wow. This past life stuff is a trip.

As I drove, my thoughts took me on a journey.

If this kind of anxiety is still inside of me … and how is it still inside of me? It's another lifetime, therefore another body. How can that be? And why hasn't it surfaced before? Is it because I'm so attached to Rhina? I feel closer to her than anyone. I thought some more about that.

Well, shit …. Have I been so detached from everyone, that nothing mattered?

"Didn't care," the nice little voice, inside my head, said. I didn't care. Well … why didn't I care? I thought of my relationships. I realized that all those men were unavailable emotionally—I didn't count the one that was *actually* unavailable—not a shining moment. Does that mean that *I* was unavailable?

So since they were unavailable, what does that do for me? Did I choose that on purpose? And if I did. Why? Did I not want a relationship? I always thought I did. I mulled that over in my head.

Until Rhina, there wasn't anyone that I thought I loved. Rhina. Within moments of meeting her, I knew. Well … maybe it took me five minutes. She is a woman after all.

I arrived home and stood in my living room. One half of my brain was still mulling things over, and the other, realized how I'd neglected my house. Because of her clients, we had spent most of our time at Rhina's. Having a girlfriend is hell on housework. I grabbed the clothes that had been sitting in the hamper and put them in the washing machine. I was surprised they didn't have mold growing on them. I then went to scrubbing the toilet. It was good therapy and a mindless task in which to think.

John and Annabelle. I had a pretty good idea that I was Annabelle in that lifetime. Incomplete love. Then I thought about Stephen and Rachael. Their love was complete. They loved each other. Why did I dream that? That dream was obviously incomplete so what was that about? I didn't know.

It was too confusing.

I quit thinking about it and put my back into scrubbing the kitchen floor on my hands and knees. After I finished cleaning the house I pulled out my homework. Papers needed graded.

Anything but past lives.

Hours later, on the couch folding clothes, I set aside my own crap enough to think of Rhina. What was up with her? I had never seen her like that. I chided myself. She was obviously going through something, but she still treated me with love and kindness, and all I did was behave like a child. I was disgusted with myself. I wanted to call her and apologize, but I thought the least I could do is to honor her request. I threw down my underwear in a heap. Why does one need to fold one's underwear anyway? I sent her a quick text, apologizing for being such a shit, and that I'd talk to her tomorrow. I stretched out and put my feet up on the coffee table. God, I missed her. My heart ached. Is it normal to miss someone so much?

I let my mind wander over various things: The night Rhina and I met, Penny, Josh, Sam ... Sam. I felt an impending doom but I put it off to ... off to ... the unknown? I thought about John and Annabelle, and Stephen and Rachael. Where does it all lead?

I couldn't come up with any answers. Like I have all the answers in all things reincarnation. Right? Hell. I didn't even know that I had *questions* until a week ago, let alone answers.

With my eyes closed, I stopped thinking of anything in particular, and just put all my thoughts in a mental pot and stirred them all together. With jumbled thoughts, I fell asleep.

I woke, in the dark, groggy and confused. Even by dream standards this was a doozy. I sat back and relived it. There were a series of pictures. A jumble of faces and places sliding in and around and on top of each other. None really making any sense. Or at least not to me. There were past, and present figments: Me, Rhina, Annabelle, Stephen, Penny, Pam. Even Lord Wilmington paid a visit. I think there were more, but that's what came to mind.

Here I am, putting faces and names, and times and places, together in dreams. Either I'm getting better at this game or ... I'm losing my mind.

I looked down, at the coffee table and the couch at my students' essays spread out and thought I should pick them up. Then, another thought passed through my brain. I blew out a breath.

What's the point? No one will see it. It felt like someone threw a spear through my heart.

Relax, I told myself. She's just taking a few days to work out her stuff. I inflated my lungs to the point of pain, then slowly let it out. I promised myself to feel better when all that air was out. I looked at the papers on the table again and I noticed one with Sam's name on it. Shit! I remembered a portion of my dream.

I flipped through the slim pickings in my kitchen. I found a can of tomato soup, a loaf of bread in the freezer, sour milk in the fridge, and three bottles of Marci's beer. A new pang of loss ripped through my heart. A sorry state of affairs most definitely. Sucking it up, I shut the door with a thud that rang of finality.

I just never thought of food. Not until Rhina. She did all the cooking and I actually missed her cooking. Huh. Until this moment I didn't think I cared about that. The doorbell rang.

On a Saturday night? What the hell?

"Who is it?"

"It's me." After a slight hesitation. "Rhina."

I flung the door open, and there she was. I was vaguely aware of a pizza box. The relief that flooded over me almost brought me to my knees. I stood there like an idiot just looking at her, with her just looking at me. I felt relief, love, shock, and heartache all at once and I could recognize those on her face.

Still in the doorway, I absentmindedly asked. "Why didn't you use your key?"

"I … I didn't know if you would want me here. I figured it was easier to slam the door in my face than to throw me out."

That brought me out of my shocked trance.

"You what? You thought I'd throw you out? Why would I want to do that?"

"Because I acted like a jerk. I feel so guilty. I should have had you stay. I'm sorry—"

"*You* acted like a jerk? Oh, honey. No. I was the stupid jerk. You have no reason to feel guilty. I threw a little tantrum and all you did was ask for a little alone time. I'm the one who needs to apologize."

We stopped talking and smiled.

"Really," I said. "I am so sorry I acted like a spoiled kid. I've never done that. I'm sorry."

"Well, apology accepted. I'm sorry too, for shutting you out," she said. I nodded.

"So … Luggio's?" I indicated the pizza.

"Peace offering."

"You brought pizza as a piece offering?" There was a moment of insecurity that flitted across her face so I said quickly. "If I hadn't already fallen in love with you, this would have tipped me over the edge." I couldn't tear my eyes from her face. She so easily put me into a trance. I couldn't think of anything but her.

"Good. So ... you think maybe I can come in?"

"Huh? Oh, jeez!" I woke up, looked at where I was and quickly ushered her inside. "Sorry. You just ..." I ran my hands through my hair. "I don't ... there are so many times I don't have words when it comes to you." I said embarrased. "It's a bit disconcerting for someone who uses her words all day long."

She stopped in the hallway, put the pizza on the end table, and turned around with her arms open. I did not hesitate. The second she had her arms around me, things righted. I buried my head against her shoulder and let out a short burst of tears. "I thought you were leaving again."

She held me tight until I quit. When she heard that I was moving through that wave, she pulled back, brushed the hair out of my face, and kissed my forehead. She then promptly put her arms around me again.

I was embarrassed. I tried to pull away but she wouldn't let me.

"I don't know why I'm being so soppy. I've never been like this." She let me pull away, but only as far as her outstretched arms.

"We've been through a lot in the last week, especially you. What do you expect?"

"Yeah, but look at you. You always hold it together."

Rhina scrunched up her face. "Do you not remember that I told you to go away this morning?"

"Yes. But you did it so politely. I was the one throwing the tantrum."

"I've just had more practice than you. That's all."

"Why *are* you here anyway? You were going to call me tomorrow."

Rhina let go of one hand, grabbed the pizza and led me to the kitchen. She gestured to the can of soup. "Because you can't cook worth beans. I didn't want you to starve."

"Uh-huh." I folded my arms and crooked an eyebrow. To give herself time to think, Rhina went in search of plates.

"I have a few trust issues." She went for the silverware drawer, and took a little too long finding just the right fork. When she turned around, she seemed a little surprised that I hadn't bolted yet. She saw that I was still waiting patiently, so she continued.

"I'm not used to people being there for me when I need it. I mean, when I was really in a bad way, I could usually find someone who would take pity on me. They meant well, but no one understood what I saw or felt. People care about me, as I care about them, but it always fell short of mutual understanding. I've never felt as though anybody 'got me.'" As she talked she dished up the pizza with her fingers and handed me the plate. "I see things so differently than most people that few really understand what it is that I'm feeling."

And she thinks I do?

"I know you don't know what I'm talking about half the time, but I also know that it's only because of ignorance, in the true sense of the word. You have this innate understanding that goes far beyond your learning to date." Okay. Far be it from me to argue.

She continued but couldn't look at me. "I didn't trust you to understand. I love you so much that I didn't want to lose that connection. That ... I didn't want to be disappointed." She looked at me with hope in her eyes, but also, with a little bit of daring. Daring me to prove her wrong. Or right.

I waited to see if she was finished.

"Well, you're right. I have no idea what you're talking about half the time, but I do understand the disappointment thing. Every guy that I kind of liked, disappointed me in the exact same way. He just didn't 'get me.'" I paused. "I can't guarantee that I'll understand everything you talk about, but I do understand your reticence about wanting to share with me." I took her hand. "Whatever happened to you today—" I changed my thought process. "Listen, I didn't handle things well this morning. It was too soon after John left Annabelle." I shook my head, in disbelief, that I actually had said that. "I thought you were leaving me again. I couldn't take it." She squeezed my hand.

"I think you understand more than you think you do. You just don't know that you do." I thought about that. What does one say to that?

"Well, I hope you're right because the last thing I want to do is disappoint you."

"Likewise," she agreed.

We ate in silence for a bit, in our own thoughts. She knew I was waiting for an explanation as to what had happened this morning.

"Kat, I don't really want to talk about this morning. I will, and I want to tell you, I'm just not sure if I can articulate what's happening to me. When I have an idea, I'll talk to you about it, okay?"

I nodded.

"So what made you come over here tonight then?"

"Simply put, I missed you." We both smiled. I'm glad I'm not the only crazy one.

"Yeah."

"I tried to deal, but everywhere I looked, there you were. I couldn't get away from you. Then, as the day went on I realized, why would I want to?" She laughed. "And I even tried to fight that. Then later, I told myself, 'Rhina. You're an idiot. Quit. Quit fighting it. Quit fighting. Give her a chance. *Give her a chance.*'" She gestured with the pizza. "So I called Luggio's." We sat in silence, then she said.

"My heart ached so bad for you. Is that normal?" I burst out laughing and told her that I had that same affliction. I got up to get us both a beer. We sat in companionable silence, holding pizza with one hand and having our fingers entwined with the other.

Later, Rhina was stretched out on the couch with her head in my lap. I was absentmindedly playing with a lock of her hair. We weren't talking much, just enjoying being together again. I just happen to glance at the stack of papers that I had straightened. A small jolt went through me.

"I had a dream earlier."

"Tell me," she said with her eyes shut.

"It was nothing specific, really. Just a jumble of events and faces. A mix of past and present. It was kind of strange, really. Flashes of faces on different bodies. They moved by so quickly that I really didn't get a good grasp on any particular thing or person." I hesitated. "Except one."

Rhina noticed my change and opened her eyes.

"Baron Halstead," I started. Rhina shifted to her side and waited, encouraging me. "Only it was a little different." I shifted uncomfortably. "He had Sam's face."

Rhina sucked in a breath and slowly blew it out.

"Wow."

"Yeah."

"Well, it's all about learning from our past, right?" she said. I started to nod, but then I realized that I had no clue. "Well, so we learn." She snickered at my dazed look. "Look at it this way—"

"Do I have to?"

"Yes. Baron Halstead."

"Baron Halstead." I steeled myself.

"Okay. What did he take from you?" I thought about it.

"The only thing he took was—" I looked at Rhina with panic. "John! You. No!" I stood up, almost dumping Rhina on the floor. "That little bastard!" I looked at Rhina and she had a shocked little smile on her face. If I wasn't so pissed I would have laughed. I gave a little crooked grin.

"See how crazy you made me today. Jeez, was that only this morning? My god, it seems like a week ago." I sagged onto the couch. "Sorry."

"Are you kidding? You were going to go to war for me. Who wouldn't want to be loved that much?"

I thought about that and it occurred to me that she was right. I would fight for her. Literally. Huh. That's new.

"You're right. I would fight for you." I turned serious. "I *would* fight for you. That's new. I've never cared enough before. It's good to know that I can care that much."

Rhina watched me closely.

"What?" I asked.

"You look different."

"How?"

"I don't know. Bigger. Brighter … more substantial somehow." Huh. What does one say to that?

I took her face in my hands.

"I don't want to talk about this anymore. I'm taking you to bed. It's been a long day." I kissed her. "And I've missed you." I took her hand and led her down the hall.

It was Sunday, so we decided to go for a drive. The day was going to be beautiful, a perfect day to be in the mountains. As we were in the kitchen, packing the cooler, I had a thought.

"What did we do before we met? I've been trying to think. It's almost like I didn't even have a life before I met you."

"Sounds like you were always busy."

"Yeah, I was, but I've been thinking a lot about that lately, since you. I was busy but I was just filling spaces. You know what I mean?" Rhina nodded. "I find myself barely remembering my life before you." She didn't say anything but her eyes asked. "I guess I didn't have a very memorable life," I said sarcastically. After saying it, I realized it was true. Wow. It's a little disconcerting to realize that your life was … mediocre. That's the word I would use.

"You look sad." She touched my arm.

"My whole life's been mediocre. It's been a sham. All this time I thought that I was "all that" because I was a professor in a college, had friends, boyfriends, busy all the time …." I was close to tears. Rhina, God bless her, just listened.

"Now that you've shown me what's real in life, I feel like there's very little in my life that I would want to keep. And to be honest, since you, there's not many of my friends that I would want to talk to either. Well, maybe a few, Marci being one, and she's gone." I tried for a little brevity. "Thank God. She'd be pissed at you, by the way." Rhina raised an eyebrow. "She'd have to fight you for time with me."

"Ah."

"My whole life has been a waste." I was knee deep in my pity party. Rhina waited to see if there was more.

"You know that's not true," she said softly.

I didn't look at her and I couldn't think of anything to say. We both let me process while we finished packing.

Was my life really a waste?

I didn't really want to look at that, but how could I not? I didn't want to lose Rhina because of my dysfunctions. Rhina. I smiled to myself. I certainly didn't know what I did there. How did I deserve her? How *did* I deserve her? No, really. How did I?—If there was ever a time to help, *now* was a good time—I sent the pseudo prayer up.

I brought the ax down on myself.

I've been a selfish, unsatisfied bitch, and a mediocre one at that.

I'm not totally selfish and not totally a bitch and not totally unsatisfied. Just enough. Just enough that guys would wonder what they did. A sharp word here, a cold remark there … I didn't even notice that I was doing it. I thought that they were just being "men." But now, looking back, I realized that it was me too. I blew out my breath. It was a heavy load indeed, to realize that I wasn't who I had thought I was.

I was thankful that Rhina was ahead of me as we walked out to the car, because I felt like I was going to cry. Again. I've never cried this much in my life. Please, God. Don't let me be mediocre for her. The prayer must have found its place because I started to hear the nice little voice again.

"You have found a reason for being unselfish. You have found a reason to be grateful. When you have achieved those, then you will no longer need to be a bitch. To know is to change. Now you know."

Huh.

I felt a weight lift off my shoulders. I watched Rhina shut the trunk and walk to the passenger side. A thought rolled through my head that was so simple, yet so huge, it almost brought me to my knees. How did I not know this?

You can change who you are.

I had slowed, almost to a stop, as the world was changing inside my head. She just stood by the door watching me over the roof of the car. Patiently waiting. Watching her watch me, with such gentleness and love, something clicked inside. I had done something right. I reached the car, and our eyes met over the roof. Maybe my life wasn't a waste after all.

"Yeah. I guess I do know that." She smiled, nodded, and got into the car.

The day was glorious. The trees were just showing hints of fall. At some point along the way, we saw a small lake with a flat rock on the far side. It had great access to the water, as it was half in. We decided that it was a good place to have a picnic.

What we found, however, was that the plan was much easier than the execution. As we went around the lake, we had to pick our way through swampy ground and fight our way through underbrush. At one point, we even had to ford a stream. We were laughing so hard, picking our way across on small boulders, trying not to fall in, that we almost fell in. But we finally made it, covered in mud. Rhina had dropped the cooler in the mud, so it was as brown as we were. We were still laughing as we crowned the rock.

"Wahoo!" she hollered, "we made it!"

I listened to the echo as it faded. I saw her glowing, and so alive, and realized that I had never really truly yelled at the top of my lungs. I faced the lake, gathered air in my lungs, and split the atoms.

And it felt good!

We hooped and hollered for a minute, then we sat down and listened to the silence.

"You know, I've never done that," I admitted.

"What?"

"This. Yell."

"What?" she asked in disbelief. She thought I was kidding.

"No. Really. I haven't. I've hardly ever raised my voice. Ever." Mediocrity at its best, I sourly made fun of myself.

Seeing the dark look on my face, she said. "I guess I've come along just in time then." She smiled and bumped me with her shoulder.

With our shoes off, we sat there in silence. While we ate, the wind died down and we enjoyed the exquisite mountains reflecting off the water. We sat in awe. I thought of Ayla, in Clan of the Cave Bear. Whenever she had passed whatever test life had thrown at her, she would find some kind of a reward. It could be a beautiful shell or rock, or whatever. I felt that this amazing view in front of us, was *my* reward for my own self-reflections today. That thought circled me around to other thoughts. What if our past lives are a reflection of us? Was Stephen like me, or, rather, was I like him? His vocation certainly paralleled mine. Rachael was a healer ... so was Rhina. Huh. It seemed there was a lot more to reincarnation than I thought, even now. It seemed the more questions I had, the more questions I had.

Much later, a black bear and her two cubs came down to the shore about halfway across the lake. We watched, fascinated, until she went back into the woods. I thanked the heavens for another gift.

"I can't believe you've never yelled for an echo," Rhina broke into my thoughts. Still in disbelief, she said, "I read this story once that will forever change my thoughts about echoes. In the story, all the rocks and cliffs and crevasses, etc., are their own being. Deep Crevasse. Sheer Cliff. Flat Shelf. Whatever. It said that *we* think that we're the ones that actually cause the echo; sound reverberation and whatnot. But this story made it sound like Deep Crevasse would catch the sound and throw it to Sheer Cliff, and they would play catch with it. Throwing the sound back and forth until they got tired, which is why echoes don't last very long." She smiled at the thought. "Because Deep Crevasse and Sheer Cliff don't get much exercise. They tire easily."

We laid down, contemplating echos, and napped.

We woke with the sun much further along in the sky.

"You know we're going to have to make our way out of here," she said.

"I know. I've been stalling."

"Well, c'mon. Let's put our big girl panties on. I sure don't want to do this in the dark. Besides, I have to go find a tree."

As we put on our shoes, we contemplated going around the other way in hopes of an easier time of it, but we didn't want to take a chance that momma and her cubs were still about. We made it back to the car in half the time, as we were experts now.

That night in bed Rhina mentioned that I seemed different. I realized she was right. I felt more settled than I ever had. I told her about my revelations that morning and mentioned my outburst last night.

"Poor Sam. He has no idea how close he came to death," Rhina joked.

"This past life stuff is a trip."

"Yes it is."

"You know, it's the thought that I would fight for you like a mother bear, believe it or not, that settled me more than anything." I pondered more about that. "I've never known that I could want, or need something so much. But in an empowering way, you know? John and Annabelle were victims. I realized today, while we were watching the bear actually, that like Josh said in his essay, I can be a victim, or I can choose not to. I made a choice today."

My skin tingled.

"I had an insight today about past lives that made me see them in a whole new light." I looked down at Rhina and brushed a lock of hair from her face. She had a pleased smile on her face. "You're enjoying this aren't you?" Her smile only got bigger and motioned me to continue.

"Well ... they're just examples, aren't they? That even if it was you in another time, that time is gone. That now, they're just stories that we can learn from. Like a parable. Only, more poignant, because well ... it's us." I looked down at her big smile. "But you already knew that."

"Well, yes. But you did say it in such a way that makes me think even more."

"I can't believe that it's barely been more than a week since we met."

"Though, if you think about it, we've known each other for thousands of years."

"Uh-huh." I leaned over and kissed her deeply.

And yet here we are, right now.

8

or the next few weeks it was business as usual. Only, it wasn't anything usual for me. On the outside, with the exception of Rhina, nothing had changed. Nobody would know that anything was different in my life. Yet on the inside, my whole world had flipped upside down, but it had flipped over so much better that I hadn't noticed anything was missing. Unless, I count the traffic. Or rather, the fact that I had traffic now. Of which I was now cursing. After a quick reconnaissance through my life, Rhina versus traffic. Okay. I accept.

Since I had the gnarly commute every day, we had actually discussed moving to my house, but most of her clients were on her side of town. So that left us in the middle again. But I have to confess, we chose Rhina's house because she had bigger closets.

Actually, Sam was different too and not in a good way. He had gotten more blatant in his remarks toward me. And speaking of that little shit, he was leaning against the gate post and gave a little wave as I pulled into faculty parking. I felt a thud in my heart. *Thud.* Definitely one of those words that sound like they are. I thought back during these last weeks. How had I been acting toward Sam? Ever since I had that dream, I'd tried to keep things as neutral as possible, but I didn't honestly know if I'd been able to do that. Had I been too curt?

Students weren't allowed in the faculty lot so he carefully waited at the gate. Maybe he's not even waiting for me, I happily thought, but that went out the window when he shifted and spoke. "Good morning, Miss Sykes."

"Good morning, Sam. A little early aren't you?" Relax. Keep it light.

"I wanted to talk to you."

"Well, next time you can wait for my office hours. In my office," I added pointedly. Relax, Kat.

I took a big breath.

"We'll talk while we walk, then I've got work to do."

"You had all weekend to work!" he blurted, sounding like a little boy throwing a tantrum.

I stopped and squared off with him and pinned him with the full force of the new me.

"My life is my own, and the next time you want to talk to me, you wait for my office hours. Understand?" I saw surprise and hurt, but what really scared me was the anger. It was only an instant but ... if looks could kill. I'd only heard that term used in jest before, but now I saw its true origin.

"Yes, Miss Sykes." The anger flitted away and his insolent smirk took its place. "I understand."

I held my stance for a moment longer, then resumed walking, trying to hide my knees shaking. So much for the new me.

"Since you're here, what did you want to talk to me about?"

He fumbled like he was searching for something real to talk about.

"My paper!" he exclaimed.

"Which paper?" I tried to remember which paper I had assigned.

"The past-life one."

I stopped abruptly.

"You waited out here at seven in the morning to talk about a paper that was assigned three weeks ago, and have had ample opportunity to talk about during office hours?"

"Well, since you put it that way." He tried for his go-to, cute face but it only pissed me off. But I'd be a fool if I didn't recognize "the pissed off" was only covering the fear. This kid scared me.

"Have I done something to you?" he asked. "You used to like me."

"Only when you stayed in class and didn't stalk me in the parking lot." I tried to be flippant, but I'm not sure it came across, because for a moment, he let his guard down and I saw the hunter. And for one quick flash I saw Baron Halstead's face. Or at least, what I assumed was the baron's face. That rattled me. I only hoped it didn't show.

Providence rolled in by way of Professor David Whitney. His silver compact stopped. He rolled down his window.

"Sykes." He nodded his greeting.

"Professor."

He acknowledged Sam with a nod, and when he looked at me his eyes were questioning. I'm not sure what mine held.

"Can you wait for me? There's been some curriculum changes for next semester and I wanted to go over them with you," he said. My knight in shining armor.

"Absolutely," I said. Sam took the hint.

"I'll just come to your office this afternoon." He walked away with a hungry, wolf-like grin. He knew he had rattled me. I stayed where I was to regain my composure.

"That looked interesting," the professor said as he walked up. "Problem?"

"Thanks, David. I'm not sure," I answered honestly as we walked. I wanted to put it aside so I asked about his weekend. He wasn't fooled but he let me persuade him.

He walked me to my office and I was grateful. "If there's a problem, you let me know immediately. Okay?" he said very seriously.

I nodded, not trusting myself to speak. I unlocked the door, dumped my belongings on my desk and paced angrily. It was hard to pace in a tiny space with furniture.

What the hell? I was pissed. Who does that little fucker think he his? I wanted to scream. It was frustrating me that I couldn't take more than two steps in any direction without bashing my shins, so I stopped in front of my window. As I looked out over the baseball field, my vision blurred and my body sizzled. Emotions that I didn't understand, and faces I didn't know, flashed through my mind's eye. The most intense anger shot through me, and I wanted to take my sword and run someone through. The moment passed and I was in my office again. I actually checked my hand to see if I even held a sword.

I felt so much anger that I had to sit down or I'd send the chair through the window. I sat in that chair and breathed, trying to calm, trying to understand. I needed to talk to Rhina. To understand. To understand what? I grabbed my phone and started to dial, then remembered that she was at my house. Thank God she didn't have any clients today and five minutes away. I grabbed my purse and left. I needed to hold her, to make sure she was … what? I stopped in the hallway. To make sure she was still there? What the hell is wrong with me?

"Sykes?" Professor Whitney came up to me with concern in his eyes. I was just standing there. "Are you okay?" He got protective. "Is it Sam?" I looked at him. Is it Sam?

"Yes. I mean no. Not really." I smiled at his expression. "I mean no. Sam just made me think of something else, that's all. I'm good." He relaxed. "Thank you, though."

"Okay. Well, if you need me you know where I am." He started to walk away.

"Yes, I do. Thanks. Listen. I forgot something at home. If I'm a little late getting back, don't call in the cavalry."

"You got it."

I quickly walked along the grounds and didn't notice Sam sitting at one of the tables, watching me. I also didn't see the hungry smirk on his face.

Rhina was baking in the kitchen. I walked straight toward her, pinned her against the counter and held on for dear life. I was so angry that if I could just hold on, I wouldn't throw something.

"Kattrina. What's wrong?" She tried to push away to look at my face but I wouldn't budge. "Are you hurt?" I shook my head in her shoulder. Relieved, she relaxed and just held me tight. Thank God for her.

After a few minutes, the anger started to recede. I pulled away, grabbed her coffee cup, sat at the table, and told her what had happened, both with Sam, and my psychotic reaction.

"I can't stay long, but I had to see you. To hold you." Rhina took my hand in hers and listened.

"What the hell happened to me?"

"My guess is that Sam triggered a cellular memory for you." She laughed at my look. "Cells retain memory from other incarnations and can make you react with emotions from *that* incarnation, making you feel like it was happening today." She could see that I still was having a hard time comprehending.

"Let me give you an example. Years ago, I knew this stunt woman. At that point in time, a movie was being released, that she had worked on. The movie was a thriller and was set on the coast. She said that most of the stunt work was in the water, so she had been cold pretty much the whole time she was on the set. Anyway, she said that when I go see it, make sure that I dress warm because it would make me feel cold. Well, when I went to see it, I didn't feel cold at all. So I realized that when the cast finally saw the finished movie, the only reason *she* felt cold, was that her body retained all those memories of being cold. Her *body* was reliving that experience and it was perceiving the movie on a whole different level." She paused.

"So it sounds like your body was going through the pain of John leaving Annabelle. And also, the fear and anger and shame of the Baron Halstead part of it. It's no wonder that you would feel all these things."

I was silent for a minute trying to wrap my brain around it.

"Okay. I can get behind the water thing because it was the same lifetime, but what about John and Annabelle? And Baron Halstead? It's a completely different lifetime, a couple of hundred years later. How does that work?" I asked frustratingly. She just shrugged.

"I don't know. I've asked myself that same question."

"You don't know?" I felt deflated. "Fat lot a good that does." She laughed at me. "If you don't know, then how do you know it's true?"

"I've been through too many personal experiences to have any other explanation. I've also seen and heard others go through their own version. And that's not including everything that I've read." She watched me giving her a *skeptical* look so she said. "I've seen some things that don't make sense, and I ask questions that I don't get the answers for. Questions just like yours." She tilted her head, "Or maybe I'm just not listening. But either way, I'm usually okay with it because …" She stopped.

"Because …?"

"Because—" She hunched her shoulders. "I have to believe that there is a perfection in the universe that we know nothing about. I just try to follow the signs and trust."

My head felt like it was in a salad spinner. I started to mock her but stopped myself. What do I know? I got up. I had to get back to work.

"I only hope that someday I have as much trust as you do." I leaned down and kissed her. "Thank you. I love you." I walked out.

As Kat left, Rhina whispered. "You have more than you know."

I was only a few minutes late, time enough to have pulled myself together. I hoped. They must have sensed something because they all behaved today. Even Sam. Which was good because, in this mood, I might have thrown him out of class.

Throughout the day I thought about the cellular memory thing. One thing didn't make any sense to me though. Stephen and Rachael. They had a happy relationship. Why would *they* have any part in my reaction? Maybe, someday, I'll know the other part of that life. Or maybe I'll never know. Today, I'll *pretend* to trust, as Rhina trusts.

In the John and Annabelle scenario, however, I could see and feel where my reactions came from. It made perfect sense that I would react like that when there was a perceived threat.

May it always be only a perception.

9

I arrived home feeling better than the last time I was here. And the aroma was amazing!

"Smells like lasagna," I yelled out, following my nose to the kitchen. "Smells amazing." I stopped, as a cold fear melded me to the jamb. In a split second I took it all in. She was sitting at the table with tears and mascara running down her face. Oh God. One hand was absent-mindedly playing with her phone, while the other ... was bandaged? She was drinking wine, and lots of it, by the looks of the empty bottle sitting at her elbow. I noticed a pile of broken glass in the sink.

Thank God there wasn't any blood. In the circumstance, I'm not sure I could've handled it. She looked so vulnerable, like she'd melt if I touched her. It was odd seeing her like this, she was always so strong.

I slowly, carefully walked to her and knelt in front of her.

"Hey, Babe," I said softly. She didn't look at me.

"I made lasagna for you. It's your favorite," she slurred.

"I see that. Thank you. You're always so sweet." I softly touched her knee and she flinched. I flinched inside. What happened?

"Babe, what happened?" I asked quietly. She slowly turned her haunted eyes toward me. Okay, now she was scaring me. My mind raced to all the places that it didn't want to go.

"My mom called." I felt relief instantly but then sobered. Something had happened. She started crying and I held her until she stopped.

"Let me get you to bed."

"I don't want to go to bed," she said, sounding like a petulant child. I smiled to myself. It was so different than her normal demeanor.

"I'll come with you," I said hopefully.

"Okay." She looked at me with such hope and sorrow that it broke my heart.

She tried to get up and almost fell over, so I mostly carried her down the hall. On the way out I glanced at the oven to make sure it was off.

It's good to know panic and practicality can co-exist.

I sat her on the bed and had to hold her up while I undressed her. Pulling back the covers was a feat. I had to roll her over, pull the blankets back, then roll her over again, all with limp limbs. It was all I could do to keep from laughing. I got her tucked in, then was going to join her, but I wanted to lock up the house for the night, which would include a really big glass of wine. I started to walk out.

"Wait!" You can't leave me!" Her little voice shook me.

"Don't worry, honey. I'm just going to lock the front door. Okay?" I sat next to her and kissed her on the forehead. "I promise I'll be back before you know it."

"Okay. You better come back." Then she was out cold.

I did my duties and hurried back. With wine. I undressed and crawled in bed. She wasn't coherent but she curled up next to me. I wrapped my arms around her and held her while she daintily snored.

After a while I shifted so that I could sit up. And drink.

What the hell had happened? I racked my brain trying to remember what she had said about her mom. Her whole family for that matter. She hadn't talked much about them. She had mentioned her mother, and a father that had left when she was six, and a brother a year younger, but that's the extent of it. I hoped it was just a family thing, and not anything that I had done this morning that had triggered this. It would do no good to worry about something that

I didn't know what I was worrying about, so I thought about *my* family.

They were a normal family doing normal jobs. I had a sister who was a bank teller, my mom was a housewife, and my dad has worked at the same warehouse job for thirty years. I knew that it wasn't their jobs that made them … what … boring? It was just how they lived their lives; the same thing…every day. Nothing changed. Midwest, middle-aged and … mediocre.

No wonder I was mediocre too. I gave myself a break.

I looked down at Rhina and my heart skipped a beat. She was so beautiful. I idly wondered what my family will think. I also realized that I didn't care. Sad, but true. We weren't angry with each other. It's just that I was so different than they wanted me to be. I laughed to myself. Now, I'm really different. Well, the good news, is that I'm one step up from mediocre. Huh. I felt slightly better. And I thought no more of it.

I kissed the top of her head and hunkered down next to her. I must have fallen asleep because sometime in the night I woke up with her on top of me.

Oh my. I really hate waking like this. I opened my eyes with her green eyes boring into mine.

"Hi, beautiful," I said.

"That's my line," she said, then promptly went back to what she was doing. I was okay with taking one for the team. She slid up and kissed me like she meant it. All other thoughts just happened to go away.

My hands meandered up and down across her incredibly soft back. My hand found my very own sweet spot; the small depression at the juncture of her lower back and her really fine ass. I loved running my hand over the fine hair that grew there.

"I love your body," I murmured.

"My line." She grabbed both my hands and drew them up over my head and held them there with one hand and ravaged my body with her other one. I gladly relinquished the control that she desperately needed, and let her have her way with me. Anything I could do to help.

After we finally made our way out of bed, we took a shower, and really didn't help the drought situation any. We walked arm in arm into the kitchen, laughing and joking. She had, efficiently, cut herself off from all thought. For a moment. The illusion of being fine, faded away when we walked into the kitchen and she saw the empty wine bottle. She turned to me.

"I'm sorry."

"No apologies," I whispered and ran my hand down her arm.

"I'm hungry. Let's eat." Okay. She was already pulling out plates, dishing up lasagna, and popping it in the microwave. I could already tell I needed a glass of wine. It was still night, right? So I started opening another bottle.

"Oh good," she said. "Can you pour me a glass too?" My eyebrows winged up. She thought about that for a moment. "Yeah. Probably better not," she agreed. She grabbed a glass of water. I watched and waited.

She joined me at the table and proceeded to play with her meal. I ate her really good lasagna and waited for her to expound. I didn't have long to wait.

"About six months ago, my father called my mom and wanted to get back together with her."

She looked at me expectantly, but I had no idea where this was going, so I kept my face blank. She seemed to realize that I didn't know anything, so she continued.

"After thirty years, he said he missed her and wanted her back. He had changed. I guess the three wives in between, had made him see the error of his ways," she said sardonically. "He had gotten a divorce, from his last wife, because he realized that he missed my mom. etc., etc. He said he had quit drinking, got his anger under control and found Jesus. She bought it hook, line and sinker." Rhina was wringing her napkin.

"He moved in. He told her he had been going to church every Sunday, and I guess it looked like he had continued to do so after he moved in. She offered to go with him but he said that he had to repent on his own. He told her he wanted to make a life with her again, so he wanted to do it right." I don't think she knew her hands had started shredding the napkin.

"I found all this out a few months ago, when she invited me over for dinner. 'Look who's here! Your father!' He tried to hug me but I told him I'd kill him if he touched me."

That one caught me by surprise. My sweet Rhina? I took one look into her eyes and realized that I didn't know her as well as I thought I did. Go figure, we've only known each other for five minutes. And again, I didn't care.

Something let go inside of me that I didn't even know I was holding. It seems I've been letting go of a lot these days. Rhina was still talking.

"He made it seem like it was my fault that I didn't want anything to do with him. Like I'm the one with the problem because *I* couldn't let it go. Blah, blah. I knew exactly why he was there. He needed a roof over his head and he was too fucking lazy to find work himself." I nonchalantly slid my napkin closer to her.

Disgusted, she took a drink of water and almost spit it out. She got up to get a wine glass, and poured herself one. I opened my mouth to say something about it, but thought better of it. I thought I was going to lose another glass the way she slammed it down.

"Today, Mom called 'just to talk' she said. She was slurring her words and I asked her what was wrong. At first she wouldn't tell me but I badgered her into it—as she knew I would—She had ended up in the emergency room. Two teeth knocked out, her face swollen and bruised. It was so swollen on one side that she could barely talk to me. I found that part out later when I called my aunt." Rhina almost broke but steeled herself. I wanted to hold her so bad; wrap her up and never let her go.

"Mom said she didn't want me to come over, didn't want to bother me. But of course, she wanted me to. She learned well from him. How to play your cards. She knew … knows … how to play me. She knew I'd come over because I'd feel so guilty if I didn't. She's always been able to get me with the guilt card. Always." Her knuckles were white.

She was silent. Her body a statue. The only movement was the slight rise of her chest, the only sound was the ticking of the clock. I waited for her to continue. The longer the silence continued, the harder it was for me to breathe; afraid of breaking the spell. I knew she wasn't done, but I didn't know what to do. I willed myself to stay rooted to the chair, when all I wanted was to wrap her up and hold her tight until it all melted away. I now understand the saying "silence hung in the air like a lead blanket."

And then it came.

"They arrested him when I was six. He used to drink, and then come home to use my mom as his punching bag. Once in a while he would come after us, but mostly took it out on her." She indicated the scar by her left eye. "You asked about my scar. Well, one night he had just opened a beer bottle and still had the cap in his hand when he hauled off and cuffed me." I jumped inside, like he had done it just this instant, in front of me. It was like watching a robot as Rhina recounted her life. Her mouth was the only thing that moved. "One night, he was hours late for dinner, with no word as to when he was coming, so Mom finally sat my brother and I down for dinner. He came home while we were eating, and got angry at her for not waiting for him. He was out of control. Dishes and food went flying. He'd never been that bad. Mom begged him to stop, not in front of us. He said—" She almost broke again. I ached to go to her but I knew I couldn't. She had to get it out. "He said that he'd give them a real show." Rhina stopped, fighting to get it out.

"He raped her right in front of us. Right there on the kitchen table. Food and broken dishes everywhere." She paused again, stealing herself. "She begged him to stop. Not in front of us she said. He hit her harder. I screamed at him that I was going to call the police. I went to the phone but he looked at me and said that if I did, then I would be next." Rhina seemed to come back to present time. She looked at me as she spoke.

"Mom looked at me as she was being pummeled with his fists and—. With mashed potatoes all over her face, she looked over at me and pleaded. Dad thought she was pleading with him so he hit her harder." Rhina looked down in shame. "I knew she was pleading with me to make the call. She looked at the phone and then back at me. She did it over and over. I couldn't move. I was terrified of what he'd do to me. When I wouldn't, she got this look on her face. Like she was disappointed. Like *she* was disappointed in me! Like I didn't have the guts!" Rhina drooped her shoulders in self-loathing. "I guess I learned well from her."

I didn't know this self-loathing person in front of me. I couldn't help but cry inwardly for this broken child. I touched her hand and she seemed to come back. "After he beat her unconscious, he passed out. I called my aunt, then she called an ambulance. She came and took my brother and me away.

"He got sent to jail for a couple of months and during that time she had filed a restraining order against him, for all the good it did, when he put her in the hospital again. He got six months that time. Oh, and anger management classes." Disgust in the system, clearly evident.

"After getting out of the hospital, mom came to live with us at my aunt's house. We kept moving so he couldn't find us. One time he tracked my aunt down through work." Rhina smiled, remembering her aunt. "You know, she was only five-two, but man, was she a pistol. She told my father that if he came around again she would cut him up in little pieces and feed him to the fishes. I guess he decided to go find someone smaller than him."

When Rhina finished she got up and tried to pace but didn't have the heart, so she stopped in front of the back door and stood, staring out into the inky black. When I saw her shoulders shaking, I came up behind her and held her tight.

After what seemed like hours, she was tired and led me down the hall. We crawled into bed and I held her all night long. I woke early and found us in the same position. She must have sensed movement because she stirred. She moved out of my arms and sat cross-legged next to me. She couldn't look at me, her head bent in shame. I reached out to touch her.

"You are so beautiful," I told her. She smiled self-consciously.

"My line." Still not looking at me.

I wasn't sure what to say so I just held her hand. This was so not the Rhina that I'd come to know. She tried to pull away from me and I realized that it was from self-pity. I wouldn't let her.

"I love you so much," I said finally. She stilled. Almost willing it to not be true, so she could be right. "Yes. It's true. You know how I know its love?" She shrugged. "I know its love because … whenever somebody I dated, fell down, or had issues, I would lose respect for them a little. Like they should be perfect. Right? I just didn't care about them anymore. I'm not sure what that says about me but …" I quickly added. "Anyway, I would move on very shortly afterward." I paused. "But with you … with you, watching you go through this, it makes me love you more. It makes me respect you more. To know what you've been through and to see what you've grown into. I am in awe of you."

She looked at me with doubt in her eyes. And hope. It almost crumbled me. I couldn't believe that the woman, sitting in front of me now, was the same woman who held me together twenty-four hours ago.

"Yes, it's true. So if this is your way of making me go away, then you've failed miserably," I said determined. Yay. A smile.

"I've never told anyone before."

"Really?" I asked. She hunched one of her shoulders. "I didn't ask. How was your mom when you saw her?"

"I didn't go," she said. What? My jaw dropped. "I'm really tired of my mother taking advantage of me. She uses guilt like a hammer, and I'm very tired of it." She sighed. "So I told her no. Of course, she put up a good fight, getting those digs in. So now, I get to feel guilty about not going." She looked at me, almost willing me to disagree with her. "I can't watch her do her life any more. She's dragging me down with her."

I shifted the covers. I shifted her legs apart and plopped myself between them, wrapping my legs around her. Then I whispered into her ear.

"I love you beyond words."

She started crying. It's a heady thing to be loved. Especially, when all your demons are slapping you in the face.

We stayed like that for a while until she evened out, then I went to make coffee. The cure all.

I came back with coffee and toast. I found her propped up with eyes closed. I stood rooted in the doorway looking at this exquisite creature and wondered how on earth she came to be sleeping in my bed.

In that split second, I saw her *Being*. Beyond the body, beyond the woman. Just another soul. I saw her, yet it wasn't really sight. It was a, kind of seeing without seeing.

And I hoped to high heaven that I didn't have to explain that to anyone.

The moment passed and I put the tray on the table and sat down next to her. We sat in silence, one hand eating toast, the other resting on each other's leg. Each in our own thoughts.

I had to work, so I made sure she was okay before I got up.

"I'm fine," she said when she saw that I was hovering. "I'm a little wrung out but the best thing I can do is go to work and have my energy flowing. It'll flow out quicker."

I had no choice but to believe her so I got ready for work. When I was putting on the finishing touches of my makeup she came in.

"I didn't ask about your day. How did it go the rest of the day?" she asked gently. I looked at her with astonishment.

"See. This is one of the *many* reasons I love you. You can go through hell and you can *still* ask how my day was. My day was fine. Thank you." I skipped a beat. "After you rescued me. It's amazing what a few hours will do."

"Yeah." She smiled. I leaned over and kissed her.

"Your lips are so amazing," I told her. She smiled and squeezed my butt and left me to finish.

My day was uneventful. I had office hours all afternoon and I kept expecting Sam to appear but he didn't. I had started seeing him around campus more often. On benches, outdoor picnic tables, walking. My heart did a little lurch every time I saw him, but even then I didn't really think anything of it. It's a campus and students walk and sit, doing whatever. They're everywhere. Had he always been there and I hadn't noticed? … or maybe he's stalking me. Get a grip, Kattrina. He's just a kid. I pushed it to the back of my head.

I was walking from the student union for lunch, when Rhina called.

"Hey, you." I couldn't help it, a big sloppy grin was plastered on my face, completely unaware of anyone or anything.

I didn't notice Sam, sitting on a bench, watching me with malice on his face.

The aroma was the first thing I noticed when I walked into Rhina's house. A good sign. Hopefully, that meant that she was all right. I'm really glad that she loves to cook because then I don't have to. After this commute it's the last thing I want to do.

I try to feel blessed for traffic, as it means Rhina is in my life, but it sure was a challenge some days. I had bought a house a mile from the college for a reason. She told me that traffic would teach me patience. I told her, very nicely, to go put it somewhere. She laughed at me.

That night, while eating dinner, she told me of her theory. I had asked if she knew why all this stuff is coming up now in our lives. Why not at any other time?

"Well, there's so many things that I could say so I'll keep it basic. *Basically,* I think it's because we're so close. We have a lot to lose. More so than either of us has had in the past. Love is such a powerful emotion that it just opened the door for … I don't know … all kinds of things to happen." She paused. "Things come up in our lives when we feel safe enough for it to do so."

I thought of that for a bit. It seemed true. I didn't have a single person that could, or would, deal with this. I think even Marci would balk.

"And since we opened the door for love, then of course, we opened it for the rest of it as well," she finished.

"Okay. That I can understand. I have another question that I've been wondering about. What happens when there's no more bad stuff? You keep telling me that we can release the energy from the past. That we can be neutral. No more loss, or panic? Does that mean our love goes away too? Will we still feel something for each other?" I was starting to feel agitated. "What if we're neutral, instead of loving each other? I've just found you, I don't want to feel neutral to you." I said in a high-pitched voice. She put her hand over my mouth.

"You are so cute." She softly laughed at me. I wanted to scream. I wasn't losing her, dammit!

"Well, you can get rid of this panic crap anytime!" I cried. "You said a person can release all of the energy from past lives, Right? Then what happens if you release energy, and all of our feelings go away? You said it would be neutral. I don't want *this* to go away!" I motioned to us.

"Okay. Let's say that we deleted all of our energy, past and present—which is highly unlikely, in this one lifetime anyway, it's a big process—but, if that happened and we became completely neutral about our pasts and all that's left is the present moment, wouldn't you think that we'd start from scratch and love each other anyway? I think so. It was instant, with us, because of our pasts together, but I think that I would have fallen for you anyway, once I met you."

"You think?" I was grasping at straws.

"Absolutely—it might have taken longer than five minutes—but I think I would have felt the same way about you. You're smart, funny, beautiful, and I generally like you. You're a good person."

I pondered this while she grabbed wine and glasses and led me into the living room. We sat in the dark sipping wine, listening to cello music, and watching the flames dance in her gas fireplace.

She didn't want to discuss any more of her life, not yet, so we didn't. I must be growing because, before, I would have pushed the issue. And what Rhina was teaching me was that everything has it's time. And I was letting Rhina have hers.

Who'da thunk?

I woke in the middle of the night and couldn't get back to sleep, and rather than wake Rhina with my restlessness, I got up and answered emails. And truth be known, I needed Marci right now.

I've been missing Marci so much these past few days. She's always been my rock-in-the-storm. Rhina was amazing in every way but I missed my rock. Although, if I told myself the truth, I'm not sure that even she would understand this storm.

An hour later, I realized that I had just dumped everything in Marci's lap. Everything. I felt better actually; my own therapy program I guess. I didn't know if she'd feel the same way about it, but ... I put my heartfelt, love you and miss you, at the end and sent it off.

Feeling lighter, I went back to bed. I was careful, but Rhina stirred anyway. She snaked an arm out and pulled me into her spoon and murmured, "You're cold, let me warm you." She held me tight so I fell asleep feeling pretty damn good.

The next morning she said that there were new polar bear cubs at the zoo and would I want to go see them? So we made plans to see them on Sunday, which also just happened to be one of the free days that the zoo offered every year.

Three days later, I arrived home and Rhina was in session, so I answered emails. Marci was finally able to respond. I laughed. Typical Marci, beating around the bush.

Kat,

Well, that was an interesting read. I don't understand half the shit you wrote about, or the woman thing, but I do know you. I've never heard you so ... involved. You were always so half-assed. I'm glad that you finally found someone, Kat. I really am. Especially since I'm not there to pick your ass up.

I'm glad I'm not there though. I think I'd be pissed and jealous. LOL.

As for the rest of it just keep your chin up. Don't let anyone tell you that you can't do, or be a certain way. And if they do, remind them.

If there's one thing that I've learned by coming here is that fear is a state of mind. It's not real. Before I came I was scared to death. I lost count of how many times I wanted to cancel.

Something kept me from it. Don't know what, but I'm grateful for it.

Once I got here I realized that all my fears were moot.

Fear is just the doorway to courage. All you have to do is walk through it.

Love,
Marci

P.S. Hi to Rhina.

God, I miss her. She always did get me.

Fear is the doorway to courage.

It didn't sound like a Marci thing to say, but I guess, if anyone would know, she would. I wondered if she'll be the same Marci when she gets back. Will *I* be the same person when she gets back?

By the time I finished answering emails, and paying bills, Rhina was out of session. We had a nice dinner and spent the rest of the evening with our respective reading material. Her, with her various energy manuals and magazines, and me with my essays to grade.

At one point, with the fire going, wine in hand, and papers everywhere, I smiled to myself. I think I'm the happiest person alive. And with a woman, no less. I shook my head in happy disbelief. Rhina looked at me and my Cheshire grin.

"What?"

"You're a woman," I stated.

"Really?"

I smiled because I knew she knew what I was talking about.

"Who'da thunk?"

"Who'da thunk"

A thought surfaced.

"Why are you a woman anyway?" I looked over and laughed at her raised eyebrow. "I mean, if what you say is true, lessons and all that, why did we come back as two women? Obviously, we know of two times where we were man and woman. Why did we choose this lifetime to come together as women?" Rhina cocked her head in thought.

"Good question. Why do you think?"

"You're asking me?" I gave her that look that said, "Fat chance of finding the answer here." I gave it a stab. "Something about some lesson. Right?"

She laughed and let me off the hook.

"Actually, I've been thinking about that. I think, at least in your case, that one of the lessons that you're working on this lifetime is 'feeling good about yourself, despite what others may think of you.' Because let's face it, being 'gay' is one of the biggest triggers for a lot of people. I think that your spirit came here to heal that piece, so your spirit made the issue so big that you couldn't gloss over it and forget about it."

I let that sink in for a while then asked her. "So what's your lesson in all this? It doesn't seem to be as big an issue for you."

"I think for me, it's more the fact that I needed to find someone who's strong enough to handle my strengths. Kind of like Rachael, I guess. *She* needed someone who could handle it. That I was lovable no matter who I was. Similar to yours but slightly different. I also need someone strong enough to be here while I deal with my guilt. Man or woman. And well, here you are. The universe pairs up people who can best help with each other's lessons." She thought some more. "Or there may be fifteen other reasons as well." She leaned over to kiss me. "Or we may *just* like each other."

"Mmmmm. But things aren't always good. Sometimes we pair up with those that hurt."

"Yes." She looked at me pointedly. "How many times have you learned from the negative?"

Too many to count. I thought of Sam. It pissed me off to think that he might be helping me.

"So what happens when we heal these lessons? Will we go back to men or what?" I asked, a little on the defensive because, dammit, I wanted *her*!

"I think that's totally up to us." She looked at me and said softly, "Stop worrying. I'm not going anywhere."

There was so much love in her eyes. How could I not believe it?

"So do you think that we're actually … gay?"

"No. I just think we love each other," she said simply.

Hmm. Relief or disappointment? Or both? Looking at this beautiful woman, I knew that it didn't matter.

We both went back to our reading, but my concentration was broken. She hadn't talked about her father again. I didn't want her to hide again, but I didn't want to push her either.

"All in due time my love," she said. "All in due time."

Crap. She did it again.

"Have you ever thought about professional poker?" I asked. She laughed.

"I can't help it. You're kind of loud." She turned to me. "Listen. I know you love me and want to help, but I'm just not ready to talk. Yet. We broke the scab. Let's let it seep. Okay?" I nodded.

"How do you do it?" I asked. "How do you stay so sane and … kind. And happy. I'm a basket case a lot of the time."

"You are not." She got serious. "I wasn't always so sane. Or happy. Or kind. I've told you of all those years of personal growth?" I nodded. "Well, now you know why." She touched my arm. "The Baron Halstead thing hit me on two levels." She let me work that out. I gasped. Lost love, *and* the abuse.

"Oh my god! I'm so sorry. I didn't even think. I'm sorry." I felt horrible. She shook her head.

"Don't worry about it. How could you have known? I didn't even put it together myself until a couple of nights ago."

"Why didn't you tell me?" I demanded.

"I'm not used to having anyone to open up to," she said defensively. "It's so much easier to keep things to myself." She got still. "No one to get scared and go away."

In that moment, all my own fears melted away. She was my only concern. I snatched up all my papers and threw them on the coffee table. I laid down and pulled her with me and wrapped my arms and legs around her in a cocoon of love.

"We've found each other, so we're done with that running scared business okay?" I said gently. She nodded, and I held her tightly as her shoulders shook.

I wish I could say that the rest of the week was uneventful, but I'd be lying. Sam was becoming an issue that would have to be addressed. He was everywhere. I went to class and he was waiting in the hallway. I went across campus and there he was. I ate lunch and there he was at the next table.

The fact that he was there was bad enough, but what made it scary was the look on his face. He always had that stupid grin but it was his eyes that gave me the creeps. They were like wolf eyes, right before it pounced. I felt like prey.

I told Professor Whitney about Sam.

"I'll talk to him," he said protectively.

"No, don't! Then he'll know that I'm worried, and that'll feed him. Besides, I don't even know that he is stalking me."

"Have you seen him this much since the beginning of the semester?"

"No."

"There you go."

"But I haven't been looking for him either. He might have been there all along and I haven't noticed. Wasn't paying attention."

"Is that what you think?"

"No." I let go of the breath I'd sort of been holding.

"Listen, I'm glad you told me. Why do you think he's doing this all of a sudden?"

"I think he's always had a slight crush on me, but I started noticing a difference when I started seeing somebody."

"Ah."

"Yeah. Listen, David, I did nothing to encourage this," I implored.

"I know, Kattrina. Half the students and faculty are in love with you and you don't even know it. That's part of your charm."

"What? Well, shit." I threw my arms up. The way he said it made me think that he was part of the half. "I wish you hadn't told me that." He shrugged and laughed.

"I told you that because not everyone's a stalker. Keep an eye on this kid and let me know if this gets worse."

I felt better after having told someone. Although, it made me squirm a little, knowing that people liked me that much, especially him. He was my friend. I felt like I wanted to shake like a dog, starting at my head all the way down to the tip of my tail.

10

"I think half the city is here," I exclaimed. The zoo's free days are great, but so are the crowds.

We couldn't go anywhere fast, so we leisurely made our way around the whole grounds, taking in all of the Mother's creatures. I loved that many zoos have changed the habitats to be more natural.

It seemed the more we walked the more I wanted to touch her. So many times I grabbed her hand, but then dropped it. It was too new for me. And there were too many people. I was a teacher, I couldn't afford to be free. Not yet. I did touch her as often as I dared, however. A touch of her arm, the small of her back as she went through a door, a slight touch of her cheek with mine as we stood next to each other.

The more we walked and the more I couldn't hold her, the more upset I got. I told her what was going on and she agreed it was hard.

"Why can't people just let other people be? Why is it so hard for others to just let love happen?"

I was frustrated. Rhina just shrugged and led me along by the elbow. "If I wasn't a teacher, I wouldn't care."

She saw the "Big Cats" section of the zoo and led us in that direction. She saw a little walkway and veered off. She led me down along a building with a gate at the end that said No Admittance.

"What are we doing?" I asked.

"Just wait and see."

"What—" She lightly shoved me behind a tree and greedily took my mouth.

Oh.

She thoroughly used me and then pulled back.

"Oh no you don't." I grabbed her lapel and pulled her back to me.

I'm not sure how long we were there but enough to realize that we were done with the zoo. I didn't want to get caught with my pants down in the bushes, so to speak. We stepped out from behind the tree onto the sidewalk and made sure all clothes were straightened. I reached up with my thumb and wiped some lipstick off her chin.

Neither saw a small group of young people walk by. One of them was lagging behind. He did a double take and saw red. "C'mon, Sam!" the rest of the group called.

"Let's go," I said hungrily. "Now!"

"Yeah." She shoved me out into the main traffic area.

We were heading to the nearest exit when we passed the tiger enclosure. I yanked her to a stop and pointed. She looked at me and smiled. We stood at the railing in awe and watched those big, beautiful cats. We forgot our need to leave.

As I watched, one of them looked straight at me and at that moment, the world shifted and I saw Rhina in tiger form through my own tiger eyes. I saw our life together. It was only a moment, but it was a lifetime.

I blinked. At least this time I knew what the hell it was. I looked at Rhina and I knew she saw the same thing. Holy shit!

"How does that happen? You saw it too?"

"Yes." She was looking at the tiger but then shifted her eyes to me.

"Ants, horses, humans ... tigers?" I said. She nodded in acknowledgment.

I put my arm through hers as we turned back to the railing; my mind elsewhere.

"Miss Sykes! Hi! What are you doing here?" Shit. Both Rhina and I froze for a split second.

Nonchalantly, with my arm only slightly pulled from hers, I turned. Angela, Josh, Alex, Penny, and crap, Sam, were standing there looking at us expectantly.

"Checking out the tigers. Aren't they amazing?" Acting like nothing was happening but a Sunday at the zoo, I extracted my arm from Rhina's and used it to gesture to everyone.

"This is Angela, Josh, Alex, Penny, and Sam in the back. They're students of mine." They all looked genuinely glad to see me. All except Sam. He had a murderous look on his face. "This is my good friend, Rhina. Are you guys enjoying the zoo? Isn't it great?" I gave a little look to Penny to say that I was happy to see her out and about with everyone. She smiled and gave a little nod.

"How good a friend are you, Rhina?" Sam asked. He tried for indifference but couldn't quite pull it off. His anger showed through. There was a stunned, awkward silence.

"Dude," Alex said.

"What? It's a legitimate question." Everyone looked at him, shocked. They saw how angry he was, even though he tried to hide it. They turned to us, confused. Then, it entered their minds.

Penny was the first one to comprehend what was happening.

"C'mon, you guys, I want to go see the penguins."

"No. I want to know," Sam demanded, "are you lesbos?"

"Sam!" Angela scolded.

With his pretense of idle curiosity gone, he pushed through the group with maliciousness on his face, straight toward me. It happened so fast I was too stunned to do anything. He ignored the cries of his friends.

"Are you a fucking dyke, Miss Sykes? Sykes the dyke?"

I stood my ground, with what I hoped was a neutral face. He came inches from me and snarled. I finally found my voice and opened my mouth to tell him off, but Josh and Alex grabbed both his arms and dragged him away with him yelling that he didn't want a dyke for a teacher, which of course drew a crowd.

"Miss Sykes, I'm so sorry." Penny was mortified. Angela was pissed. They walked up to us.

"It's okay, Penny. It wasn't your fault," I said in a shocked monotone.

"We all knew he had a crush on you. We teased him about it, but I never thought he would be like this," Angela explained. She took a good look at Rhina, and then back at me and smiled.

"Love the soul, not the vessel?" she asked rhetorically. "C'mon, Penny. Let's go see if we can drown Sam."

They walked away, Penny looking like she wanted to drown herself, and Angela, smiling, called in support, "You're the coolest, Miss Sykes!"

The whole interaction took only a few minutes, but I felt like I had just gone a few rounds. This is what shell-shocked must feel like. I couldn't move, couldn't think, couldn't speak.

"What just happened?" I heard Rhina ask. All I could do is shake my head.

She grabbed my hand and pulled me forward. "Let's go home." My heroine.

All the way to the car, I played the picture of Sam's face in my head, how murderous it was. It kept reminding me of something, but I couldn't remember what. Ugly thoughts flooded in and wouldn't stop. Thoughts about losing my job, losing Rhina. What my kids will think of me. What my friends will think of me. By this time tomorrow the whole school will know … What *does* Rhina think of me?

My mind went into overdrive. Problems that were never problems before became mountains.

I started envisioning worst-case scenarios. By the time I got to the car I was shaking.

We got in and Rhina asked if I was okay. I had to rein in my brain and took a moment to consider. I swiped my shaky hands through my hair.

"Define okay." I was shaking so bad that it took three tries to put the key in the ignition.

"Babe," she called through the fog. She grabbed my hand. "Babe."

"Don't!" I snapped. Then more softly. "Please. Just don't."

"Okay then. You should let me drive."

My first reaction was to reject the offer, but after looking at my shaking hands, I thought it was probably a good idea. I nodded and opened the door. I didn't touch her, didn't even look at her as we walked around the car.

As we drove, she tried to hold my hand, but I pulled it away. Part of my brain registered that it wasn't Rhina's fault but I couldn't help it. I felt a wave of shame wash over me like I'd never known.

I drowned in my own thoughts as we drove to her house.

I felt so helpless. The anger I felt almost choked me. I looked at Rhina and the thought raced through my brain—not again. Just when I thought I had everything I could ever want, it's taken from me. Only a small part of my brain registered that it wasn't really the case, but the rest of my body was reacting like it *was* the case.

Rhina didn't know what to do or say so she just drove in silence. The voices in her own head clamoring to make themselves heard. Guilt. She knew it wasn't rational, but she felt responsible for the situation that they were now in. Because of her, Kat's job may be in jeopardy. She should have been more careful. She didn't really take Kat's concerns seriously. Hers is a different world. I should've paid more attention. Why didn't I speak up at the zoo? Why did I just stand there? Only a tiny part of her realized that there was really nothing that she could've said, but that small part couldn't be heard over the rest of the din in her head.

We pulled up in front of Rhina's house. She led me up the walk, but when we reached her beautiful door, I stopped. I was mad at her, yet I wasn't. I was mad at me, yet I wasn't. I was mad, helpless, and confused and I didn't know why. I didn't know how the hell any of this fit together.

I now knew why Rhina had to be alone that day. I needed to … I don't know … something.

I had a feeling about something so vague that I couldn't get a handle on it. Something about, "together."

"I have to go," I said. She whipped around.

"What? Why?" The desperate look in her eyes made me pale, but I couldn't help it. I had to go. I didn't understand. The only thing I wanted more than to be held by her, was to run away from her.

MONICA SCHUSTER

"Please," she begged. "Don't do this. We can figure this out together."

I was already walking down the sidewalk. In a fog.

I'm not sure how I got home. Maybe I was a truck driver in another lifetime, I thought derisively.

I was striding up my front walk arguing with myself, "You know, my life was just fine before all this crap!"

Of course, that nice, little voice, sitting on my shoulder, said, "No, it wasn't."

"Shut up!" I said out loud as I opened the door.

The neighbor looked up from watering his flowers.

I walked straight to the fridge, grabbed a beer, and plopped myself on the couch. I continued my thoughts that had started in the car.

Me, Rhina, Annabelle, John, Rachael, Stephen, Baron Halstead, Sam. How did they fit together? Round and round in my head they turned. I felt like I was on the teacup ride at the state fair.

I finally couldn't stand it.

"Stop it!" I yelled to an empty house. I sat up, looking around me. I saw the couch underneath me, the matching chair, coffee table, end tables, lamps, TV, the pictures on the walls. I noticed the layer of dust on everything and told myself that I needed to clean my house. I woke up a bit. I need to clean my house.

Now!

I was in the here and now. "Here and now!" I yelled to the dust mites. I started to pace. "This is stupid! There's just the here and now! There is no Baron Halstead. Or Annabelle, or John, or Stephen, or Rachael. There's just me and Rhina! And that fucking Sam!"

Then why do I feel so desperate?

I stopped pacing. I stood in my living room, in silence. Listening to that damn clock. Tick, tick, tick. I thought of the *Tell Tale Heart*. I snorted to myself. This would've made a perfect Poe book.

For a long time I stood there listening to the tick of the clock. The steady beat of the metronome transported me to an alternate place in my psyche. For one brief moment, past and present melded into one. Like putting layers upon layers of those clear plastic sheets that one used on the old projectors. Each layer had a different face, but added together, they made up a totally different entity. Each layer significantly recognizable, yet all part of the totality.

In that one brief moment in time, I saw everything so clearly. I saw all of us. I saw the multitude of lives and lifetimes. How many were there? … hundreds … I don't know. I felt, in that one moment, that the answers were all swirling around in front of me, just waiting for me to reach up and grasp their meaning.

I shifted back to this dimension—or rather, I think I could call it this dimension—anyway, I arrived back in my living room.

I saw all the pieces of the puzzle, or in this case, the people in the puzzle, and I understood. I realized why I was so frustrated. I had never really trusted my relationship with Rhina. I was always waiting for the other shoe to drop. It was so instantaneous, so … karmic and part of the strange, that if things were normal, would she even be here? I always had this warped sense that someone, or something, was going to come in and steal her away again. Our relationship couldn't possibly be real because none of this other stuff seemed real. But now I understood how we fit together. We learn the same lessons no matter what lifetime we're in. I can meld Stephen, Annabelle and I, all together and get the same person. Me. And like Penny said that day, it's just different facets of me. So the issues I have now, are just the same issues I had then. Whichever lifetime I was in.

Exhausted, but more at peace, I sat on the couch. I had to talk to Rhina. Shit. Rhina. I felt so bad. I hope she understood. I'm counting on it. She picked up on the first ring.

"Are you okay?" she asked.

"Yeah," I said softly, "but I wasn't before." There was silence on the other end.

"Are you there?"

"Yes. I'm just listening." I heard her voice crack.

"I'm sorry. I shouldn't have bolted like that."

"No. I'm sorry," she said quickly. "I feel so guilty."

"You? Why should you be sorry? There's no reason for you to feel guilty."

"Because, I just didn't think there was a worry. I didn't put enough credence to your fears. I just didn't—"

"You mean you just didn't buy into my fears? You didn't let me get all freaky about everything? And when I did, you just let me cry on your shoulder? You have no reason to feel guilty," I put it simply. There was silence.

"Well, if you put it like that …." She paused. "Now, I know how you felt that day when I said I needed to be alone."

"Like it was over."

"Yeah."

"I can only imagine what you thought. I was acting pretty bizarre. I'm sorry. I love you." I heard a sigh on the other end. "Wanna hear a Poe tale?"

"A what?" Rhina asked. I told her what happened.

"I don't know. I think it was all too much for me. Too new. Too many new thoughts. Too many loose ends that I couldn't name or see how they fit together. And to be honest, I wasn't a hundred percent sure that I believed any of this. I thought I was, but now I see that I wasn't," I admitted.

"And since we met, it's been nothing *but* that, and you didn't trust *us*, because of it."

"Yes." Relief flooded my being that she understood.

"How do you feel now?" she asked. I sighed.

"I feel good." I searched for words. "I've been thinking about it. It felt so amazing to be with you. I couldn't believe it. But I see now that I was just holding my breath, waiting for someone to say, 'Ha! Just kidding!' You know what I mean?"

"Yes, I do."

We sat in companionable silence for a bit.

"I miss you," I said.

"I know. I miss you too." We laughed because it was so stupid.

"I can't believe that it was only this afternoon that we were together. We're such saps."

"You want me to come over?"

"Yes ... but no. It's late. You don't need to drive across town. We're big girls. We can handle a night alone. I'll be thinking of you lying next to me though."

"Me too. I'm glad you called. I was pulling my hair out. I'm so sorry I didn't see the signs."

"We've got to figure out where that guilt thing comes from." I threw her a bone, "Sweetie, you have nothing to be sorry for. If anything, I'm the one that needs to be saying sorry for bringing you into all my drama." She snickered.

"It's so strange to be with someone who isn't so willing to blame me for everything," she said and I laughed.

"I suppose you're going to say something about some lesson, right?" I mocked her.

"I wasn't, but now that you mention it." We were both smiling, I could hear it in her voice.

"Let's make a pact," I said.

"Okay."

"The next time one of us gets the urge to run, let's not. Sooner or later, we won't have another house to run to." I paused. "You do still want to live together. Right?" I asked hopefully.

"Yes. Absolutely. Silly."

"Phew. Good. Okay. So we won't have anywhere else to run to, so let's practice on running to each other instead." Rhina was silent so I continued. "I mean, neither of us has had any real stability in relationships. Right?" In my mind's eye I could actually see her nodding. Weird. "Well, let's practice. *No more running.*"

Silence.

"Hello." Silence. "Rhina?" I panicked. "Rhina!"

"I'm here." She sniffled.

"Jeez. You can't do that to me," I said relieved. "I'm going under the assumption that you're crying because it's a good thing."

"I can't believe we've found each other," Rhina whispered. I heard her blow her nose.

"So ... is that a yes?" I asked hesitantly.

"Yes. Yes. Yes."

"Thank God." I sighed. I could hear her laughing on the other end. "You know you're killing me, right?"

We finished up with us feeling pretty damn good about ourselves. I was kind of wired, so sleep was out of the question. Freed from all my anxiety about Rhina, and the characters of my past, my mind planted itself right here in the present. They may all fit together, but the only thing I can do anything about is the present. So I thought of Sam, and what I was going to do about him.

I grabbed a glass of wine, and missing Rhina's fireplace, lit some candles and turned off all the lights. I plopped myself on the couch again. With feet up on the coffee table, blanket covering me, I let my mind wander. What's up with Sam? Why is he here? What do I need to see about my life? Jeez, I sound like Rhina. I liked that.

Thinking of Sam made me so mad I had to set my glass on the table; I didn't need to lose another one. I tried to calm down but I couldn't. I thought of an exercise that Rhina had showed me. Deep breathing. Simple, right? Not so much. I tried but my breath kept catching in anger. *Okay, Kitten! It's breathing! You've been doing it your whole life. Girl up!* I started breathing purposefully. Concentrating on just my breath.

In. out. In. Out. In. Ou—

11

*A*s I rode across the valley I was relaxed. I wished that Rachael and Meerina could have joined me. The day was beautiful. When we leave here, I'll make sure we take a few days longer to our next destination. They had worked hard and deserved some time. As I got closer to the castle, I could hear the bells clanging, but still didn't think anything of it, until I was greeted with mayhem. People were shouting and rushing to and fro, carrying what looked like their belongings. Guards were yelling, rounding the villagers up and forcing them toward the gate. I waylaid a small boy who was running by and asked him what was happening.

"Lady Pembroke died, sir. My lord is beside himself. He ordered everyone out of the castle." The boy ran away. Shite. My gut seized up.

I started to make my way to our room, floundering upstream through the river of people. I had to dodge, as people were running haphazardly, overloaded with belongings. I turned and saw Meerina, and then my Rachael, running toward me. I let go a sigh of relief, but when I saw Meerina's face, I seized up again. There was a grave panic in both their eyes, but the absolute terror I saw in Meerina's made my blood turn to ice.

Parting the way for them, I led them back to our room. Meerina directed Rachael to pack their belongings, and for me to come help her outside. Rachael started to object, but Meerina turned stern.

"Do it!" That alone made Rachael panic even more, but did what she was told. "Just one bag each." Meerina shoved me outside. Once we were out of earshot she spun me around.

"You must get her out," she demanded quickly.

"Of course—"

"No! You *must* get her out. No matter what happens. Get her out."

"What's—"

"No time to explain. Do what you have to." The look in her eyes scared me beyond anything I'd ever felt.

"Meerina. What's—"

"She's going to fight you. Don't let her. We have to go." She tried to push me back inside.

"Meerina—"

"No time. Just promise me." I hesitated, not knowing what was happening. She jerked me and yelled at me. "Promise me!"

"I promise."

"No matter what," she repeated. I nodded.

She shoved me back into the room. Rachael gave us a confused look but remained silent. We helped her finish packing and left. As we hurried, Meerina told us to cover our heads and keep them down as we immersed ourselves in the throng heading for the gate. Suddenly, we heard someone yell.

"There. There they are!" We all looked up in time for us to see one of the lady's chamber maids pointing at us. Guards swooped down on us immediately. They grabbed the chamber maid as well. It all happened so fast I couldn't think straight.

I swore and I tried to wring the maid's neck, but the guards held me tight. I gave her a murderous stare. She had to yell over the noise of the crowd.

"I'm so sorry," she pleaded to Meerina. "He said I had to or he'd kill my family. I'm so sorry." A guard ripped her away from us. There were three guards for the three of us. One for Meerina and two on either side of Rachael and me.

Meerina turned and looked at me. Pleading with me. What was I supposed to do? We were being hauled away by guards. She kept trying to get away from them. She fought. She jumped, squirmed and kicked so much that the guard who was holding Rachael, let go to help with Meerina. I noticed a horse and rider coming our direction.

"Now!" Meerina screamed, as he came broadside to us.

As she screamed loud, she jumped and kicked harder. The rider was preoccupied with watching Meerina. Fear and adrenalin overtook me, and I tripped our guard, grabbed Rachael, flung her over my shoulder and shoved the rider off the horse, all before the guards could contemplate what was happening. By the time they had their wits, I had climbed on and was speeding toward the gate. There was shouting and people diving out of the way. Rachael screamed at me to go back. She was screaming so loud, and kicking so hard, it was all I could do to hold on.

I was bearing down, before the guards at the gate knew what was happening. By the time they grasped the situation, we neared and they ordered the gate shut. My back was being pelted, and I thought the guard's arrows had found their mark, but it was only Rachael pummeling me with her fists. At the gate, the horse hit the crowd, who were trying to get out of the way. The guards were scrambling, trying to get the gates closed. The horse reared and everyone scattered or fell. One guard tripped and fell against the other. Remembering the look of terror in Meerina's eyes was the only reason I was able to hold on. I couldn't let her down. I couldn't let Rachael down.

The gate was falling as we passed under.

"Stop, you bastard!" Rachael was yelling. "Stop!" She was sobbing. "Stop! We have to go back." Then she suddenly stopped and slumped over my back and was silent.

I briefly wondered what had happened, then I felt a searing pain in my side. The arrows. I urged the horse faster. I couldn't worry about the pain. I couldn't even worry about Rachael. I heard yelling, and bells clanging; it wouldn't be long before the guards followed. We dodged the masses, as the road was filled with the exiled.

I slowed slightly as we entered a wooded area. I wanted to leave the road but I didn't trust any of the dislodged people to keep silent. They would say anything for a price.

Then, I saw my chance. There was a stream as the road took a sharp turn. The thicket was so dense that you couldn't see through it. I turned into the stream on the left side of the road. All anyone saw was me going left. I traveled up the stream, then doubled back to the curve. Hiding in the thicket, so no one could see me. Impatiently, I waited until there was a break in the crowd. I could hear screaming coming from down the road, in the direction of the castle. Soldiers! They were coming and coming fast. I could hear the horses.

The people up ahead on the road heard the soldiers coming so they started running. It was now or never. I crossed over the road quickly and hid in the thicket on the downstream side of the road, praying that no one saw. I was holding my breath as I heard the horses pass. I heard more screaming, then a whip, then a whelp, then a voice.

"They went in the water," a scared voice answered. My heart stopped.

"Which way?" I heard a gruff voice ask.

"Upstream."

Upstream. Thank God. I heard the splashing get further away. I urged my horse deeper into the woods. As the sun rode higher in the sky I wanted to stop, but I didn't dare. The horse needed rest, and I couldn't even think about Rachael right now. I slowed the horse, but kept on.

With the immediate danger behind us, my mind wandered down very dark roads. I couldn't keep from worrying about Rachael. If it wasn't for the occasional moan from her I'd have thought that she was dead. I thought about Meerina as well. She had been taken prisoner. We had been taken prisoner. Why? Now, Rachael and I were convicts. What had happened? Meerina had warned me. What did she know that the rest of us didn't?

My side was becoming extremely painful. The horse needed rest, and Rachael needed help. I wanted to stop so badly, but I couldn't. I had promised Meerina. Rachael had to stay safe. The longer I rode the more angry I became. I needed to stop, dammit! But seeing Meerina's face in my mind, I pushed on. I couldn't let her down.

We had traveled all day and dusk was beginning to set in. Chilled and dizzy, I had to stop. I found a clearing by a stream with a rock overhang that would help hide us. When I was finally able to lay Rachael in the alcove, I felt the punch in my gut to see two arrows, and she was covered in blood. One arrow was in her upper arm and the other was in her shoulder just below the neck. She had taught me how to check the pulse. Weak. I cursed as I left her laying there. I needed to secure our camp for the night and couldn't tend to her. We could not be found and darkness was falling fast.

Thank God for small wonders, the guards missed my carving knife which I always carried in my belt. I was becoming delirious, but I could not stop. I stumbled around and cut enough branches to hide the alcove. The saddle needed to be taken off the horse for fear of immediate recognition. Finally, when camp was camouflaged as much as possible, it was almost full dark. I could finally take care of Rachael.

I hurried to her, almost falling to my knees, my own loss of blood forcing me to move slower than I wanted. As I moved her to the stream, that movement tore my shirt away from my own dried blood. I snarled quietly while I shut my pain down. I gently washed the blood off her beautiful face, wishing there was more that I could do. She licked her lips in thirst, and I cursed at losing my belongings and grabbed a nearby leaf to use as a cup.

I propped her head in my lap as I held up the leaf. She smacked her lips as the water slid through them. I cursed the maid. I cursed Lord Pembroke. I cursed the guards. I wanted to yell in frustration at the absurdity of it all. I couldn't help Rachael like this so I banked down my feelings. If I didn't get her treated she would die. I feared I was already too late.

I broke the arrows at the wound, leaving the shafts sticking out. She had told me once that someone could bleed to death if they didn't know what they were doing, so I left them in. I thanked God that she wasn't awake. She murmured, but that was it. I cut my shirt into strips and washed and bandaged her wounds as best I could. I carried her to the shelter and layed her gently down.

I went back to the stream and in my own haze and dizziness, washed and dressed my own wound. The arrow, thankfully, just skimmed me but it had left a sizable hole. The horse snickered so I went to him and thanked him for helping us. He had saved our lives. Stiff and sore, worried and angry, I saw to the horse, then took the branches and covered the opening, and when I was satisfied that no one could readily see, I crawled in next to Rachael. I fell asleep before my head hit the ground.

I woke to the sun shining through the branches. As I looked out, making sure no one was about, Rachael restlessly stirred. She was burning with fever. I cursed, and I cursed myself for not paying more attention when Rachael had talked of plants. I needed help. I brought her to the water and slid more down her throat. I untethered the horse, who snorted in greeting. So ever thankful, I gave him a pat and a hug as I saddled him. "Thank you, big fella. We would die without you."

I sat Rachael in front of me as we rode north toward a village in which we knew the healer; a woman named Ohna. When our business at the castle was completed, Meerina was to teach some of the priestess healing techniques to her. I had briefly met Ohna a few times, but Rachael and Meerina were much closer to her.

Mid-morning I began to see signs of life. I stopped at a small farm to ask directions to where Ohna lived. They inquired about Rachael's wounds, or more to the point, the arrows in them. I told them that we had gotten caught in a crossfire between the castle guards and some convicts that had escaped. I don't know if they believed me but what else was I to tell them?

The word had spread and Ohna was waiting outside her cottage as we rode up. "Bring her inside," she commanded. Her assistant was a small boy of about ten.

I laid Rachael on the table which Ohna had already set up. She immediately undid the bandages. I started to explain but she shushed me.

"Damien, go check to see if the water is hot." He left on a run. She turned to me. "Do not speak here," she whispered. "I know what has happened," she said quickly when she saw the panic in my eyes.

"You have nothing to fear from me. Meerina was like family. And this one here," she motioned to Rachael, "I was present when she was born. Always had the knack, and like a daughter to Meerina." She had been deftly removing the bandages and arrows as she spoke. It relaxed me some.

When the boy came back with a pail of hot water, Ohna began treating Rachael's wounds. I sat in a chair against the wall and promptly fell asleep.

I tried to jump up when Ohna started to work her magic on my side. When I saw who she was, I fell back into my chair. I winced, as she washed my wound with something that burned. I enquired about Rachael.

"She'll be fine. You did a fine job cleaning her wounds. I gave her something that will keep her from getting septic and make her rest. She's resting peacefully now." She talked to me in quiet, calm words. I began to feel calmer, then I remembered the horse.

"Relax." She pushed me back down. "I had the boy take care of the horse hours ago. You're safe. For now, anyway." I must have looked mistrustful. "Relax boy. If I was going to turn you in you'd already be gone. You've been asleep for hours." I wanted to talk but she shook her head. "Can you walk?" she asked. I nodded.

When we were well away from the cottage we talked.

"Tell me everything," she said.

I told her everything.

"I feared that might happen."

"What? What might happen? Why did they try to imprison us? I don't understand. Meerina and Rachael did everything they could!" She touched my arm.

"I know. I know that Meerina would've given her own blood to save that woman if it would have helped."

"Then what? Why did they take her? Us?"

Ohna didn't say anything for a bit.

"Stephen, this isn't just about Meerina. Or Lord Pembroke, even. They've been slowly gaining popularity in the towns and countryside."

"Who?"

"The Church. They're after the devil worshipers."

"Devil worshipers? What does that have to do with Rachael and Meerina?"

"The church is after anyone who says they can heal. Herbs or otherwise."

"I don't understand. What does that have to do with devil worship?"

"It doesn't."

"But—"

"They're saying it does." I tried to speak, but she stopped me. "Somewhere along the way, the church decided that only the priests can heal or talk to God."

"That's ridiculous!"

"Yes, it is. But since they've got the power, they can say and do whatever they want." She went on to say that healers of all kinds were being rounded up and being tortured and burned as witches.

I couldn't believe what I was hearing. It was so unfathomable to me. I started thinking of all the bits and pieces I'd been hearing throughout the castle, about witches and burnings, etc. My stomach churned. I didn't equate that with Rachael or Meerina. They heal with plants! What does that have to do with worship of any kind? Ohna was speaking again.

"Meerina had mentioned something like this might happen when she came through last spring. She had premonitions about things to come, but since those events were so far away, she thought we might be safe here."

"Meerina had said that Lady Pembroke was sick long before this. Even before they had sent for her. Why are they punishing her? The devil obviously got to Lady Pembroke long before Meerina did," I said derisively.

"She couldn't save her."

"The lady was too far gone. It wasn't Meerina's fault!" I cried.

"I know." She sighed. "Lord Pembroke is hurting. He doesn't want to blame himself. If he had acted sooner she might have lived. He has to blame somebody."

"Misplaced as it is, I actually understand that kind of thinking, but devil worship?"

"He must have heard about what's happening in the church, as well, and in his rage and pain decided that it was a good excuse. He can blame the devil."

"But Meerina has done nothing but good. How could he possibly ..." I couldn't finish.

"I know," she said sadly.

I thought of the witches being burned at the stake. I stopped.

"Is he saying she's a witch?" I cried out.

Ohna looked down.

"Are they to burn her?" I paled. "We have to go back! We have to do something!"

"You can't do anything."

"We have to tell them she's not a witch!"

"You will be taken prisoner. Although, you yourself might get off easy. You might just get hanged." She paused to see if any of this was sinking in. "Rachael will be burned," she said deliberately.

"What if I go, just me?" I beseeched.

"Are you deaf?" she yelled. "What have I been trying to tell you? They will lock you up and kill you! Then what will happen to Rachael? They'll hunt her like a dog. Meerina saved you both. She wanted Rachael to live, and she wanted you to be there for her! Meerina did what she had to so that you both could live. Don't throw that away," she said more softly. "I appreciate that you want to save her, but just know there is nothing more you can do for Meerina." I couldn't think. I couldn't look at Ohna any longer. I turned and looked upon the land.

"But they're going to burn her at the stake!" I cried to the heavens, wondering what God would let this happen. She put a hand on my shoulder.

"I know," she said in anguish. "The only thing for you to do now is to take Rachael far away and keep her safe. It's the only thing that Meerina would have wanted." I nodded with head hanging.

"You can't tell Rachael. It'll kill her." Resigned, helpless, and utterly devastated, I stood there, looking at the future with blind eyes, knowing I had to find the resolve to keep Rachael alive. They'll be looking for us all over the land. We turned around and stopped. There, in front of us, was Rachael.

"So you were going to keep this from me."

Neither of us said anything. What was there to say? She looked like I had betrayed her.

"I can't believe you were going to keep this from me."

"We wanted to wait until you were stronger," Ohna explained. She moved toward Rachael, but Rachael put her hands up.

"Aunt Meerina is going to be burned at the stake and you two decide to do nothing. And not even tell me about it?" Rachael was incredulous.

"Rachael. There's nothing we can do."

"We can go back."

"No, we can't." I was trying to be firm but I wasn't doing a very good job of it. I tried to go to her but she threw her arms up.

"No! I will not have a coward near me!"

"Rachael—"

"No." She turned to walk away.

"They have the power to do anything they want. There's nothing we can do to save her," I said, trying to convince myself.

"So you won't even try." She turned around. I said nothing. "Coward."

"We'll die trying."

"I'd rather be dead then. Right next to her."

"You can't mean that," I said.

"We serve together, we die together," she dictated. "I can't leave her to die alone …" her voice caught, "at the stake." She turned back to the hut. "I'm going back to the castle."

"What? You can't!" I ran after her. She tried to shove me away, but I held her arms tight. She looked so pale. "Meerina wanted you out of harm's way." Rachael didn't want to listen. "When we went outside, while you packed, do you know what she said to me? She told me, that no matter what happened, that I was to get you out. She made me promise to get you out." Rachael just stared at me.

"That was her wish. She knew it would come to this." My voice broke. "She knew."

We were silent. She turned back to the cottage. I let her go.

"You must have known, as well, working in the castle with her. You must have heard something."

Her step hitched and then she collapsed. Ohna ran past me.

"Bring her inside. She shouldn't have been up."

Ohna made her comfortable while I helplessly watched. I hovered, so she chased me outside to do chores. I checked periodically, but the healer managed quite well without me. When nightfall came, she went to sleep in her cot while I dropped into the chair next to Rachael's bed.

I woke, sometime in the night, and with eyes still shut, I reached out to Rachael. She was gone. I bolted out of my chair and out the door.

"Ohna!" She was up fast and followed me out the door.

"Check the barn!" she yelled.

I sprinted to the barn, hoping to God, that Rachael had just wanted some fresh air. I reached the barn and found one of Ohna's horses gone. Oh god. Oh please, God. I grabbed the guard's horse and quickly saddled him. I wouldn't have bothered but it would be easier to carry her back with a saddle. I wasn't sure that she would even survive the trip to the castle.

Ohna met me at the door. She gave me two small, colored vials.

"The green will make her sleep." She looked at me pointedly. She knew Rachael would fight. "Apply the red to the wound. It will help with infection. Please get to her, Stephen." She didn't need to tell me twice. I bolted.

I rode hard in the dark. It killed me to eventually slow down to save the horse. We had taken such a circuitous route to get here, I had no way of knowing how long it would take by road. I traveled for, what seemed like hours, until I could see the subtle change in the light. Shite. We were running out of time. I had counted on the dark to hide us, provided I found her, but even that was failing.

In my panic, I spurred the horse on again. I rounded the curve and I could see the castle at the far end of the valley. It was still a ways off, but close enough that I could see the fires burning. The horse, sensing its home, galloped faster yet.

Halfway across the valley I noticed a rider that looked like it was listing and barely holding on. Hope sprang forth as I raced forward. I pulled up alongside. There are no words that could describe the relief that flooded me.

"Rachael."

She looked at me with glassy eyes and pitched forth into my arms.

With her horse in tow, we reached the woods and pulled off. It was too light to travel the road safely. It was still dark in the woods so we traveled through them until the sun poked through the leaves, warming the air. I found a clearing by the stream. Horses and all, we needed rest. I laid Rachael near the stream and checked her bandages. She was bleeding so I pulled out the red container.

I finished and she started to stir, licking her lips. I found a large leaf and gave her water. I couldn't believe I was here again. She opened her eyes a slit, then they flew open. When she saw it was me she relaxed and tried to sit up.

"What are you doing? Where are we? I have to get to the castle!" She tried to fight me, but she was too weak and soon gave up.

"Please," she broke. "I have to go see her," she cried.

"I can't let you." I felt small, but I willed myself to stay strong.

"Stephen. Please, if you love me you'll let me go." I didn't see the logic in that so I kept quiet.

In desperation, she grabbed my shirt.

"Please!" She became distraught, kicking and screaming.

"Rachael." I held her down. "Stop this! What is the matter with you?" I yelled at her. I didn't understand. "It's too late. There's nothing we can do!" She stopped fighting and looked at me with dead eyes, and was so still, that I thought she had died. I yelled, and cursed God, at the top of my lungs. Then I saw her chest rise. The fit had so exhausted her there was no need for the green vile.

When the horses were rested, we continued. We rode slowly as to disturb Rachael as little as possible. We arrived at Ohna's hut at dusk. Profoundly relieved, she ushered me inside.

"Thank God you found her."

"Barely. She was almost there." When I laid her down, I noticed she was covered in blood. "She's lost so much blood."

"It was providence that she left. The guards showed up while you were gone." I paused and digested that.

"Will she be okay?"

"She will if we can keep her down," she said sarcastically. "If she won't stay in bed we'll have to tie her." She grabbed me. "I mean it Stephen. She has to stay down!" I nodded heavily.

The next two days were spent restlessly doing chores: chopping wood, combing horses, sorting and drying herbs, all interspersed with sitting by her side. For hours, I would sit and hold her hand. One of us had to be with her at all times.

During her feverish moments, she would babble and get so excited, that we had to sedate her with herbs that Ohna had made ready. By the third day, she didn't seem to be getting better. I was worried.

"Ohna. Why isn't she getting better? Has she lost too much blood?"

She put an arm on my shoulder as I sat next to Rachael.

"I don't know, son." I looked at her quizzically. "Her wounds are healing, yet she seems to be wasting away." She looked at me seriously. "What happened at the castle?" I didn't know what she was talking about. "Something happened. The times when she talks in her sleep. What does she say?"

I grasped what she was thinking.

"Just pieces mostly. Something about a gift. She says my name. Plenty of time. Need to go back. I'm sorry. It's my fault." I stopped, understanding dawning. "My god. She thinks it's her fault."

Ohna nodded.

"Ohna. It's not true!" I pleaded. "Even if she hadn't gone back, for whatever it was, they had the gate watched. They were already looking for us. It wouldn't have mattered," I desperately tried to explain.

"There's no need to explain to me. She's the one you have to convince."

"How?"

"Talk to her. Convince her."

"Convince me of what?"

We both whipped around. Rachael looked like death. Her skin was so pale and thin, I could almost see her veins. Even before this she was thin, still trying to gain the weight from when she was sick, but she had lost so much more now, she was almost like a skeleton. She was wasting away before my eyes. I tried not to break at the agony in her eyes. The hell.

Ohna gave me a look that said, "Convince her or else" and left us. I started right in.

"Meerina's death was not your fault!" Fire sprang into her eyes at me trying to talk her out of her pain and guilt.

"What do you know? You weren't there," she said angrily. Even in her weakened state she was a force. I admired her for that.

"You talk in your sleep." She had that betrayed look in her eye. By me. By herself. I tried again. "You couldn't have known. It wasn't your fault. Lord Pembroke wanted heads to roll. They would have gotten to her no matter what you did. They were watching for her." I implored her to see the truth. "For you."

She had momentarily found strength from somewhere.

"You don't understand. I didn't take it seriously. She was trying to hurry. She tried to make me hurry but I laughed." Rachael fought the tears. "I laughed. I said it would be all right. She tried to stop me." She started crying. "I laughed." I let her cry it out. Then I tried again.

"It wouldn't have mattered," I said softly but matter-of-factly.

"Don't you see?" She implored me to understand her guilt. She grabbed my shirt. Her eyes haunted. "We could've gotten out the gate. We could've run. Hid from the soldiers." She lost her strength, finally letting her secret out. "Now, it's too late." She closed her eyes and I thought she had passed out again, but she whispered one more thing. "And now, when I close my eyes, I hear her screams, and see her charred flesh."

With that, she slid under again. Away from her pain.

I layed my head down on Rachael's hand in utter despair, also seeing Meerina's charred body. Ohna came in and put her hand on my shoulder.

"I can't help her, can I?" The blood drained from my face.

"Guilt is a powerful weapon."

The next day Ohna sent Damien and me into the village for supplies. While we were there we overheard a few lads talking about a witch burning at the castle. A big event. They were laughing about witches squirming and screaming while the flames took hold. Damien held me back from killing them. It sounded like it had already happened. I felt shame at not being there for her, even though it was impossible.

Damien sat me down and told me to behave. He was leaving for a bit and left me to burrow in my sorrows.

When he came back he had more information. He said that Meerina and two others, had been detained and tortured, all week, and the burning was to happen tomorrow. Tomorrow! Something inside me sparked.

A seed had planted itself in my brain. All the way back to the cottage I cultured that seed.

That evening I sat holding Rachael's hand. I knew what I had to do. I held her frail hand to my cheek and whispered, "I'm losing you." I sobbed.

Later, I played storyteller, reliving the stories of our travels together. Rachael's hand was so slight, I could barely feel it.

Ohna watched and listened for a while then left. She came back with some roots and dried plants. I asked her what she was doing.

"If you're going back there you'll need a disguise." I gave her a questioning look.

"It's written all over your face." She softened. "And it's your way to cope. You feel helpless, so going back gives you some power. You won't rest until you do … and she'll die anyway." She walked to me. "And Meerina was like a mother to you too," she said softly. She ran her fingers through my hair. "So let's get you outside and cut your hair."

When I looked back at Rachael, she had opened her eyes and heard everything. She squeezed my hand, though I barely felt it. She closed her eyes and I followed Ohna outside.

People gave me a wide berth as I went through the castle gates. While Ohna had cut my hair, she told Damien to rub pig manure on my robe. My hair was short and light brown, and I had rotted teeth by the time Ohna was done with me. No one would recognize me, and with the stench, we made sure no one wanted to.

I had said my good-byes before I left. There was a good chance Rachael would be dead when I came back. I weighed that with the fact that she may not survive if I didn't go—such was the weapon of guilt. Rachael needed to know, that Meerina knew, that they were free. It was all I could do for Rachael. She couldn't go herself.

I hung in the back of the crowd until they brought the three "witches" out and tied them to their stakes. My insides twisted to see that strong woman battered and broken. And then the ultimate evil; burned alive. I almost threw up thinking about it.

I think the devil is on the wrong side of the rope.

I was getting angry, standing there, watching. I had to reign in my emotions for fear of giving myself away. That would do none of us any good. They would search for Rachael, and Ohna now too.

I easily maneuvered myself to the front. I guess no one liked pig.

I reached into the folds of my smock and brought out Rachael's bright colored healing bag that Meerina had made for her. I wanted her to recognize me. I wanted her to know that she wasn't alone.

When they came to light her fire, I willed her to open her eyes. She did. She didn't see me at first, but as her eyes locked onto something colorful, she recognized it. Her eyes flew to mine and recognized me.

Her eyes beseeched mine, asking, "Is she okay?" I gave her a slight smile and nod. Relief flooded her being. Her "daughter" was safe. And the extra pain she endured for helping them escape wasn't for not. Confidence surged through her body, fire spit in her eyes and she raised her head in defiance. Meerina was back. We locked eyes as the flames took hold. Tears rolled down my face long after her screams were gone.

12

$\mathcal{I}$ woke with my hair plastered to my face and swimming in tears. I was staring at my unlit ceiling fixture—there was something strange about it. It took me a moment to realize that it was from the twentieth century! Rachael! Rhina! I bolted upright.

As my seventeenth-century mind melded with my twentieth-century mind I calmed. Rhina was okay. She was home sleeping in her bed. I could not get the picture of Rachael out of my mind. So pale and weak, so near to death. And Meerina. Oh god. Meerina. My mind flashed back to Meerina as the flames licked at her. And her screams. Oh man. I squirmed. Dread flooded my being. I scrubbed my face with my hands and stood up. Rhina. I needed Rhina. I grabbed my keys and left.

The dream, vision, whatever, released its mental hold slowly as I drove. It was the only time I was glad of the commute. By the time I reached Rhina's house I felt almost normal. Almost.

I let myself in and when I reached her bedroom and saw her there, and heard her beautiful, soft snore, I collapsed against the jamb in body-numbing relief. So much for almost normal. I hadn't realized, until that moment, that I had expected her to be the pale, frail, almost dead Rachael.

I tried to sob in silence, but on some level of her psyche, she heard me because she woke and called my name. She saw the onslaught coming and opened her covers just in time for me to dive in.

Once I was in her arms a new dam broke. I wondered, idly, how many dams can one person have? I shook and blubbered while she hadn't a clue; the last time we spoke I was fine.

"Babe. What's wrong?" she asked gently. I was crying so hard I couldn't say anything. Besides, what would I say?

"Okay. Are you hurt?" Reassurance. I could give her that. I shook my head. She let out a relieved sigh.

"Okay. Good." She waited a bit then said, "Then I'll just hold you until you get done blathering enough to tell me what's going on."

I snorted in kind of a half-cry, half-laugh. I'm sure it was the desired effect. She held me tight. Then the laugh seed grew, and the next thing I knew, I was laughing hysterically, like a hyena. Ants, horses, humans, tigers ... hyenas. That random thought sent me into more hysterics. I sat up.

Rhina watched me with that half smile that said I-really-want-to-be-part-of-the-joke-but-I'm-happy-to-see-you-laughing. I couldn't not touch her. Even though I couldn't see her through the veil of happy tears, I couldn't let go. My hand clamped onto her leg. Every time I thought I had calmed down enough to tell her what was going on, I would start laughing again. She had just propped herself up on her pillows and watched me with that patient, loving look in her eyes.

May I always see it there, I thought.

I finally sobered. I wiped my tears and grabbed her hand and entwined our fingers. She waited patiently. I opened my mouth to say something sweet.

"I gotta pee!" popped out.

This made both of us laugh. I laughed into the bathroom, until I looked in the mirror. Holy crap! I looked like a train wreck. I did my business, then scrubbed my face with cold water. My robe was hanging on the back of the door, so I undressed.

I sat cross-legged next to her. The soft light of her lamp flooded the room with a gentle glow. I gazed at her; whole, healthy and happy. She gazed back with that wise look that I'd come to love. I wanted to kiss her and hold her tight, but I didn't think I could handle that yet. I felt wrung out, like I'd just ran a marathon, but I was actually surprised to notice that I felt a little lighter too. Huh.

I closed my eyes and retold every detail. I could hear her, at different times, sniffling and blowing her nose, but I didn't stop. When I finished, I couldn't look at her. I just kept a hand on her leg as her body shook.

Long after she stopped crying, I opened my eyes. I'm sure they mirrored the haunted look that was in hers. We just stared at each other for a long while. Then she said the only thing she could say; she pulled open the covers for me to crawl in.

Neither of us moved to turn off the light. Demons were too easy to see in the dark.

At some point I heard her murmur, "Guilt is a powerful weapon." We just held each other until, eventually, we both nodded off.

We both woke, and still had no idea what to say to each other, so we just lay in each other's arms. It was Monday morning so I couldn't stay in bed. Neither of us could speak, so we just treated each other tenderly, a gentle touch while getting coffee, entwining fingers while eating, her hand on my back as I brushed my teeth.

I tried to think about how I was going to handle Sam, and what I assumed, was going to be a shit storm, but too much had happened since then. I couldn't concentrate on the present. I knew I had to, but couldn't. And honestly, I couldn't care less.

On the way to work I called Pam. I wasn't sure what I was going to say, but ...

"Pam. It's Kat. Hi."

"Kat! Oh my god! I was going to call you today," she blurted. "I'm so sorry. Penny told me what happened yesterday."

Was that only yesterday? So much for reliving the past. Here's to diving into the present.

"Good, then I don't have to explain," I said, relieved. Pam didn't say anything for a beat.

"I'm sorry, Kat. Sam's been telling everyone you're a dyke. And yesterday, before they parted ways, he told the rest of them he was going straight to the dean and tell him everything," Pam sounded so sad.

That all-too-familiar, helpless feeling, reared its ugly head again.

"Penny said they all tried to calm him down and to talk him out of whatever he was going to do, but he was inconsolable."

I thought of Baron Halstead. Throw that in with thwarted teenage hormones and you have a very damaging combination. Pam was still talking.

"Penny did say that Sam was the only one that had a problem. Everyone else was supportive."

Pam started laughing. "I guess Angela was going to rip his hair out. Alex and Josh had to hold her back.

I pictured that scene and it made me laugh as well.

"Thanks, Pam. I needed that." Then reality set in. "But unfortunately, I'm sure there's plenty of people that will be more than happy to agree with him." I sighed.

"I'm sorry, Kat." Pam said.

"Thanks for the heads up." I didn't want to think about it anymore. "But I actually called for another reason. Got a minute?" I told her the Reader's Digest version.

"So I can see how it all fits together. Why things show up in present time, and how they relate to the past, but what do you do with it? Other than a quick trip to the asylum, what good is that information?" I asked. Pam laughed.

"Well, yeah, there is that." She got serious. "To put it simply, you release it."

"I release it." Sure, I thought. "That's helpful," I said evenly. Pam laughed again.

"All that past stuff is energy trapped in our cells. They call it cellular memory." Pam explained.

I thought of the stunt woman that Rhina had talked about.

"Yeah. Rhina spoke a little about cellular memory but that's pretty much it. So tell me. What does it mean to release it? And why do I need to?"

"Well, to release it means that your body doesn't have those memories in it to react to. It's kind of like a computer. When you want to upload a new program, you have to offload the old program in order for the new program to work properly. Right?"

"Right."

"Same thing. An example would be: If you had an intense fear of water—with no present-life cause—and if you release that energy out of your cells, then most likely your fear of water will no longer be there."

"That fear will just be gone?"

"Essentially … yes. Though, I've simplified it greatly and there may be many layers to the process, like an onion. And there also may be different issues intertwined with each other as well, but basically . . . that is the process."

"Okay. So do we *need* to release it?"

Pam thought for a moment gathering her thoughts.

"Do you need to release it? No. But life can be much lighter if you do."

"So what do you do, flip a switch or something, and it all flows out?" I asked. She laughed.

"Wow! Don't I wish," she said. "Well, actually I don't wish."

"What do you mean?" I asked. Pam thought for a moment.

"Well, say you're standing below a dam. Picture that the water represents the energy of all of your past lives."

"Okay."

"If you're standing there when they release *all* the water you'd be obliterated, right?" She must have seen my nod over the ether, because she continued on. "But if we can let that energy, or water, out a little bit at a time, we can release it in a manageable amount. It may knock us over but we can still get up.'"

"Okay. I'm with you but what are past lives for? Why do we need them? Can't we just deal with our crap in this lifetime?"

"Absolutely. We can. It can be harder sometimes though. You've had your baggage hit you in the face, right?"

"Right."

"How hard was it to function like that?"

"Like walking in mud."

"Exactly. So, looking at past lives can be easier, because they're 'out there.' Far removed. You know how it's easier to deal with other people's problems? Like that. It's removed." She paused. I remembered Penny had said a similar thing that first day. "Also, it can answer some questions that mainstream therapy doesn't deal with. That fear of water example I talked about?"

"Yeah."

"A woman I know, had this insane fear of water, with no knowledge of where that fear came from. She'd gone through years of therapy without any results. After just one energy session with me, finding, and working with that particular lifetime where the fear of water originated, she was able to go near the water and then eventually, swim. She is now the swim coach at a local high school. We had a few sessions after that to help her integrate, but basically, it's that easy."

"No kidding?"

"I know. Granted, her years of therapy probably helped her deal with it all, but yeah, it's pretty amazing stuff."

I thought about my dream and voiced that it didn't seem so removed.

"Well, I think that what you experienced was an extreme case. More of a vision really. But regardless, the process is the same. It's all an opportunity to release energy. Whether it's from this lifetime or a past one."

"What's the endgame?"

"I'm sure Rhina's talked about learning lessons, right?"

"Yes."

"Sometimes a lesson is so huge that we can't begin to deal with it all in one lifetime. Sometimes we can, but sometimes it's just easier doing it in small lumps. Sounds like your helplessness complex might be one of those. The more energy you release in a particular lesson, in a particular lifetime, then the less you need to release later." I was silent so she continued on. "I'm simplifying this immensely, so I'm sure I've created more questions than answers." Understatement. Clear as mud.

"You said, though, that we don't need to delve into any past lives."

"Right. It's just another way to do it. A story we can learn from."

"Okay. So how do you release it? Can I do it? Or do I need someone to do it?"

"Rhina can definitely. But I can show you both how to release it."

"I can do it?"

"Absolutely. But to tell you the truth it's easier for someone to help you. Even skilled energy workers find it difficult at times. Even they ask for help."

"Help," I croaked. She laughed. I was turning my thoughts around in my head so I didn't notice Sam standing by the gate.

"I'd be happy to help."

"Great. How about tonight?"

I was busy gathering my belongings, and then my thoughts, so I didn't notice Sam until I was halfway across the lot. I immediately came back to the present. My step hitched and an instant reaction of dread followed. Getting rid of this dread would be nice, I thought. He saw the hitch and I received a smirk for it. I would love to wipe *that* off his face.

I pretended nothing was out of the ordinary, and I saw Dave exiting the building toward me. Thank goodness. I concentrated on watching him and not Sam.

"Hey, Kat."

"Hi, Dave." Neither of us acknowledged Sam as we walked right past.

"Miss Sykes," he said. Dave and I turned.

"Oh, hi, Sam. I didn't see you standing there." My knees were shaking. He opened his mouth to say something as he walked toward us. I cut him off. "My office hours are between ten and twelve today. Talk to me then," I said over my shoulder as we continued walking. I didn't see Sam's face turn an angry red. I waited until I was out of earshot.

"Thanks, Dave. I owe you one."

"No problem. I heard a few things so I was keeping a look out."

"How bad is it?"

"Scale of one to ten?"

"Sure."

He thought for a moment. He changed his tactics. Not Good.

"Let me put it another way." He skipped a beat. "I hope you have some very thick skin."

"Ugh. Tell me."

"It's all over the school that you're a lesbo." He added quickly, "Their words not mine."

I absorbed that.

"I know hearts are being broken all over the school." He tried to joke. It fell flat. We arrived at my office.

"C'mon in." We both sat with the desk between us. I made a quick decision. I gave him a brief synopsis.

"Wow! What else is there to say, but wow!"

"Yeah. Ditto." I sighed. "So what does this mean?"

"Job-wise?" He picked up the threads quickly and gave it some thought. "I honestly don't know. You're a really good teacher, so hopefully, nothing. Plus, with the political climate being what it is, they don't want to be sued." He got up. "I have class, but I'll keep my ears open for anything afoot."

"Thank you." I got an idea, and joked.

"You know. We could stay in here half the day and give them something else to think about. Muddy the waters a bit."

He laughed and tried to joke, but it fell just shy of the mark.

"I would love that, but my wife might disagree and you're too nice to be disemboweled."

I laughed and wondered how big a shoe I had just shoved in my mouth.

"Thanks again, Dave. It's good to know chivalry is not dead."

I had class as well. I started walking down the hall with, what I hoped, was confidence. It was very hard with the concrete blocks on my feet. Some students were openly staring and others weren't so open. I felt like I was in the Coliseum, ready to be eaten by the tigers. The irony of that made me smile.

I noticed a few girls staring at me. Then that totally helpless feeling enveloped me. Everyone is against me. How can I fight that?

I've never realized how long the hallway was.

Marci came to mind. I wonder if she wore concrete blocks when she boarded the plane. Then, what it felt like when she took them off. I was hoping I would have the same experience. I remembered her words.

Fear is the doorway to courage. Fear is the doorway to courage. Fear is … shit

I'm thinking I need a bigger door.

With my "helpless" knees shaking, I drew in a big breath and opened my classroom door. I was a few minutes late so my students were already in their seats.

"Good morning, everyone," I said brightly. I got hellos back in various shades. So far so good.

"I hope you guys had a good weekend. Let's dispense with the pleasantries and get started. Open your books." They were participating very nicely. At least the rumor mill was good for something. I was writing on the board.

"Hey, Miss Dykes. I mean Miss Sykes. Can I ask a question?" Sam asked. I froze.

Some of the class were silent, holding their breath. Others were quick to speak out in support.

"Jesus, Sam. Grow the fuck up!" Alex spoke.

"C'mon, Sam," Josh said.

"You childish dirtbag!" Angela roared—that was my personal favorite—and others spoke up as well.

"Don't you guys care that she's a dyke?" Sam yelled.

I turned around. All the rage, helplessness, loss, and the fear—the full range of emotions that have been rearing their ugly heads lately—must have been on my face, because the silence in the room was palpable. With my eyes on Sam's, I slowly walked to the front of my desk. Even Sam squirmed. I was afraid that if I raised my voice, I would eviscerate him, so it was dead, cold, calm.

"Samuel Henry Jackson, if you can't keep your personal feelings out of the classroom, then you should leave." I could feel the temperature of the room drop. A few squirmed.

Sam locked eyes with me, challenging me, but he soon backed down. He had lost, in so many ways and he knew it. Humiliated, he started gathering his things.

"Fine, but this isn't over," he cried his last ditch effort as he made his way to the door.

"Sam, there is nothing to *be* over."

With that, I turned back to the board, shutting him out. He stopped at the door.

"I'm sure the dean will want to know everything. Including that time when you didn't follow curriculum." Then he left. I stood poised at the board.

A few in the class had some choice remarks about Sam. The rest were silent.

I was about to continue writing, but decided to turn around instead.

"Anyone else?" I waited a beat. Listened to the stunned silence. "Good." Then turned back to the board.

It took me a bit to reel in my emotions but the kids were engaging, so in the context of teaching, I came back quicker than expected.

The class ended and I started erasing the board for my next class. A few left but most of them remained seated. I turned and lifted an eyebrow, waiting for them to explain.

No one really knew what to say; they just looked around, hoping someone else would speak up.

This is what solidarity looks like in teenagers.

"Miss Sykes. Whatever that dip-shit Sam says to the dean," Angela stood up and the rest of the class followed suit, "we support you," and they all agreed. The scene from *Dead Poets Society* came to mind, when they all stood on their desks. I tried not to think about what finally happened to the Robin Williams character.

I was too choked up to really say anything. I just watched them file out, larger than when they walked in.

Penny was the last. She walked up to me, gave me a hug and walked out. I stood there, not moving, until my next class started straggling in. Then I was forced to continue like normal. I called Rhina at lunch time, to ask her if she was available tonight and to give her a quick rundown of events. I was holding it together surprisingly well, right up until the time when I got an email from the dean. I was to go to his office at nine o'clock in the morning. Fear raced through my blood. It's happening again. They're taking everything away. My knees almost buckled on the way out to my car.

13

hy? Why do I lose every time? They take everything! My thoughts ran amuck. All the way to Rhina's house, doom reigned. I thought of all the negative things that could happen: Laughing stock of the school, losing my job, losing my house, losing my friends, even losing Rhina because I had no job. Over and over my thoughts spiraled down and down. Part of my brain knew it was ludicrous, but I couldn't stop. What the hell was happening to me? I've never been like this.

I was a wreck by the time I reached Rhina's. She met me at the door and I immediately threw up all over her—metaphorically speaking, of course—she tried, for a while, to support me and talk me out of it but I was too far gone. But even Rhina had a breaking point.

"That's enough!" she snapped. It had the desired effect. My head snapped up.

"Stop that wheel right now!" She stood in front of me with hands on hips. "First of all, who do you think you are, telling me that I'm going to leave you because you lost your job? What kind of crap is that? Second of all, you're a great teacher and your students love you." She started pacing around in frustration. "If you lose your job, so what? That school doesn't deserve you!"

"It's my job!" I whined like a little kid.

"There are other jobs!"

"I worked hard for this one!" I was getting hysterical.

"There are other jobs!"

"I need this one!"

"Why?" She hurled at me. I couldn't say anything. I stood there floundering in my own thoughts.

"Why do you need this one?" she softened a bit. She walked to me and stood in front of me. "Tell me what would happen if you lost your job."

My negative mood went to the first negative thought I could think of.

"I would have to find another teaching position." I began to see a flicker then lost it. "But what if I can't find one. I'll lose my house." I started to panic and Rhina rolled her eyes.

"Weren't we planning on selling one of our houses anyway?" she countered.

"But what if I can't find one here?"

"What if?" I was starting to feel that she was guiding me somewhere, but it was too much in my face to see it. I was getting frustrated.

"C'mon, can't we just drop it?" I whined.

"No. What would happen if you couldn't find another job here?" she demanded. I snarled.

"Okay!" I capitulated. "I'll play along. I would look elsewhere. But your job is—"

"Don't worry about me. I can work anywhere."

"But—"

"Shush. You would look elsewhere ..."

"We could sell both houses and go elsewhere." I was beginning to see the daylight. Just a pin prick. "What if I couldn't find any colleges that wanted to hire me?"

"What if?"

With a heavy sigh I thought about that.

"I guess I could teach high school." That pinprick was getting bigger. "But I really like teaching at the college level."

"Why?" Rhina wasn't letting off.

"I like shaping young minds. Taking old information and making it usable for today."

"Couldn't you do that with high school students?"

I tilted my head in thought. Yes.

"Any age?" she asked. I nodded. "Sounds like you like teaching, period. Isn't that right?"

I nodded. I could feel the box of my limited world, slowly crumbling.

"Okay. What if we couldn't find our respective jobs anywhere?"

My throat closed. What if they won't hire me, anywhere? What if they won't hire me? There's the helplessness again. "They'll take everything!"

"Who's *they*? And what are *they* going to take?" she inquired.

My life! My freedom! I started to answer, but then I realized that I didn't know who *they* were. And what were *they* trying to take anyway? Rhina patiently watched the wheels turning in my head. *They*.

"*They?*" I inquired. Rhina just shrugged. "Who the hell are *they* anyway?" She smiled, seeing that I was putting everything together.

I thought of Rachael and Stephen, and Annabelle and John. Maybe in their world, *they* had power. But if one wanted out they could've run away. It would have been harder, but … now, *they* are different. At least, in this country. I could do anything I wanted.

I could do anything I wanted.

I could do anything I wanted. Anywhere.

The walls of my box came tumbling down.

"I can do anything I want. And *they* aren't anyone at all. *They* are in my head … And in my past lives," I joked. "That mediocre life I've led." I couldn't believe it. "Oh my god!" I felt myself floating. She nodded and smiled.

"You've been worried about this since we've met. *They* are going to take me away. Subconsciously, *they've* been there the whole time, right between us. It's that helpless mode. You've been a victim. Now, you're seeing that there's nothing to take. You can do anything to survive. *They* can't take that away. No one can." She paused and stood in front of me. "They can't take me away." She repeated softly, making sure that I got it. "They can't take me away."

My body started to shake uncontrollably. I was cold, but not. It was kind of freaking me out.

"What is this?" I asked.

"It's okay," she said. "it's that helpless victim energy leaving your body, your cells."

"Why am I shaking though?"

"I don't know. Everyone moves energy in their body slightly differently. It just energy moving and flowing." She paused, looked at me, remembering who she was talking to. "Okay. You know when you have a hose lying there in the grass, and you turn on the water, and the hose bucks and jumps with the water going through it?" I nodded. "Well, it's the same thing. Water is just energy too." I pondered that.

"Pam said you would probably know about this."

"Yes. It's just energy." She grabbed a blanket off the couch and covered me with it while I shook. "She said that you would probably ask."

"You talked to Pam?"

"Yes. I went over there. I had a major guilt trip this morning after you called … It's all my fault. Blah, blah. She helped me work through it. It helped that you had called so I didn't have to explain everything to her."

"Tell me." I listened to her as I continued shaking.

She told me that they had worked a similar process, as that which Rhina had just done with me; breaking down of the boxes.

"What am I guilty of here? … Blah, blah." She gestured to us. "Anyway, I got to a similar conclusion that you just did. We're not helpless, or guilty. You're not helpless, and I'm not guilty. Like with Rachael. Pam and I delved into that lifetime a bit more. I learned, that there were early warning signs that Meerina didn't heed. They could've gotten out but Meerina was too stuck in her ways and too absorbed in her 'needing' to heal Lady Pembroke, even when she knew it was pointless to keep trying. Her ego had gotten in the way. And on that fateful day, when Rachael delayed by going back, well, it was nothing that Meerina hadn't done before that. They both had. Neither thought anything of it until that day. Rachael *and* I, can let go of my guilt." She stood there looking at me, willing me to understand what she was saying.

"My mom is weak, and my dad's an asshole. I don't need to be guilty for that. I don't need to be guilty of someone else's failings." She looked at me, and seemed deep in thought. "And I find it fascinating that both of us did this huge breakthrough work on the same day."

"Why do you think that is?"

"I don't know. There could be so many reasons. Karma. Timing. Our need to be level-headed for what's to come. Planets are aligned. All of the above. I don't know." She shrugged.

"What do you mean, timing?"

"Well, I believe that nothing is left to chance. I think that you and I, still in spirit form—before we incarnated—planned this whole thing. Our spirits said, 'Okay, we need to learn these lessons, so at this particular time in our lives, we're going to meet and work our lessons together.'"

I just looked at her with a dead stare. She laughed at me.

"So what about Pam tonight?" I said.

She let me change the subject. Baby steps.

"She said we didn't have to go tonight unless you wanted to. She told me what you were after and gave me some helpful tools." I watched her give me the once over with eagle eyes. "And to tell you the truth, I think you've just done what you needed to do."

I took that in. I breathed deep, and for the first time, noticed how good it smelled.

"What's for dinner? It smells great. I'm starved."

After dinner, we sat at the table sipping wine. I was in a pensive mood so I didn't say much. But finally, I spoke. "I'm sorry I've been such a basket case. I don't understand it. I've never been this unstable in my life."

"You've told me that you've lived a pretty mediocre life up to now, right?" she asked. I nodded.

"You're starting to live life more fully. When you live safely like you have, it's comfortable. When you move beyond the safety zone it becomes uncomfortable."

"So basically, I have to get used to being uncomfortable?" I asked resigned.

"Well ... pretty much."

"Great."

"Of course, it doesn't have to be like that all the time. Don't worry, sooner or later, it gets easier, and it doesn't feel uncomfortable, hardly at all." She gave me her biggest smile. "Besides. Being uncomfortable is where you find all the juicy bits."

"Hardly at all." Great. I stood up. "Well, it's certainly been juicy so far." I held out my hand. "Speaking of juicy, I'm going to bed and I want you to come with me."

The next morning, Rhina and I talked strategy for my meeting. As we were talking I realized that I felt lighter. Not so jittery. Like I could actually *help* myself. Very different than "helpless."

The thought of losing my job still rubbed me wrong but it didn't make me crazy. Mainly, it just pissed me off. I mentioned that to Rhina and she said that it was a good sign, instead of being so full of fear. I also mentioned that I still had the helpless feelings, just not to the extent that I had.

"You may not have released all of it. Or maybe it's bumping up against some other issues that you have. Who knows? Nothing around energy is cut and dried. Or it may just take practice. You may have those same initial knee-jerk reactions, but then when you realize that the emotions from those reactions are gone, that's when you're able to train your body to react differently. Hence, practice." I thought of the woman with the fear of water. Once the fear was gone I wondered how long it took her to actually swim. To train her body to *like* water.

"Well, here's to training like crazy then."

She came to wrap her arms around me.

"All I know is that you drive *me* crazy." She showed me what she meant. She kissed me good.

When I was starting to get hot and bothered, and my mind was good and well away from the issues at hand, I quizzed her, "Is this your strategy, to make my brain so fuzzy that I forget about it?"

"The thought crossed my mind."

"Well"—I was starting to sweat—"it's working." We continued our exploration so much that I wanted to head down the hall instead of to work. "Okay. Making me hot and bothered is"—I pulled away, then thought better of it—"a really good strategy." I attacked her lips. "Okay. Okay. We have to stop." I pulled away and said breathlessly. "I mean it." I laughed as she kept trying.

We finally relinquished the hold we had on each other. She leaned her forehead on mine.

"You'll be fine."

"As long as I know I've got you in my corner."

"Of course you do. But even if you didn't, you'd be fine."

I gave her a quizzical look.

"There's no hidden meaning. All I'm saying is that you're stronger than you think you are."

I thought about that and nodded. I definitely felt stronger.

"No matter what happens, I'm here for the long haul. I'm not going anywhere." She kissed me at the door.

"You know, that's the first time that I've heard you say that without that little voice saying 'I'm going to lose her.' It feels good," I said. She smiled at me.

"Good luck. Call me when you're done."

"First thing."

Nothing like a traffic jam to ruin a good itch.

When I left the house I felt strong, but the longer I was in the car, the more agitated I got. So much for being strong, I thought. By the time I got to work I was a mess again. But at least I wasn't in the tailspin that I was in yesterday. That was something. Fear is the doorway to courage. Fear is the doorway to courage. Fear ….

I noticed a small group of students by the gate. I recognized Alex, Josh, Angela, and Penny, and … wow!, half my freshman class! There was a hail from all of them as I got out of my car. They walked over to me.

"Hey, Miss Sykes!"

"Hey, what are you guys doing here?"

"We heard about the meeting this morning," Angela spoke. I felt a little choked and didn't say anything. All I could do was look at them and nod.

"We just wanted to say that Sam's wrong. He shouldn't have gone to the dean," Alex stressed.

"What a dickhead," Erin exclaimed! Everyone was taken back. In the past, Erin had spoken less often than Penny had. In fact I was even surprised he was there. We all laughed.

"We just wanted to let you know that we're behind you. No matter what," Penny said.

"Thanks, Penny. Thank you, all."

As we walked into the school, the conversation was light and we were joking and playing with each other. It was just what I needed. They walked me to my office so that I could dump my things. I told them all to go to class and they wished me luck.

"Thank you, guys. I'll see you later. Don't forget to read your chapters!" I laughed at their good natured groans. As they walked away Alex let out a war cry.

"Death to the establishment!" Laughter followed him down the hall.

As I locked my door, I snickered at the remark. Death to the establishment. The school system.

I started thinking about Rachael and Stephen, and Annabelle and John. They were at the mercy of the establishment. That establishment was not merciful.

I am not at the mercy of the establishment.

I stopped walking.

It's a different time. Different place. I could always wonder what someone else would do, would take. Or I could give them nothing to take. I am not my job. It doesn't define me. If they take that away then they just take one avenue away. I'll just go find another avenue!

Rhina said that Meerina had chances to get away, but she hadn't taken them. She had other avenues. Annabelle and John could've run away but they chose helplessness instead. The law of the land was very different back then. Difficult but not impossible. They took the path of helplessness. *I* chose helplessness. But not anymore. I choose power.

I choose power.

"Miss Sykes?" David interrupted my thought process. "What are you doing?" He gestured around him. I had stopped in the middle of the hall, staring off into space and students were gawking. My smile was self-deprecating. I must have looked like an idiot.

"Just thinking."

"You better think your way a little faster. They're waiting."

"They're?"

"Sam's there too."

Sam. Shit.

"Good luck. We're all rooting for you."

"Thanks."

I continued walking. Baron Halstead was part of the establishment. I was the victim, or rather, Annabelle was. I'm not Annabelle. I'm not Stephen. I'm me. I could let others choose my path for me. Or I could make my own.

I thought of Josh and his paper. How he watched his brother die and then drowned in his "victim." He then chose not to drown.

I stood at the gate. This is not about Rachael or Stephen, or the dean, or the baron, or my job, or Sam, or anyone else. It's not about the past. They're just here to point me in the direction that I need to go. This is about me. Right this moment. Making a choice to live under my own rules, no matter what. To be at the mercy of no one. I finally got what all the information is for. And why.

My body tingled, every hair stood on end. Blood surged through my veins. For the first time in my life, I finally understood power. My own.

I stood at the gate to my own destiny.

I didn't wait for permission.

I knocked and opened the door.

Dean Barriston was behind his desk, and Sam was in a chair. When he saw me he smirked. The little pissant.

My initial reaction to him was to have a hiccup in my step, but with each step, I realized that it was a conditioned response. Just like Rhina had said. My reaction to him, with every passing second, went from hiccup, then to acknowledgment, then neutrality, then swung the pendulum into contempt. No, I'm wrong. Let's just call a spade a spade. I was pissed as hell. It felt good, instead of the insidious fear that had been haunting me. I acknowledged Sam like nothing was amiss.

"Hi, Sam. Dean Barriston." Sam's smile downgraded, seeing that I didn't seem upset.

"Miss Sykes," Dean Barriston countered. "Please be seated." I stayed where I was. The dean questioningly looked at me then gestured toward Sam. He had opened his mouth to say something, but I was too mad to wait to hear what he had to say.

"Why is he here? I want him out of here. He's done nothing but disrupt my class, and my life, mind you. To say nothing of him stalking me. And now this." I turned toward Sam.

"That's not—" Sam bolted out of his chair.

"Out. Now!" I said it very loud and stern. I looked toward the dean. "You and I can talk about whatever business you think needs to be discussed, but I will not do it with one of my students. As far as I'm concerned, there is no reason for him to be here."

I waited for an answer. Dean Barriston gave me a long, considering look. Sam just glared at me.

"Sam, will you please step outside," he said, still looking at me.

Ouch. If looks could kill. Sam glared all the way to the door. When he was gone, Dean Barriston considered me further.

"I seem to remember a version of you that was a little … nicer," he said with a little humor in his voice. I gave him a slight smile because, well … true statement.

"Yes, well … I've been dealing with a few things lately." I gave him a look that he understood that Sam was one of those things.

"That's what I understand." He considered me. Once again he started to say something, but I cut him off.

"Why was he here? How could you bring him in here and discuss … anything?"

He waited until I was done, and then waited a bit more to see if I really was done. "Miss Sykes. You were five minutes early, and you barged in without knocking, well, in a fashion, then you proceeded to ramrod my guest. And he *was* a guest. No matter what has transpired, he was in here at my behest. *And* I was just about to ask him to leave when you barged in," he said very calmly. Quite opposite of me. Didn't I feel like an ass. I cleared my throat, and sat.

"I'm sorry. You're right. I did barge in," I said matter-of-factly. It felt great. I apologized for what I needed to and nothing else. And the great thing is that I didn't feel the need to go further. Before I would have sat there, and *not* insist that Sam leave, and then I might have felt like I needed to apologize for being upset.

I felt strong. Apologies don't have to take someone's soul. Huh. How cool is that?

He waited for me to say more. He saw that I was done and continued on. Though, he looked at me like I had two heads. Obviously, I had thrown him for a loop, as much as I had thrown myself for one.

"Yes, well, things have been brought to my attention."

"Sir, I have no idea what those things are, so I'd love for you to bring them to my attention." I was picking a fight and I knew it. But I was pissed, dammit!

I wasn't mad at him. He was just doing his job, but I was pissed. It actually felt good to be pissed. He opened his mouth to say something but he changed his mind and changed tactics.

"I hear you went a little off curriculum for a while."

"If you are referring to past lives. Yes sir, I did. For a day and a half. Or did I?" I adjusted myself in the chair. "The assignment was to write what they knew about past lives, or reincarnation. Then, if they could, they were supposed to tie it in with the Roman Empire, which *was* part of the curriculum. And since the *past* is what we call *history*, I'm really not sure that I was all that far off."

The dean contemplated me. He shook his head like he was in an altered state.

"Stretching it maybe ...." he said, with a slight seesaw motion with his hand. "So what prompted this foray into reincarnation?" he asked idly.

"I don't know. It just came across my path and I thought it was worth looking into." I shrugged and was curt.

"And it doesn't have anything to do with a particular relationship?"

Sticky subject. I vowed to myself, that Rhina would not be a mental pawn in any of this.

"Does it matter?" I asked curtly.

"Well ..." He was stammering. I don't think he had expected me to be so combative. "Only, in so much as ..." He didn't know what to say.

"What?" I was not going to make it easy on him.

"Rumor has it—"

"Sam, has it?"

"*Rumor* has it that you're seeing another woman."

"Are you asking me if I'm a dyke?" I asked angrily. He shrugged. "Does it matter who I date?"

"Well, our bylaws—"

"Your bylaws say that there will be no discrimination, of any kind. So I ask you again. Why does it matter who I date? If there is no reason to ask then there is no reason to answer."

"Why are you so angry, Miss Sykes?"

"Because I resent the fact that some snot-nose little kid, can run crying to mommy when he can't get his way. He's had a crush on me since the very beginning."

"And did you do anything to encourage him?"

"Of course not!"

"Relax, Miss Sykes. I'm just asking."

I realized that I was getting a little too excited so I calmed myself down.

"I'm sorry, sir." I sat back in my chair and blew out my breath. "I'm just very tired of living my life according to someone else's rules."

"I see that." He was smiling, like he knew something that I didn't. I cocked my head in curiosity. He just kept on smiling.

"What?" I asked.

"Oh nothing," he said, smiling.

"Is there something that you want from me, sir?"

"It seems to me that you've found everything that you need." He just kept smiling, like he had swallowed that damn cat. I waited for him to say more but he just sat there, smiling.

"Okay then." Curious as hell, I planted my hands and pushed myself up. "Is there anything else?" This was so strange it completely took me off guard.

"No."

"You're not going to criticize me?"

"No. why on earth would I do that?"

"I … uh, thought that because I went off into other subjects and because of the rumors …."

"Did you think that you were here because you were in trouble of some sort?" He seemed honestly confused. I was dumbfounded and shrugged in the affirmative. "Miss Sykes, now it is my turn to apologize. I am very sorry that you got that impression." I must have looked completely confused because he laughed a bit. "I was just curious about how you were finding things these days. What your thoughts were about what's been going on. How you were."

His relaxed demeanor helped me relax as well. I answered him with the only way I knew how.

"Honestly, sir. I have been finding things very interesting." I held out my hands in complete surrender. "And that's all I got." He laughed and clasped his hands together.

"Terrific. That's terrific. I'm glad to hear it," he said it like he truly meant it. Like it was exactly what he was waiting for. I'm not sure how I knew that particular aspect but there it was.

We sat in companionable silence. I was probably more stunned than companionable but who was I to quibble with myself. I got up to go.

"Is there anything else?"

"No. You may go if you wish." It seemed like he wasn't done yet but I didn't know what else to say. It was one of those times when you either have to talk about nothing and go, or you have to stay and talk about everything. I didn't know which one so I chose the former.

"Okay, then. This has been … interesting," I said with a smile. He laughed again.

"All right. But you might want to keep to the curriculum. Just to keep things simple," he said with a grin.

"Yes, sir." I smiled. "I'll do that." I started to the door, but I changed my mind and turned back. I guess I did have something to say. "For the record sir. It was a spur of the moment thing … but it changed their lives," I said with conviction.

"I know," he said.

"Sir?"

He picked up a stack of letters.

"Letters from students, all writing to say how their lives are different because of that 'day and a half.'"

I didn't know what to say. I stood with my mouth open. Again.

"When you stand for who you are, it's amazing who shows up." He paused. "Good or bad."

I saw him in a new light. He had a certain look in his eyes that I had never noticed. I didn't know why, but at that moment I thought of Meerina. I regained some of my composure.

"So … maybe we should offer a class on reincarnation then?" I said smiling.

He guffawed, greatly amused.

"No," he said, shooting me down.

"Too much?" I quipped.

"Too much, too soon." He reached behind him and grabbed a book off the shelf.

"Here. Here is a book that you might enjoy." He held it out for me. *Many Lives Many Masters*.

"Is this what I think it is?" I was shocked. Reincarnation?

He nodded. He got up and walked me to the door.

"Read it, then let me know what you think. My wife and I will have you over to discuss it. It's a favorite topic of ours." He paused. "You can bring your … friend."

I looked him in the eye and jumped.

"She would like that."

He nodded. We shook hands with understanding. He closed the door behind me. It's amazing who shows up when *you* do.

Sam walked up to me. Good or bad.

"What he say?" He had that smirk again. Obviously, he thought things were much worse than they really were. I met him eye to eye.

"Whatever you have, or think you have, going on in that little head of yours, it's done." I pointed to the dean's door. "This is done." I walked past him.

"This isn't over," he said, grasping.

"What, Sam? What's not over? There was never *anything* to *be* over." I walked back to him and got inches from his face. "Leave it alone or I will bury you," I said quietly and walked away. And promptly forgot about him.

I still had twenty minutes before class so I took a walk. It was a nice, sunny day. The sun on my face felt like breath.

I called Rhina. I kept it short, saying I'd give her the details later. I just wanted to breathe. Then I thought of something. Something still didn't make sense to me. The puzzle I'd been weaving, still had a piece missing. Hoping she'd be available, I called Pam. I told her what had transpired with the dean, then asked her my question.

"So when Annabelle walked off that day vowing she'd never be helpless again, didn't *she* deal with it? Why am I dealing with it in this lifetime? And Stephen. Didn't he go back, even at great risk? Why am I dealing with helplessness in this lifetime, if they did in theirs?"

"That is a great question. OMG. That is such a great distinction." Pam was excited. "First of all, Annabelle didn't "deal" with it, she just shoved down all her feelings. She became strong in order to *not* be something else." I wasn't quite getting it so she tried something else. "Okay. When you stood at the door, at the dean's, what did you feel?" Pam asked. I thought about that.

"Well, it wasn't necessarily a feeling. It was more a recognition of who I already was." Huh. "That I am the culmination of all my strengths and weaknesses, and with all that information, I actually chose what my future will look like. I am not at the mercy of anyone." It clicked into place. "I see where you're going with this. I accepted my weaknesses and still chose. I didn't shove them under and decide to go the other way." Wow, did I just say all that?

"Yes." I could hear her exultation in the phone. "That's exactly right."

"Okay, so what about Stephen?"

"That's a little different, but as I see it, he went back because of Rachael. Yes, he loved Meerina, but it was really because of Rachael. If he didn't go, she'd die anyway because her guilt would eat her alive. If he didn't go and she survived, their marriage would never have survived her guilt," Pam surmised.

"So therefore, he went for Rachael. It wasn't really *his* choice," I deduced.

"Exactly." Pam paused. "Kat, I have to say this. You are not the same person I met weeks ago. In the short time that you've been on this roller coaster of a path, it's been amazing to watch. You've jumped right in and went with it—"

"Right along with my tantrums and pity parties and my anger," I said.

"That's part of it. You've jumped in with both feet and never looked back. Sure, you may have wanted to, but really, you just trusted the process and hung on for dear life, and now look where you are."

I thought about what Rhina had said about trust. I thought about what my life had been like lately, and honestly, it *must* have been trust, because I really didn't have a clue how I would've hung on otherwise. I thanked her and hung up. I guess Rhina was right. I must have more trust than I thought.

I thought of Marci and I remembered that night at her party. I had wondered if I would be able to step up to the plate. I had my answer. I had walked through the door. Marci would be proud.

May it always be that way.

My classes went better than anticipated. If I were a fly on the wall I would say that everything was the same, but what the fly couldn't see was how everything was different. I felt stronger, taller, faster. Like nothing could stop me. Like no person could trip me.

I left work feeling invincible. Euphoric.

Then I hit traffic.

My euphoria quickly dissipated as I spewed some choice words. Okay, maybe I'm at the mercy of traffic. I tried deep breathing and the mantra "It only bothers me if I let it. It only bothers ... blah, blah."

I took a deep breath and let it out slowly. I only wanted to hold Rhina.

Even thinking of her felt differently. Stronger. Stronger because *I* was stronger. Like I was finally able to hold up my side of the table.

She met me at the door with open arms and I held on tight. Not in a needy way, like I'd been feeling lately, but a solid bond. She could feel it.

She leaned back and looked into my eyes.

"You did something today," she said knowingly.

I nodded, and that's all I needed to say. She kissed me, and we walked arm in arm to the kitchen.

"I made lasagna."

The End
For now

ABOUT THE AUTHOR

*M*onica Schuster lives her life wherever she hangs her hat and by the seat of her pants. Her training has included hospitality, construction, acting, modeling, spiritual ministry, psychic training (which includes past-life regressions), and teaching at the psychic institute where she studied, until she left to follow her own path through life. From there she became a truck driver and has driven all over the United States and Canada, and then for several years in Yellowstone National Park, where her love of the hospitality industry reasserted itself. That, in turn, led her to the last frontier, where she became a tour guide/bus driver in Juneau and Skagway, Alaska for two summers.

Where she is now is anyone's guess, but through all of her adventures, her spiritual path has been the one constant that has led her through the bonfires of life. Healing and self-discovery have always come first when making life's decisions, so following her intuition to her "next step" has never steered her wrong and has led her in amazing directions.

Writing has always been one of the true loves in Monica's life, and although she's written many stories starting at a young age, this is her first published novel.

CPSIA information can be obtained
at www.ICGtesting.com
Printed in the USA
FFHW021243281018
48984895-53230FF

9 781642 140422